KT-222-752

CHILDREN'S CLASSICS

Around the World in Eighty Days

JULES VERNE

Around the World in Eighty Days

PARRAGON

Around the World in Eighty Days
A Parragon Classic

This edition published in 1993 by
Parragon Book Service Ltd
Avonbridge Industrial Estate
Atlantic Road, Avonmouth
Bristol BS11 9QD

Printed and bound in Great Britain by
BPCC Paperbacks Ltd
Member of BPCC Ltd

CHAPTER 1

In which Phileas Fogg and Passepartout accept each other—the one as Master, the other as Servant

In the year 1872, the house No. 7 Saville Row, Burlington Gardens—the house in which Sheridan died, in 1814—was inhabited by Phileas Fogg, Esq., one of the most singular and most noticed members of the Reform Club of London, although he seemed to take care to do nothing which might attract attention.

This Phileas Fogg, then, an enigmatic personage, of whom nothing was known but that he was a very polite man, and one of the most perfect gentlemen of good English society, succeeded one of the great orators that honour England.

An Englishman Phileas Fogg was surely, but perhaps not a Londoner. He was never seen on 'Change, at the Bank, or in any of the counting-rooms of the "City." The docks of London had never received a vessel fitted out by Phileas Fogg. This gentleman did not figure in any public body. His name had never sounded in any Inns of Court, nor in the Temple, nor Lincoln's Inn, nor Gray's Inn. He never pleaded in the Court of Chancery, nor the Queen's Bench, nor the Exchequer, nor the Ecclesiastical Courts. He was neither a manufacturer, nor a trader, nor a merchant, nor a gentleman farmer. He was not a member of the Royal Institution of Great Britain, or the London Institution, or the Artisan's Association, or the Russell Institution, or the Literary Institution of the West, or the Law Institute, or that Institute of the Arts and Sciences, placed under the direct patronage of Her Gracious Majesty. In fact, he belonged to none of the numerous societies that swarm in the capital of England, from the Harmonic to the Entomological Society, founded principally for the purpose of destroying hurtful insects.

Phileas Fogg was a member of the Reform Club, and that was all.

Should anyone be astonished that such a mysterious gentleman should be among the members of this honourable institution, we will reply that he obtained admission on the recommendation of Baring Brothers, with whom he had an open credit. Thence a certain appearance due to his cheques being regularly paid at sight by the debit of his account current, which was always to his credit.

Was this Phileas Fogg rich? Undoubtedly. But the best informed could not say how he had made his money, and Mr. Fogg was the last person to whom it would have been proper to go for information. He was by no means extravagant in anything, neither was he avaricious, for when money was needed for a noble, useful, or benevolent purpose, he gave it quietly, and even anonymously. In short, no one was less communicative than this gentleman. He talked as little as possible, and seemed much more mysterious than silent. But his life was open to the light, but what he did was always so mathematically the same thing, that the imagination, unsatisfied, sought further.

Had he travelled? It was probable, for none knew the world better than he; there was no spot so secluded that he did not appear to have a special acquaintance with it. Sometimes, in a few, brief, clear words, he would correct the thousand suppositions circulating in the Club with reference to travellers lost or strayed; he pointed out the true probabilities, and so often did events justify his predictions that he seemed as if gifted with a sort of second sight. He was a man who must have travelled everywhere, in spirit at least.

One thing was certain, that for many years Phileas Fogg had not been from London. Those who had the honour of knowing him more intimately than others, affirmed that no one could pretend to have seen him elsewhere than upon the direct route, which he traversed every day to go from his house to the Club. His only pastime was reading the papers and playing whist. He frequently won at this quiet game, so very appropriate to his nature; but his winnings never went into his purse, and made an important item in his charity fund. Besides, it must be remarked, that Mr. Fogg evidently played for the sake of playing, not to win. The game was for him a contest, a struggle against a difficulty; but a motionless, unwearying struggle, and that suited his character.

Phileas Fogg was not known to have either wife or children—which may happen to the most respectable people—neither relatives nor friends—which is more rare, truly. Phileas Fogg lived alone in his house in Saville Row, where nobody entered. There was never a question as to its interior. A single servant sufficed to serve him. Breakfasting and dining at the Club, at hours fixed with the utmost exactness, in the same hall, at the same table, not entertaining his colleagues nor inviting a stranger, he returned home only to go to bed, exactly at midnight, without ever making use of the comfortable chambers which the Reform Club puts at the disposal of its favoured members. Of the twenty-four hours he passed ten at his residence either sleeping or busying himself at his toilet. If he walked, it was invariably with a regular step in the entrance hall with its Mosaic floor, or in the circular gallery, above which rose a dome with blue-painted windows, supported by twenty Ionic columns of red porphyry. If he dined or breakfasted, the kitchens, the buttery, the pantry, the dairy of the Club furnished his table from their succulent stores; the waiters of the Club, grave personages in dress-coats and shoes with swanskin soles, served him in a special porcelain and on fine Saxon linen; the Club decanters of a lost mould contained his sherry, his port, and his claret, flavoured with orange flower water and cinnamon; and finally the ice of the Club, brought at great expense from the American lakes, kept his drinks in a satisfactory condition of freshness.

If to live in such conditions is to be eccentric, it must be granted that eccentricity has something good in it!

The mansion of Saville Row, without being sumptuous, recommended itself by its extreme comfort. Besides, with the unvarying habits of the occupants, the number of servants was reduced to one. But Phileas Fogg demanded from his only servant an extraordinary and regular punctuality. This very day, the second of October, Phileas Fogg had dismissed James Forster—this youth having incurred his displeasure by bringing him shaving-water at eighty-four degrees Fahrenheit, instead of eighty-six—and he was waiting for his successor, who was to make his appearance between eleven and half-past eleven.

Phileas Fogg, squarely seated in his armchair, his feet close together like those of a soldier on parade, his hands resting on his knees, his body straight, his head erect, was watching the hand of the clock move—a complicated mechanism which indicated the hours, the minutes, the seconds, the days, the days of the month, and the year. At the stroke of half-past eleven Mr. Fogg would, according to his daily habit, leave his house and repair to the Reform Club.

At this moment, there was a knock at the door of the small parlour in which was Phileas Fogg.

James Forster, the dismissed servant, appeared.

"The new servant," said he.

A young man, aged thirty years, came forward and bowed.

"You are a Frenchman, and your name is John?" Phileas Fogg asked him.

"Jean, if it does not displease Monsieur," replied the newcomer. "Jean Passepartout, a surname which has clung to me and which my natural aptitude for withdrawing from a business has justified. I believe, sir, that I am an honest fellow; but to be frank, I have had several trades. I have been a travelling singer; a circus rider, vaulting like Leotard, and dancing on the rope like Blondin; then I became professor of gymnastics, in order to render my talents more useful; and in the last place, I was a sergeant fireman at Paris. I have among my papers notes of remarkable fires. But five years have passed since I left France, and wishing to have a taste of family life, I have been a valet in England. Now, finding myself out of a situation, and having learned that Monsieur Phileas Fogg was the most exact and the most settled gentleman in the United Kingdom, I have presented myself to monsieur with the hope of living tranquilly with him, and of forgetting even the name of Passepartout."

"Passepartout suits me," replied the gentleman. "You are recommended to me. I have good reports concerning you. You know my conditions?"

"Yes, sir."

"Well, what time have you?"

"Twenty-two minutes after eleven," replied Passepartout, drawing from the depths of his pocket an enormous silver watch.

"You are slow," said Mr. Fogg.

"Pardon me, monsieur, but it is impossible."

"You are four minutes too slow. It does not matter. It suffices to state the difference. Then, from this moment—twenty-nine minutes after eleven o'clock a.m., this Wednesday, October 2,1872, you are in my service."

That said, Phileas Fogg rose, took his hat in his left hand, placed it upon his head with an automatic movement, and disappeared without another word.

Passepartout heard the street door close once; it was his new master going out; then a second time; it was his predecessor, James Forster, departing in his turn. Passepartout remained alone in the house in Saville Row.

CHAPTER 2

In which Passepartout is Convinced that he has Found his ideal

"Upon my word," said Passepartout to himself, "I have known at Madame Tussaud's good people as lively as my new master!"

It is proper to say here that Madame Tussaud's "good people"' are wax figures, much visited in London, and who, indeed, are only wanting in speech.

During the few minutes that he had interviewed Phileas Fogg, Passepartout had examined his future master, rapidly but carefully. He was a man that might be forty years old, of fine handsome face, of tall figure, which a slight corpulence did not disparage, his hair and whiskers light, his forehead compact, without appearance of wrinkles at the temples, his face rather pale than flushed, his teeth magnificent. He appeared to possess in the highest degree what physiognomists call "repose in action," a quality common to those who do more work than talking. Calm, phlegmatic, with a clear eye and immovable eyelid, he was the finished type of those cool-blooded Englishmen so frequently met in the United Kingdom, and whose somewhat academic posture Angelica Kauffman has marvellously reproduced under her pencil. Seen in the various acts of his existence, this gentleman gave the idea of a well-balanced being in all his parts, evenly hung, as perfect as a Leroy or Earnshaw chronometer. Indeed Phileas Fogg was exactness personified, which was seen clearly from "the expression of his feet and his hands," for with man, as well as with the animals, the limbs themselves are organs expressive of the passions.

Phileas Fogg was one of those mathematically exact people, who, never hurried and always ready, are economical of their steps and their motions. He never made one stride too many, always going by the shortest route. He did not give an idle look. He did not allow himself a superfluous gesture. He had never been seen moved or troubled. He was a man of the least possible haste, but he always arrived in time. However, it will be understood that he lived alone, and, so to speak, outside of every social relation. He knew that in life one must take his share of friction, and as frictions retard, he never rubbed against anyone.

As for Jean, called Passepartout, a true Parisian of Paris, he had sought vainly for a master to whom he could attach himself, in the five years that he lived in England and served as a valet in London. Passepartout was not one of those Frontins or Mascarilles, who, with high shoulders, nose high in air, a look of assurance, and staring eye, are only impudent dunces. No, Passepartout was a good fellow, of amiable physiognomy, his lips a little prominent, always ready to taste or caress, a mild and serviceable being, with one of those good round heads that we like to see on the shoulders of a friend. His eyes were blue, his complexion rosy, his face fat enough for him to see his cheek-bones, his chest broad, his form full, his muscles vigorous, and he possessed a herculean strength which his youthful exercise had splendidly developed. His brown hair was somewhat tumbled. If the ancient sculptors knew eighteen ways of arranging Minerva's hair, Passepartout knew of but one for fixing his own: three strokes of a large tooth-comb, and it was dressed.

The most meagre stock of prudence would not permit of saying that the expansive character of this young man would agree with that of Phileas Fogg. Would Passepartout be in all respects exactly the servant that his master needed? That would only be seen by using him. After having had, as we have seen, quite a wandering youth, he longed for repose. Having heard the exactness and proverbial coolness of the English gentlemen praised, he came to seek his fortune in England. But until the present, Fate had treated him badly. He had not been able to take root anywhere. He had served in ten different houses. In every one the people were capricious and irregular, running after adventures or about the country— which no longer suited Passepartout. His last master, young Lord Longsferry, Member of Parliament, after having passed his nights in the Haymarket oyster rooms, returned home too frequently on the shoulders of policemen. Passepartout wishing, above all things, to be able to respect his master, ventured some mild remarks, which were badly received, and he left. In the meantime, he learned that Phileas Fogg, Esq., was hunting for a servant. He made some inquiry about this gentleman. A person whose existence was so regular, who never slept in a strange bed, who did not travel, who was never absent, not even for a day, could not but suit him. He presented himself, and was accepted under the circumstances that we already know.

At half-past eleven, Passepartout found himself alone in the

Saville Row mansion. He immediately commenced its inspection, going over it from cellar to garret. This clean, well-ordered, austere, Puritan house, well organised for servants, pleased him. It produced the effect upon him of a fine snail-shell, but one lighted and heated by gas, for carburetted hydrogen answered both purposes here. Passepartout found without difficulty, in the second story, the room designed for him. It suited him. Electric bells and speaking-tubes put it in communication with the lower stories. On the mantel an electric clock corresponded with the one in Phileas Fogg's bed-chamber, both beating the same second at the same instant. "That suits me, that suits me!" said Passepartout.

He observed also in his room a notice fastened above the clock. It was the programme for the daily service. It comprised—from eight o'clock in the morning, the regular hour at which Phileas Fogg rose, until half-past eleven, the hour at which he left his house to breakfast at the Reform Club—all the details of the service, the tea and toast at twenty-three minutes after eight, the shaving-water at thirty-seven minutes after nine, the toilet at twenty minutes before ten, etc. Then from half-past eleven in the morning until midnight, the hour at which the methodical gentleman retired—everything was noted down, foreseen, and regulated. Passepartout took a pleasure in contemplating this programme, and impressing upon his mind its various directions.

As to the gentleman's wardrobe, it was in very good taste, and wonderfully complete. Each pair of pantaloons, coat or vest, bore a regular number, which was also entered upon a register, indicating the date at which, according to the season, these garments were to be worn in their turn. The same rule applied to his shoes.

In short, in this house in Saville Row—which, in the time of the illustrious but dissipated Sheridan, must have been the temple of disorder—its comfortable furniture indicated a delightful ease. There was no study, there were no books, which would have been of no use to Mr. Fogg, since the Reform Club placed at his disposal two libraries, the one devoted to literature, the other to law and politics. In his

12

bed-chamber there was a medium-sized safe, whose construction protected it from fire as well as from burglars. There were no weapons in the house, neither for the chase, nor for war. Everything there denoted the most peaceful habits.

After having minutely examined the dwelling, Passepartout rubbed his hands, his broad face brightened, and he repeated cheerfully: "This suits me! This is the place for me! Mr. Fogg and I will understand each other perfectly. A home-body, and so methodical! A genuine automaton! Well, I am not sorry to serve an automaton!"

CHAPTER 3

In which a conversation takes place which may cost Phileas Fogg dearly

Phileas Fogg had left his house in Saville Row at half-past eleven, and after putting his right foot before his left foot five hundred and seventy-five times, and his left foot before his right foot five hundred and seventy-six times, he arrived at the Reform Club, a spacious and lofty building in Pall Mall, which cost not less than three millions to build.

Phileas Fogg repaired immediately to the dining-room, whose nine windows opened upon a fine garden with trees already gilded by autumn. There, he took his seat at his regular table where the plate was awaiting him. His breakfast consisted of a side-dish, a boiled fish with Reading sauce of first quality, a scarlet slice of roast beef garnished with mushrooms, a rhubarb and gooseberry tart, and a bit of Chester cheese, the whole washed down with a few cups of that excellent tea, specially gathered for the stores of the Reform Club.

At forty-seven minutes past noon, this gentleman rose and turned his steps towards the large hall, a sumptuous apartment, adorned with paintings in elegant frames. There, a servant handed him *The Times* uncut, the tiresome cutting of which he managed with a steadiness of hand which denoted great practice in this difficult operation. The reading of this journal occupied Phileas Fogg until a quarter before four, and that of the *Standard*, which succeeded it, lasted until dinner. This repast passed off in the same way as the breakfast, with the addition of "Royal British Sauce."

At twenty minutes before six, the gentleman reappeared in the large hall, and was absorbed in the reading of the *Morning Chronicle*.

Half an hour later, various members of the Reform Club entered and came near the fireplace, in which a coal fire was burning. They were the usual partners of Phileas Fogg; like himself, passionate players of whist—the engineer, Andrew Stuart; the bankers, John Sullivan and Samuel Fallentin; the brewer, Thomas Flanagan; Gauthier Ralph, one of the directors of the Bank of England—rich and respected personages, even in this Club, counting among his members the *élite* of trade and finance.

"Well, Ralph," asked Thomas Flanagan, "how about that robbery?"

"Why," replied Andrew Stuart, "the bank will lose the money."

"I hope, on the contrary," said Gauthier Ralph, "that we will put our hands on the robber. Detectives, very skilful fellows, have been sent to America and the Continent, to all the principal ports of embarkation and debarkation, and it will be difficult for this fellow to escape."

"But you have the description of the robber?" asked Andrew Stuart.

"In the first place, he is not a robber," replied Gauthier Ralph seriously.

"How, is he not a robber, this fellow who has abstracted fifty-five thousand pounds in bank-notes?"

"No," replied Gauthier Ralph.

"Is he, then, a manufacturer" said John Sullivan.

"The *Morning Chronicle* assures us that he is a gentleman."

The party that made this reply was no other than Phileas Fogg, whose head then emerged from the mass of papers heaped around him. At the same time, he greeted his colleagues, who returned his salutation. The matter under discussion, and which the various journals of the United Kingdom were discussing ardently, had occurred three days before, on the 29th of September. A package of bank-notes, making the enormous sum of fifty-five thousand pounds, had been taken from the counter of the principal cashier of the Bank of England. The Under-Governor, Gauthier Ralph, only replied to anyone who was astonished that such a robbery could have been so easily accomplished, that at this very moment the cashier was occupied with registering a receipt of three shillings and sixpence, and that he could not have his eyes everywhere.

But it is proper to be remarked here—which makes the robbery less mysterious—that this admirable establishment, the Bank of England, seems to care very much for the dignity of the public. There are neither guards nor gratings; gold, silver, and bank-notes being freely exposed, and, so to speak, at the mercy of the first comer. They would not suspect the honour of anyone passing by. One of the best observers of English customs relates the following: He had the curiosity to examine closely, in one of the rooms of the bank, where he was one day, an ingot of gold, weighing seven to eight pounds, which was lying exposed on the cashier's table; he picked up this ingot, examined it, passed it to his neighbour, and he to another, so that the ingot, passing from hand to hand, went as far as the end of a dark entry, and did not return to its place for half an hour, and the cashier had not once raised his head.

But on the twenty-ninth of September, matters did not turn out quite in this way. The package of bank-notes did not return, and when the magnificent dock, hung above the "drawing office" announced at five o'clock the closing of the office, the Bank of England had only to pass fifty-five thousand pounds to the account of profit and loss.

The robbery being duly known, agents, detectives, selected

15

from the most skilful, were sent to the principal ports—Liverpool, Glasgow, Havre, Suez, Brindisi, New York, etc., with the promise, in case of success, of a reward of two thousand pounds and five per cent of the amount recovered. Whilst waiting for the information which the investigation, commenced immediately, ought to furnish, the detectives were charged with watching carefully all arriving and departing travellers.

As the *Morning Chronicle* said, there was good reason for supposing that the robber was not a member of any of the robber bands of England. During this day, the twenty-ninth of September, a well-dressed gentleman, of good manners, of a distinguished air, had been noticed going in and out of the paying room, the scene of the robbery. The investigation allowed a pretty accurate description of the gentleman to be made out, which was at once sent to all the detectives of the United Kingdom and of the Continent. Some hopeful minds, and Gauthier Ralph was one of the number, believed that they had good reason to expect that the robber would not escape.

As may be supposed, this affair was the talk of all London and throughout England.

It was discussed, and sides were taken vehemently for or against the probabilities of success of the city police. It will not be surprising, then, to hear the members of the Reform Club treating the same subject, all the more that one of the Under-Governors of the Bank was among them.

Honourable Gauthier Ralph was not willing to doubt the result of the search, considering that the reward offered ought to sharpen peculiarly the zeal and intelligence of the agents. But his colleague, Andrew Stuart, was far from sharing this confidence. The discussion continued then between the gentlemen, who were seated at a whist table, Stuart having Flanagan as a partner, and Fallentin Phileas Fogg. During the playing the parties did not speak, but between the rubbers the interrupted conversation was fully revived.

"I maintain," said Andrew Stuart, "that the chances are in favour of the robber, who must be a skilful fellow!"

"Well," replied Ralph, "there is not a single country where he can take refuge."

"Pshaw!"

"Where do you suppose he might go?"

"I don't know about that," replied Andrew Stuart, "but after all, the world is big enough."

"It was formerly," said Phileas Fogg in a low tone. Then he added: "It is your turn to cut, sir," presenting the cards to Thomas Flanagan.

The discussion was suspended during the rubber. But Andrew Stuart soon resumed it, saying:

"How, formerly? Has the world grown smaller perchance?"

"Without doubt," replied Gauthier Ralph. "I am of the opinion of Mr. Fogg. The world has grown smaller, since we can go round it now ten times quicker than one hundred years ago. And, in the case with which we are now occupied, this is what will render the search more rapid."

"And will render more easy, also, the flight of the robber."

"It is your turn to play, Mr. Stuart," said Phileas Fogg.

But the incredulous Stuart was not convinced, and when the hand was finished, he replied: "It must be confessed, Mr. Ralph, that you have found a funny way of saying that the world has grown smaller! Because the tour of it is now made in three months—"

"In eighty days only," said Phileas Fogg.

"Yes, gentlemen," added John Sullivan, "eighty days, since the section between Rothal and Allahabad, on the Great Indian Peninsular Railway, has been opened. Here is the calculation made by the *Morning Chronicle*:

From London to Suez via Mont Cenis and Brindisi, by rail and steamers	7 days
From Suez to Bombay, steamer	13 days
From Bombay to Calcutta, rail	3 days
From Calcutta to Hong-Kong (China) steamer	13 days
From Hong-Kong to Yokohama (Japan) steamer	6 days
From Yokohama to San Francisco, steamer	22 days
From San Francisco to New York, rail	7 days
From New York to London, steamer and rail	9 days

80 days"

"Yes, eighty days!" exclaimed Andrew Stuart, who, by inattention, made a wrong deal, "but not including bad weather, contrary winds, shipwrecks, running off the track, etc."

"Everything included," replied Phileas Fogg, continuing to play, for this time the discussion no longer respected the game.

"Even if the Hindus or the Indians tear up the rails!" exclaimed Andrew Stuart, "if they stop the trains, plunder the cars, and scalp the passengers!"

"All included," replied Phileas Fogg, who, throwing down his cards, added: "Two trumps."

Andrew Stuart, whose turn it was to deal, gathered up the cards, saying:

"Theoretically, you are right, Mr. Fogg, but practically—"

"Practically also, Mr. Stuart."

"I would like very much to see you do it."

"It depends only upon you. Let us start together."

"Heaven preserve me!" exclaimed Stuart, abut I would willingly wager four thousand pounds that such a journey, made under these conditions, is impossible."

"On the contrary, quite possible," replied Mr. Fogg.

"Well, make it, then!"

"The tour of the world in eighty days?"

"Yes!"

"I am willing."

"When?"

"At once. Only I warn you that I shall do it at your expense."

"It is folly!" cried Stuart, who was beginning to be vexed at the persistence of his partner. "Stop! let us play rather."

"Deal again, then," replied Phileas Fogg, "for there is a false deal."

Andrew Stuart took up the cards again with a feverish hand; then suddenly, placing them upon the table, he said:

"Well, Mr. Fogg, yes, and I bet four thousand pounds!"

"My dear Stuart," said Fallentin, "compose yourself It is not serious."

"When I say—'I bet,'" replied Andrew Stuart, "it is always serious."

"So be it," said Mr. Fogg, and then, turning to his companions, continued: "I have twenty thousand pounds deposited at Baring Brothers. I will willingly risk them—"

"Twenty thousand pounds!" cried John Sullivan. "Twenty thousand pounds, which an unforeseen delay may make you lose."

"The unforeseen does not exist," replied Phileas Fogg quietly.

"But, Mr. Fogg, this period of eighty days is calculated only as a minimum of time?"

"A minimum well employed suffices for everything."

"But in order not to exceed it, you must jump mathematically from the trains into the steamers, and from the steamers upon the trains!"

"I will jump mathematically."

"That is a joke."

"A good Englishman never jokes when so serious a matter as a wager is in question," replied Phileas Fogg. "I bet twenty thousand pounds against who will that I will make the tour of the world in eighty days or less—that is, nineteen hundred and twenty hours, or one hundred and fifteen thousand two hundred minutes. Do you accept?"

"We accept," replied Messrs. Stuart, Fallentin, Sullivan, Flanagan, and Ralph, after having consulted.

"Very well," said Mr. Fogg. he Dover train starts at eight forty-five. I shall take it."

"This very evening?" asked Stuart.

"This very evening," replied Phileas Fogg. Then he added, consulting a pocket almanac, "since to-day is Wednesday, the second of October, I ought to be back in London, in this very saloon of the Reform Club, on Saturday, the twenty-first of December, at eight forty-five in the evening, in default of which the twenty thousand pounds at present deposited to my credit with Baring Brothers will belong to you, gentlemen, in fast and by right. Here is a cheque of like amount."

A memorandum of the wager was made and signed on the spot by the six parties in interest. Phileas Fogg had remained cool. He had certainly not bet to win, and had risked only these twenty thousand pounds—the half of his fortune—because he foresaw that he might have to expend the other half to carry out this difficult, not to say impracticable, project. As for his opponents, they seemed affected, not on account of the stake, but because they had a sort of scruple against a contest under these conditions.

Seven o'clock then struck. They offered to Mr. Fogg to stop playing, so that he could make his preparations for departure.

"I am always ready," replied this tranquil gentleman, and dealing the cards, he said: "Diamonds are trumps. It is your turn to play, Mr. Stuart."

CHAPTER 4

In which Phileas Fogg surprises Passepartout, his Servant, beyond measure

At twenty-five minutes after seven, Phileas Fogg having gained twenty guineas at whist, took leave of his honourable colleagues, and left the Reform. Club. At ten minutes of eight, he opened the door of his house and entered.

Passepartout, who had conscientiously studied his programme, was quite surprised at seeing Mr. Fogg guilty of the inexactness of appearing at this unusual hour. According to the notice, the occupant of Saville Row ought not to return before midnight precisely.

Phileas Fogg first went to his bedroom. Then he called "Passepartout!"

Passepartout could not reply, for this call could not be addressed to him, as it was not the hour.

"Passepartout," Mr. Fogg called again without raising his voice much.

Passepartout presented himself

"It is the second time that I have called you," said Mr. Fogg.

"But it is not midnight," replied Passepartout, with his watch in his hand.

"I know it," continued Phileas Fogg, "and I do not find fault with you. We leave in ten minutes for Dover and Calais."

A sort of faint grimace appeared on the round face of the French-man. It was evident that he had not fully understood.

"Monsieur is going to leave home?" he asked.

"Yes," replied Phileas Fogg. "We are going to make the tour of the world."

Passepartout, with his eyes wide open, his eyebrows raised, his arms extended, and his body collapsed, presented all the symptoms of an astonishment amounting to stupor.

"The tour of the world!" he murmured.

"In eighty days," replied Mr. Fogg. "So we have not a moment to lose."

"But the trunks?" said Passepartout, who was unconsciously swinging his head from right to left.

"No trunks necessary. Only a carpet-bag. In it two woollen shirts and three pairs of stockings. The same for you. We will purchase on the way. You may bring down my mackintosh and travelling cloak, also stout shoes, although we shall walk but little or not at all. Go."

Passepartout would have liked to make reply. He could not. He left Mr. Fogg's room, went up to his own, fell back into a chair, and making use of a common phrase in his country, he said: "Well, well, that's pretty tough. I who wanted to remain quiet!"

And mechanically he made his preparations for departure. The tour of the world in eighty days! Was he doing business with a madman? No. It was a joke, perhaps. They were going to Dover. Good. To Calais. Let it be so. After all, it could not cross the grain of the good fellow very much, who had not trod the soil of his native country for five years. Perhaps they would go as far as Paris, and, indeed, it would give him pleasure to see the great capital again. But, surely, a gentleman so careful of his steps would stop there. Yes, doubtless; but it was not less true that he was starting out, that he was leaving home, this gentleman who, until this time, had been such a home-body!

By eight o'clock, Passepartout had put in order the modest bag which contained his wardrobe and that of his master; then, his mind still disturbed, he left his room, the door of which he closed carefully, and he rejoined Mr. Fogg.

Mr. Fogg was ready. He carried under his arm *Bradshaw's Continental Railway Steam Transit and General Guide*, which was to furnish him all the necessary directions for his journey. He took the bag from Passepartout's hands, opened it, and slipped into it a heavy package of those fine bank-notes which are current in all countries.

"You have forgotten nothing.?" he asked.

"Nothing, monsieur."

"My mackintosh and cloak?"

"Here they are."

"Good; take this bag," and Mr. Fogg handed it to Passepartout. "And take good care of it," he added, "there are twenty thousand pounds in it."

The bag nearly slipped out of Passepartout's hands, as if the twenty thousand pounds had been in gold, and weighed very heavy.

The master and servant then descended, and the street door was double-locked. At the end of Saville Row there was a carriage stand. Phileas Fogg and his servant got into a cab, which was rapidly driven towards Charing Cross Station, at which one of the branches of the South Eastern Railway touches. At twenty minutes after eight the cab stopped before the gate of the station. Passepartout jumped out. His master followed him, and paid the driver. At this moment a poor beggar woman, holding a child in her arms, her bare feet all muddy, her head covered with a wretched bonnet, from which hung a tattered feather, and a ragged shawl over her other torn garments, approached Mr. Fogg, and asked him for help.

Mr. Fogg drew from his pocket the twenty guineas which he had just won at whist, and giving them to the woman, said:

"Here, my good woman, I'm glad to have met you." Then he passed on.

Passepartout had something like a sensation of moisture about his eyes. His master had made an impression upon his heart.

Mr. Fogg and he went immediately into the large sitting-room of the station. There Phileas Fogg gave Passepartout the order to get two first-class tickets for Paris. Then returning, he noticed his five colleagues of the Reform Club.

"Gentlemen, I am going," he said, "and the various vises put upon a passport which I take for that purpose will enable you on my return, to verify my journey."

"Oh! Mr. Fogg," replied Gauthier Ralph, "that is useless. We will depend upon your honour as a gentleman."

"It is better so," said Mr. Fogg.

"You do not forget that you ought to be back—" remarked Andrew Stuart.

"In eighty days," replied Mr. Fogg. "Saturday, December 21, 1872, at quarter before nine p.m. *Au revoir*, gentlemen."

At forty minutes after eight, Phileas Fogg and his servant took their seats in the same compartment. At eight forty-five the whistle sounded, and the train started.

The night was dark. A fine rain was falling. Phileas Fogg, leaning back in his corner, did not speak. Passepartout, still stupefied, mechanically hugged up the bag with the bank-notes.

But the train had not passed Sydenham, when Passepartout uttered a real cry of despair!

"What is the matter" asked Mr. Fogg.

"Why—in—in my haste—my disturbed state of mind, I forgot— —"

"Forgot what?"

"To turn off the gas in my room."

"Very well, young man," replied Mr. Fogg coldly, "it will burn at your expense."

CHAPTER 5

In which a new Security appears on the London Exchange

Phileas Fogg, in leaving London, doubtless did not suspect the great excitement which his departure was going to create. The news of the wager spread first in the Reform Club, and produced quite a stir among the members of the honourable circle. Then from the Club it went into the papers, through the medium of the reporters, and from the papers to the public of London and the entire United Kingdom. The question of "the tour of the world" was commented upon, discussed, dissected, with as much passion and warmth as if it were a new Alabama affair. Some took sides with Phileas Fogg, others—and they soon formed a considerable majority—declared against him. To accomplish this tour of the world otherwise than in theory and upon paper, in this minimum of time, with the means of communication employed at present, it was not only impossible, it was visionary. *The Times*, the *Standard*, the *Evening Star*, the *Morning Chronicle*, and twenty other papers of large circulation, declared against Mr. Fogg. The *Daily Telegraph* alone sustained him to a certain extent. Phileas Fogg was generally treated as a maniac, as a fool, and his colleagues were blamed for having taken up this wager, which impeached the soundness of the mental faculties of its originator. Extremely passionate, but very logical, articles appeared upon the subject. The interest felt in England for everything concerning geography is well known. So there was not a reader, to whatever class he belonged, who did not devour the columns devoted to Phileas Fogg.

During the first few days, a few bold spirits, principally ladies, were in favour of him, especially after the *Illustrated London News* had published his picture, copied from his photograph deposited in the archives of the Reform Club. Certain gentlemen dared to say, "Humph! why not, after all? More extraordinary things have been seen!" These were particularly the readers of the *Daily Telegraph* But it was soon felt that this journal commenced to be weaker in its support.

In fact, a long article appeared on the seventh of October, in the *Bulletin* of the Royal Geographical Society. It treated the question from all points of view, and demonstrated clearly the folly of the enterprise. According to this article, everything was against the traveller, the obstacles of man and the obstacles of nature. To succeed in this project, it was necessary to admit a miraculous agreement of the hours of arrival and departure, an agreement which did not exist, and which could not exist. The arrival of trains at a fixed hour could be counted upon strictly, and in Europe, where relatively short distances are in question; but when three days are employed to cross India, and seven days to cross the United States, could the elements of such a problem be established to a nicety? The accidents to machinery, running of trains off the track, collisions, bad weather, and the accumulations of snows, were they not all against Phileas Fogg? Would he not find himself in winter on the steamers at the mercy of the winds or of the fogs? Is it then so rare that the best steamers of the ocean lines experience delays of two or three days? But one delay was sufficient to break irreparably the chain of communication. If Phileas Fogg missed only by a few hours the departure of a steamer, he would be compelled to wait for the next steamer, and in this way his journey would be irrevocably compromised. The article made a great sensation. Nearly all the papers copied it, and the stock in Phileas Fogg went down in a marked degree.

During the first few days which followed the departure of the gentleman, important business transactions had been made on the strength of his undertaking. The world of betters in England is a more intelligent and elevated world than that of gamblers. To bet is according to the English temperament; so that not only the various members of the Reform Club made heavy bets for or against Phileas Fogg, but the mass of the public entered into the movement. Phileas Fogg was entered like a racehorse in a sort of stud book. A bond was issued, which was immediately quoted upon the London Exchange. "Phileas Fogg" was "bid" or "asked" firm or above par, and enormous transactions were made. But five days after his departure, after the appearance of the article in the *Bulletin* of the Geographical Society, the offerings commenced to come in plentifully. "Phileas Fogg" declined. It was offered in bundles. Taken first at five, then at ten, it was finally taken only at twenty, at fifty, at one hundred!

Only one adherent remained steadfast to him. It was the old paralytic, Lord Albemarle. This honourable gentleman, confined to his armchair, would have given his fortune to be able to make the tour of the world, even in ten years. He bet five thousand pounds in favour of Phileas Fogg, and even when the folly as well as the uselessness of the project was demonstrated to him, he contented himself with replying: "If the thing is feasible, it is well that an Englishman should be the first to do it."

The adherents of Phileas Fogg became fewer and fewer; everybody, and not without reason, was putting himself against him; bets were taken at one hundred and fifty and two hundred against one, when, seven days after his departure, an entirely unexpected incident caused them not to be taken at all.

At nine o'clock in the evening of this day, the Commissioner of the Metropolitan Police received a telegraphic dispatch in the following words:

"SUEZ TO LONDON.
"Cowan, Commissioner of Police, Central Office, Scotland Square: I have the bank robber, Phileas Fogg. Send without delay warrant of arrest to Bombay, British India.
"FIX, *Detective*."

The effect of this dispatch was immediate. The honourable gentleman disappeared to make room for the banknote robber. His photograph, deposited at the Reform Club with those of his colleagues, was examined. It reproduced, feature by

26

feature, the man whose description had been furnished by the commission of inquiry. They recalled how mysterious Phileas Fogg's life had been, his isolation, his sudden departure; and it appeared evident that this person, under the pretext of a journey round the world, and supporting it by a senseless bet, had had no other aim than to mislead the agents of the English police.

Chapter 6

In which the Agent, Fix, shows a very proper impatience

These are the circumstances under which the dispatch concerning Mr. Phileas Fogg had been sent:

On Wednesday, the ninth of October, there was expected at Suez, at eleven o'clock a m., the iron steamer *Mongolia*, of the Peninsular and Oriental Company, sharp built, with a spar deck, of two thousand eight hundred tons burden, and nominally of five hundred horse-power. The *Mongolia* made regular trips from Brindisi to Bombay by the Suez Canal. It was one of the fastest sailers of the line, and always exceeded the regular rate of speed, that is, ten miles an hour between Brindisi and Suez, and nine and fifty-three hundredths miles between Suez and Bombay.

Whilst waiting for the arrival of the *Mongolia*, two men were walking up and down the wharf, in the midst of the crowd of natives and foreigners who come together in this town, no longer a small one, to which the great work of M. Lesseps assures a great future.

One of these men was the Consular agent of the United Kingdom, settled at Suez, who, in spite of the doleful prognostications of the British Government, and the sinister predictions of Stephenson, the engineer, saw English ships passing through this canal every day, thus cutting off one-half the old route from England to the East Indies around the Cape of Good Hope.

The other was a small, spare man, of a quiet, intelligent, nervous face, who was contracting his eyebrows with remarkabe persistence. Under his long eyelashes there shone very bright eyes, but whose brilliancy he could suppress at will. At this moment he showed some signs of impatience, going, coming, unable to remain in one spot.

The name of this man was Fix, and he was one of the detectives, or agents of the English police, that had been sent to the various seaports after the robbery committed upon the Bank of England. This Fix was to watch, with the greatest care, all travellers taking the Suez route, and if one of them seemed suspicious to him, to follow him up whilst waiting for a warrant of arrest Just two days before Fix had received from the Commissioner of the Metropolitan Police the description of the supposed robber. It was that of the distinguished and well-dressed gentleman who had been noticed in the paying-room of the bank. The detective, evidently much excited by the large reward promised in case of success, was waiting then with an impatience easy to understand, the arrival of the *Mongolia*

"And you say, Consul," he asked for the tenth time, "this vessel cannot be behind time?"

"No, Mr. Fix," replied the Consul. "She was signalled yesterday off Port Said, and the one hundred and sixty kilometres of the canal are of no moment for such a vessel I repeat to you that the *Mongolia* has always obtained the reward of twenty-five pounds given by the Government for every gain of twenty-four hours over the regulation time."

"This steamer comes directly from Brindisi?" asked Fix.

"Directly from Brindisi, where it took on the India mail; from Brindisi, which it left on Saturday, at five o'clock p.m. So have patience; it cannot be behind-hand in arriving. But really I do not see how, with the description you have received, you could recognise your man, if he is on board the *Mongolia*"

"Consul," replied Fix, awe feel these people rather than know them. You must have a scent for them, and the scent is like a special sense, in which are united hearing, sight, and smell. I have in my life arrested more than one of these gentlemen, and, provided that my robber is on board, I will venture that he will not slip from my hands."

"I hope so, Mr. Fix, for it is a very heavy robbery."

"A magnificent robbery," replied the enthusiastic detective. "Fifty-five thousand pounds! We don't often have such windfalls! The robbers are becoming mean fellows. The race of Jack Sheppard is dying out! They are hung now for a few shillings!"

"Mr. Fix," replied the Consul, "you speak in such a way that I earnestly wish you to succeed; but I repeat to you that, from the circumstances in which you find yourself, I fear that it will be difficult. Do you not know that, according to the description you have received, this robber resembles an honest man exactly?"

"Consul," replied the detective dogmatically, "great robbers always resemble honest people. You understand that those who have rogues' faces have but one course to take to remain honest, otherwise they would be arrested. Honest physiognomies are the very ones that must be unmasked. It is a difficult task, I admit; and it is not a trade so much as an art."

It is seen that the aforesaid Fix was not wanting in a certain amount of self-conceit.

In the meantime the wharf was becoming lively little by little. Sailors of various nationalities, merchants, shipbrokers, porters, and fellahs, were coming together in large numbers. The arrival of the steamer was evidently near. The weather was quite fine, but the atmosphere was cold from the east wind. A few minarets towered above the town in the pale rays of the sun. Towards the south, a jetty of about two thousand yards long extended like an arm into the Suez roadstead. Several fishing and coasting vessels were tossing upon the surface of the Red Sea, some of which preserved in their style the elegant shape of the ancient galley.

Moving among this crowd, Fix, from the habit of his profession, was carefully examining the passers-by with a rapid glance.

It was then half-past ten.

"But this steamer will never arrive!" he exclaimed on hearing the port clock strike.

"She cannot be far off," replied the Consul.

"How long will she stop at Suez" asked Fix.

"Four hours. Time enough to take in coal. From Suez to Aden, at the other end of the Red Sea, is reckoned thirteen hundred and ten miles, and it is necessary to lay in fuel."

"And from Suez this vessel goes directly to Bombay?"

"Directly, without breaking bulk."

"Well, then," said Fix, "if the robber has taken this route and this vessel, it must be in his plan to disembark at Suez, in order to reach by another route the Dutch or French possessions of Asia He must know very well that he would not be safe in India, which is an English country."

"Unless he is a very shrewd man," replied the Consul. "You know that an English criminal is always better concealed in London than he would be abroad."

After this idea, which gave the detective much food for reflection, the Consul returned to his office, situated at a short distance. The detective remained alone, affected by a certain nervous impatience, having the rather singular presentiment that his robber was to be found aboard the *Mongolia*—and truly, if this rascal had left England with the intention of reaching the New World, the East India route, being watched less, or more difficult to watch than that of the Atlantic, ought to have had his preference.

Fix was not long left to his reflections. Sharp whistles announced the arrival of the steamer. The entire horde of porters and fellahs rushed towards the wharf in a bustle, somewhat inconveniencing the limbs and the clothing of the passengers. A dozen boats put off from the shore to meet the *Mongolia* Soon was seen the enormous hull of the *Mongolia* passing between the shores of the canal, and eleven o'clock was striking when the seamer came to anchor in the roadstead, while the escaping of the steam made a great noise. There was quite a number of passengers aboard. Some remained on the spar-deck, contemplating the picturesque panorama of the town; but the most of them came ashore in the boats which had gone to hail the *Mongolia*.

Fix was examining carefully all those that landed, when one of them approached him, after having vigorously pushed back the fellahs who overwhelmed him with their offers of service, and asked him very politely if he could show him the office of the English consular agent. And at the same time this passenger presented a passport upon which he doubtless desired to have the British *visé*. Fix instinctively took the passport, and at a glance read the description in it. An involuntary movement almost escaped him. The sheet trembled in his hand. The description contained in the passport was identical with that which he had received from the Commissioner of the Metropolitan Police.

"This passport is not yours?" he said to the passenger.

"No," replied the latter, "it is my master's passport."

"And your master?"

"Remained on board."

"But," continued the detective, "he must present himself in person at the Consul office to establish his identity."

"What, is that necessary?"

"Indispensable."

"And where is the office?"

"There at the corner of the square," replied the detective, pointing out a house two hundred paces off.

"Then I must go for my master, who will not be pleased to have his plans deranged!"

Thereupon the passenger bowed to Fix and returned aboard the steamer.

31

CHAPTER 7

Which shows once more the uselessness of Passports in Police Matters

The detective left the wharf and turned quickly towards the Consul's office. Immediately upon his pressing demand he was ushered into the presence of that official.

"Consul," he said, without any other preamble, "I have strong reasons for believing that our man has taken passage aboard the *Mongolia*," and Fix related what had passed between the servant and himself with reference to the passport.

"Well Mr. Fix," replied the Consul, "I would not be sorry to see the face of this rogue. But perhaps he will not present himself at my office if he is what you suppose. A robber does not like to leave behind him the tricks of his passage, and besides the formality of passports is no longer obligatory."

"Consul," replied the detective, "if he is a shrewd man, as we think, he will come."

"To have his passport *viséd*?"

"Yes. Passports never serve but to incommode honest people and to aid the flight of rogues. I warrant you that his will be all regular, but I hope certainly that you will not *visé it*"

"And why not? If his passport is regular I have no sight to refuse my *visé*."

"But, Consul, I must retain this man until I have received from London a warrant of arrest."

"Ah, Mr. Fix, that is your business," replied the Consul, "but I—I cannot—"

The Consul did not finish his phrase. At this moment there was a knock at the door of his private office, and the office boy brought in two foreigners, one of whom was the very servant who had been talking with the detective. They were, indeed, the master and servant. The master presented his passport, asking the Consul briefly to be kind enough to vise it. The latter took the passport and read it carefully, while Fix, in one corner of the room, was observing or rather devouring the stranger with his eyes.

When the Consul had finished reading, he asked:

"You are Phileas Fogg, Esq.?"

"Yes, sir," replied the gentleman.

"And this man is your servant.?"

"Yes, a Frenchman named Passepartout."

"You come from London.?"

"Yes."

"And you are going?"

"To Bombay."

"Well, sir, you know that this formality of the *visé* is useless, and that we no longer demand the presentation of the passport?"

"I know it, sir," replied Phileas Fogg, "but I wish to prove by your *visé* my trip to Suez."

"Very well, sir."

And the Consul having signed and dated the passport, affixed his seal, Mr. Fogg settled the fee, and having bowed coldly, he went out, followed by his servant.

"Well?" asked the detective.

"Well," replied the Consul, "he has the appearance of a perfectly honest man!"

"Possibly," replied Fix; "but that is not the question with us. Do you find, Consul, that this phlegmatic gentleman resembles, feature for feature, the robber whose description I have received?"

"I agree with you, but you know that all descriptions—"

"I shall have a clear conscience about it, replied Fix. "The servant appears to me less of a riddle than the master. Moreover, he is a Frenchman, who cannot keep from talking. I will see you soon again, Consul."

The detective then went out, intent upon the search for Passepartout.

In the meantime Mr. Fogg, after leaving the Consul's house,

had gone towards the wharf. There he gave some orders to his servant; then he got into a boat, returned on board the *Mongolia*, and went into his cabin. He then took out his memorandum book, in which were the following notes:

"Left London, Wednesday, October 2, 8.45 p.m.

"Arrived at Paris, Thursday, October 3, 7.20 am.

"Left Paris, Thursday, 8.40 am.

"Arrived at Turin, via Mont Cenis, Friday, October 4, 6.35 am.

"Left Turin, Friday, 7.27 a.m.

"Arrived at Brindisi, Saturday, October 5, 4 p.m.

"Set sail on the *Mongolia*, Saturday, 5 p.m.

"Arrived at Suez, Wednesday, October 9, 11 a.m.

"Total of hours consumed, 158 1-2; or in days, 6 1-2 days."

Mr. Fogg wrote down these dates in a guide-book arranged by columns, which indicated, from the 2nd of October to the 21st of December—the month, the day of the month, the day of the week, the stipulated and actual arrivals at each principal point, Paris, Brindisi, Suez, Bombay, Calcutta, Singapore, Hong-Kong, Yokohama, San Francisco, New York, Liverpool, London, and which allowed him to figure the gain made or the loss experienced at each place on the route. In this methodical book he thus kept an account of everything, and Mr. Fogg knew always whether he was ahead of time or behind.

He noted down then this day, Wednesday, October 9, his arrival at Suez, which agreeing with the stipulated arrival, neither made a gain or a loss. Then he had his breakfast served up in his cabin. As to seeing the town, he did not even think of it, being of that race of Englishmen who have their servants visit the countries they pass through.

CHAPTER 8

In which Passepartout perhaps talks a little more than is proper

Fix had in a few moments rejoined Passepartout on the wharf, who was loitering and looking about, not believing that he was obliged not to see anything.

"Well, my friend," said Fix, coming up to him, "is your passport *viséd*?"

"Ah! it is you, monsieur," replied the Frenchman. "Much obliged. It is all in order."

"And you are looking at the country?"

"Yes, but we go so quickly that it seems to me as if I am travelling in a dream. And so we are in Suez?"

"Yes, in Suez."

"In Egypt?"

"You are quite right, in Egypt."

"And in Africa?"

"Yes, in Africa?"

"In Africa?" repeated Passepartout. "I cannot believe it. Just fancy, sir, that I imagined we would not go farther than Paris, and I saw this famous capital again between twenty minutes after seven and twenty minutes of nine in the morning, between the northern station and the Lyons station, through the windows of a cab in a driving rain! I regret it! I would have so much liked to see again Pere Lachaise and the Circus of the Champs-Elysees!"

"You are then in a great hurry?" asked the detective.

"No, I am not, but my master is. By the bye, I must buy some shirts and shoes! We came away without trunks, with a carpet-bag only."

"I am going to take you to a shop where you will find everything you want."

"Monsieur," replied Passepartout, "you are really very kind."

And both started off. Passepartout talked incessantly.

"Above all," he said, "I must take care not to miss the steamer!"

"You have the time," replied Fix, "it is only noon!"

Passepartout pulled out his large watch.

"Noon. Pshaw! It is eight minutes of ten!"

"Your watch is slow!" replied Fix.

"My watch! A family watch that has come down from my great-grandfather! It don't vary five minutes in the year. It is a genuine chronometer."

"I see what is the matter," replied Fix. "You have kept London time, which is about two hours slower than Suez. You must be careful to set your watch at noon in each country."

"What! I touch my watch!" cried Passepartout. "Never."

"Well, then, it will not agree with the sun."

"So much the worse for the sun, monsieur! The sun will be wrong then!"

And the good fellow put his watch back in his fob with a magnificent gesture.

A few moments after Fix said to him: "You left London very hurriedly then.?"

"I should think so! Last Wednesday, at eight o'clock in the evening, contrary to all his habits, Monsieur Fogg returned from his Club, and in three-quarters of an hour afterwards we were off."

"But where is your master going, then?"

"Right straight ahead! He is making the tour of the world!"

"The tour of the world!" cried Fix.

"Yes, in eighty days! On a wager, he says; but, between ourselves, I do not believe it. There is no common sense in it. There must be something else."

"This Mr. Fogg is an original genius?"

"I should think so."

"Is he rich?"

"Evidently, and he carries such a fine sum with him in fresh money on the route! And he doesn't spare his money on the route! Oh! but he has promised a splendid reward to the engineer of the *Mongolia,* if we arrive at Bombay considerably in advance!"

"And you have known him for a long time, this master of yours?"

"I," replied Passepartout, "I entered his service the very day of our departure."

The effect which these answers naturally produced upon the mind of the detective, already strained with excitement, may easily be imagined

This hurried departure from London so short a time after the robbery, this large sum carried away, this haste to arrive in distant countries, this pretext of an eccentric wager, all could have no other effect than to confirm Fix in his ideas. He kept the Frenchman talking, and learned to a certainty that this fellow did not know his master at all, that he lived isolated in London, that he was called rich without the source of his fortune being known, that he was a mysterious man, etc. But at the same time Fix was certain that Phileas Fogg would not get off at Suez, but he was really going to Bombay.

"Is Bombay far from here?" asked Passepartout.

"Pretty far," replied the detective. "It will take you ten days more by sea"

"And where do you locate Bombay?"

"In India"

"In Asia?"

"Of course."

"The deuce! What I was going to tell you—there is one thing that bothers me—it is my burner."

"What burner.?"

"My gas-burner, which I forgot to turn off, and which is burning at my expense. Now, I have calculated that it will cost me two shillings each twenty-four hours, exactly sixpence more than I earn, and you understand that, however little our journey may be prolonged—"

Did Fix understand the matter of the gas? It is improbable. He did not listen any longer, and was coming to a determination. The Frenchman and he had arrived at the shop. Fix left his companion there making his purchases, recommending him not to miss the departure of the *Mongolia*, and he returned in great haste to the Consul's office. Fix had regained his coolness completely, now he was fully convinced.

"Monsieur," said he to the Consul, "I have my man. He is passing himself off as an oddity, who wishes to make the tour of the world in eighty days."

"Then he is a rogue," replied the Consul, "and he counts on returning to London after having deceived all the police of the two continents."

"We will see," replied Fix.

"But are you not mistaken?" asked the Consul once more.

"I am-not mistaken."

"Why, then, has this robber insisted upon having his stopping at Suez confirmed by a *visé?*"

"Why? I do not know, Consul," replied the detective; "but listen to me." And in a few words he related the salient points of his conversation with the servant of the said Fogg.

"'Indeed," said the Consul, "all the presumptions are against this man. And what are you going to do?"

Send a dispatch to London with the urgent request to send to me at once at Bombay a warrant of arrest, set sail upon the *Mongolia*, follow my robber to the Indies, and there, on British soil, accost him politely, with the warrant in one hand, and the other hand upon his shoulder."

Having coolly uttered these words, the detective took leave of the Consul, and repaired to the telegraph office. Thence he dispatched to the Commissioner of the Metropolitan Police, as we have already seen. A quarter of a hour later Fix, with his light baggage in his hand, and besides well supplied with money, went on board the *Mongolia*, and soon the swift steamer was threading its way under full head of steam on the waters of the Red Sea.

CHAPTER 9

In which the Red Sea and the Indian Ocean show themselves Propitious to Phileas Fogg's designs

The distance between Suez and Aden is exactly thirteen hundred and ten miles, and the time-table of the company allows its steamer a period of one hundred and thirty-eight hours to make the distance. The *Mongolia* whose fires were well kept up, moved along rapidly enough to anticipate her stipulated arrival. Nearly all the passengers who came aboard at Brindisi had India for their destination. Some were going to Bombay, others to Calcutta, but via Bombay, for since a railway crosses the entire breadth of the Indian peninsula, it is no longer necessary to double the island of Ceylon.

Among these passengers of the *Mongolia*, there were several officials of the Civil Service and army officers of every grade. Of the latter, some belonged to the British Army, properly so-called, the others commanded the native Sepoy troops, all receiving high salaries, since the Government has taken the place of the powers and charge of the old East India Company; sub-lieutenants receiving £280; brigadiers, £2400; and generals, £4000. The emoluments of officials in the Civil Service are still higher: Simple assistants in the first rank get £480; judges, £2400; the president judges, £10,000; governors, £12,000; and the governor-general more than £24,000.

There was good living on board the *Mongolia*, in this company of officials, to which were added some young Englishmen, who, with a million in their pockets, were going to establish commercial houses abroad. The purser, the confidential man of the company, the equal of the captain on board the ship, did things up elegantly. At the breakfast, at the lunch at two o'clock, at the dinner at half-past five, at the supper at eight o'clock, the tables groaned under the dishes of fresh meat and the relishes, furnished by the refrigerator, and the pantries of the steamer. The ladies, of whom there were a few, changed their toilet twice a day. There was music, and there was dancing also when the sea allowed it.

But the Red Sea is very capricious and too frequently rough, like all long, narrow bodies of water. When the wind blew either from the coast of Asia, or from the coast of Africa, the *Mongolia*, being very long and sharp built, and struck amidships, rolled fearfully. The ladies then disappeared; the pianos were silent; songs and dances ceased at once. And yet, notwithstanding the squall and the agitated waters, the steamer, driven by its powerful engines, pursued its course without delay to the straits of Bab-el-Mandeb.

What was Phileas Fogg doing all this time? It might be supposed that, always uneasy and anxious, his mind would be occupied with the changes of the wind interfering with the progress of the vessel, the irregular movements of the squall threatening an accident to the engine, and in short, all the possible injuries, which, compelling the *Mongolia* to put into some port, would have interrupted his journey.

By no means, or, at least, if this gentleman thought of these probabilities, he did not let it appear as if he did. He was the same impassible man, the imperturbable member of the Reform Club, whom no incident or accident could surprise. He did not appear more affected than the ship's chronometers. He was seldom seen upon the deck. He troubled himself very little about looking at this Red Sea, so fruitful in recollections, the spot where first historic scenes of mankind were enacted. He did not recognise the curious towns scattered upon its shores, and whose picturesque outlines stood out sometimes against the horizon. He did not even dream of the dangers of the Gulf of Arabia, of which the ancient historians, Strabo, Arrius, Artemidorus, and others, always spoke with dread, and upon which the navigators never ventured in former times without having consecrated their voyage by propitiatory sacrifices.

What was this queer fellow, imprisoned upon the *Mongolia* doing? At first he took his four meals a day, the rolling and pitching of the ship not putting out of order his mechanism, so wonderfully organised. Then he played at whist. For he found companions as devoted to it as himself: a collector of taxes, who was going to his post at Goa; a minister, the Rev. Decimus Smith, returning to Bombay; and a brigadier-general of the British Army, who was rejoining his corps at Benares. These three passengers had the same passion for whist as Mr. Fogg, and they played for entire hours, not less quietly than he.

As for Passepartout, sea-sickness had taken no hold on him. He occupied a forward cabin, and ate conscientiously. It must be said that the voyage made under these circumstances was decidedly not unpleasant to him. He rather liked his share of it. Well fed and well lodged, he was seeing the country, and besides, he asserted to himself that all this whim would end at Bombay. The next day after leaving Suez it was not without a certain pleasure that he met on deck the obliging person whom he had addressed on landing in Egypt.

"I am not mistaken," he said on approaching him with his most amiable smile; "you are the very gentleman that so kindly served as my guide in Suez?"

"Indeed," replied the detective, "I recognise you! You are the servant of that odd Englishman—"

"Just so, Monsieur—?"

"Fix."

"Monsieur Fix," replied Passepartout. "Delighted to meet you again on board this vessel. And where are you going?"

"Why, to the same place as yourself, Bombay."

"That is first rate! Have you already made this trip?"

"Several times," replied Fix. "I am an agent of the Peninsular Company."

"Then you know India?"

"Why—yes," replied Fix, who did not wish to commit himself too far.

"And this India is a curious place?"

"Very curious! Mosques, minarets, temples, fahirs, pagodas, tigers, serpents, dancing girls! But it is to be hoped that you will have time to visit the country?"

41

"I hope so, Monsieur Fix. You understand very well that it is not permitted to a man of sound mind to pass his life in jumping from a steamer into a railway car and from a railway car into a steamer, under the pretext of making the tour of the world in eighty days! No. All these gymnastics will cease at Bombay, don't doubt it."

"And Mr. Fogg is well?" asked Fox in a most natural tone.

"Very well, Monsieur Fix, and I am too. I eat like an ogre that has been fasting. It is the sea air."

"I never see your master on deck."

"Never. He is not inquisitive."

"Do you know, Mr. Passepartout, that this pretended tour in eighty days might very well be the cover for some secret mission—a diplomatic mission, for example!"

"Upon my word, Monsieur Fix, I don't know anything about it, I confess, and really I wouldn't give a half-crown to know."

After this meeting, Passepartout and Fix frequently talked together. The detective thought he ought to have close relations with the servant of this gentleman Fogg. There might be an occasion when he could serve him. He frequently offered him, in the barroom of the *Mongolia*, a few glasses of whisky or pale ale, which the good fellow accepted without reluctance, and returned even so as not to be behind him—finding this Fix to be a very honest gentleman.

In the meantime the steamer was rapidly getting on. On the 13th they sighted Mocha, which appeared in its enclosure of ruined walls, above which were hanging green date trees. At a distance, in the mountains, there were seen immense fields of coffee trees. Passepartout was delighted to behold this celebrated place, and he found, with its circular walls and a dismantled fort in the shape of a handle, it looked like an enormous cup and saucer.

During the following night the *Mongolia* passed through the Straits of Bab-el-Mandeb, the Arabic name of which signifies "The Gate of Tears," and the next day, the 14th, she put in at Steamer Point, to the north-west of Aden harbour. There she was to lay in coal again. This obtaining fuel for steamers at such distances from the centres of production is a very serious matter. It amounts to an annual expense for the Peninsular Company of eight hundred thousand pounds. It has been necessary, indeed, to establish depots in several ports, and in these distant seas coal reaches as high as from three to four pounds per ton.

The *Mongolia* had still sixteen hundred and fifty miles to make before reaching Bombay, and she had to remain four hours at Steamer Point, to lay in her coal. But this delay could not in any way be prejudicial to Phileas Fogg's programme. It was foreseen. Besides, the *Mongolia* instead of not arriving at Aden until the morning of the 15th, put in there the evening of the 14th, a gain of fifteen hours.

Mr. Fogg and his servant landed. The gentleman wished to have his passport *viséd* Fix followed him without being noticed. The formality of the *visé* through with, Phileas Fogg returned on board to resume his interrupted play. Passepartout, according to his custom, loitered about in the midst of the population of Somalis, Banyans, Parsees, Jews, Arabs, Europeans, making up the twenty-five thousand inhabitants of Aden. He admired the fortifications which make of this town the Gibraltar of the Indian Ocean, and some splendid cisterns, at which the English engineers were still working, two thousand years after the engineers of King Solomon. "Very singular, *very* singular" said Passepartout to himself on returning aboard. "I see that it is not useless travel, if we wish to see anything new."

At six o'clock p.m. the *Mongolia* was ploughing the waters of the Aden harbour, and soon reached the Indian Ocean. She had one hundred and sixty-eight hours to make the distance between Aden and Bombay. The Indian Ocean was favourable to her, the wind kept in the north-west, and the sails come to the aid of the steam. The ship well balanced, rolled less. The ladies, in fresh toilets, reappeared upon the deck. The singing and dancing recommenced. Their voyage was then progressing under the most favourable circumstances. Passepartout was delighted with the agreeable companion whom chance had procured for him in the person of Fix.

On Sunday, the 20th of October, towards noon, they sighted the Indian coast. Two hours later, the pilot came aboard the *Mongolia* The outlines of the hills blended with the sky. Soon the rows of palm trees which abound in the place came into distinct view. The steamer entered the harbour formed by the islands of Salcette, Colaba, Elephanta, Butcher, and at half-past four she put in at the wharves of Bombay. Phileas Fogg was then finishing the thirty-third rubber of the day, and his partner and himself, thanks to a bold manoeuvre, having made thirteen tricks, wound up this fine trip by a splendid victory. The *Mongolia* was not due at Bombay until the 22nd of October. She arrived on the 20th. This was a gain of two days, then, since his departure from London, and Phileas Fogg methodically noted it down in his memorandum-book in the column of gains.

CHAPTER 10

In which Passepartout is only too happy to get off with the loss of his shoes

No one is ignorant of the fact that India, this great reversed triangle whose base is to the north and its apex to the south, comprises a superficial area of fourteen hundred thousand square miles, over which is unequally scattered a population of one hundred and eighty millions of inhabitants. The British Government exercises a real dominion over a certain portion of this vast country. It maintains a Governor-General at Calcutta, Governors at Madras, Bombay, and Bengal, and a Lieutenant-Governor at Agra.

But British India, properly so-called, counts only a superficial area of seven hundred thousand square miles, and a population of one hundred to one hundred and ten millions of inhabitants. It is sufficient to say that a prominent part of the territory is still free from the authority of the Queen; and, indeed, with some of the rajahs of the interior, fierce and terrible, Hindu independence is still absolute. Since 1756—the period at which was founded the first English establishment on the spot to-day occupied by the City of Madras—until the year in which broke out the great Sepoy insurrection, the celebrated East India Company was all-powerful. It annexed little by little the various provinces, bought from the rajahs at the price of annual rents, which it paid in part or not at all; it named its Governor-General and all its civil or military employees; but now it no longer exists, and the British possessions in India are directly under the Crown. Thus the aspect, the manners, and the distinctions of race of the peninsula are being changed every day. Formerly they travelled by all the old means of conveyance, on foot, on horseback, in carts, in small vehicles drawn by men, in palanquins, on men's backs, in coaches, etc. Now, steamboats traverse with great rapidity the Indus and the Ganges, and a railway crossing the entire breadth of India, and branching in various directions, puts Bombay at only three days from Calcutta.

The route of this railway does not follow a straight line across India The air-line distance is only one thousand to eleven hundred miles, and trains, going at only an average rapidity, would not take three days to make it; but this distance is increased at least one-third by the arc described by the railway rising to Allahabad, in the northern part of the peninsula In short, these are the principal points of the route of the Great Indian Peninsular Railway. Leaving the island of Bombay, it crosses Salcette, touches the main land opposite Tannah, crosses the chain of the Western Ghauts, runs to the north-east as far as Burhampour, goes through the nearly independent territory of Bundelkund, rises as far as Allahabad, turns towards the east, meets the Ganges at Benares, turns slightly aside, and descending again to the south-east by Burdidan and the French town of Chandernagor, it reaches the end of the route at Calcutta.

It was at half-past four p.m. that the passengers of the *Mongolia* had landed in Bombay, and the train for Calcutta would leave at precisely eight o'clock. Mr. Fogg then took leave of his partners, left the steamer, gave his servant directions for some purchases, recommended him expressly to be at the station before eight o'clock, and with his regular step which beat the second like the pendulum of an astronomical clock, he turned his steps towards the passport office. He did not think of looking at any of the wonders of Bombay, neither the city hall, nor the magnificent library, nor the forts, nor the docks, nor the cotton market, nor the shops, nor the mosques, nor the synagogues, nor the Armenian churches, nor the splendid pagoda of Malebar Hill, adorned with two polygonal towers. He would not contemplate either the masterpieces of Elephanta, or its mysterious hypogea, concealed in the southeast of the harbour, or the Kanherian grottoes of the Islands of Salcette, those splendid remains of Buddhist architecture! No, nothing of that for him. After leaving the passport office, Phileas Fogg quietly returned to the station, and there had dinner served. Among other dishes, the landlord thought he ought to recommend to him a certain giblet of "native rabbit," of which he spoke in the highest terms. Phileas Fogg accepted the giblet and tasted it conscientiously; but in spite of the spiced sauce, he found it detestable. He rang for the landlord.

"Sir," he said, looking at him steadily, "is that rabbit.?"

"Yes, my lord," replied the rogue boldly, "the rabbit of the jungles."

"And that rabbit did not mew when it was killed?"

"Mew! oh, my lord! a rabbit! I swear to you—"

"Landlord," replied Mr. Fogg coolly, "don't swear, and recollect this: in former times, in India, cats were considered sacred animals. That was a good time."

"For the cats, my lord?"

"And perhaps also for the travellers!"

After this observation Mr. Fogg went on quietly with his dinner.

A few minutes after Mr. Fogg, the detective Fix also landed from the *Mongolia*, and hastened to the Commissioner of Police in Bombay. He made himself known in his capacity as detective, the mission with which he was charged, his position towards the robber. Had a warrant of arrest been received from London? They had received nothing. And, in fact, the warrant, leaving after Fogg, could not have arrived yet.

Fix was very much out of countenance. He wished to obtain from the Commissioner an order for the arrest of this gentleman Fogg. The director refused. The affair concerned the metropolitan government, and it alone could legally deliver a warrant. This strictness of principles, this rigorous observance of legality is easily explained with the English manners, which, in the matter of personal liberty, does not allow anything arbitrary. Fix did not persist, and understood that he would have to be resigned to waiting for his warrant. But he resolved not to lose sight of his mysterious rogue whilst he remained in Bombay. He did not doubt that Phileas Fogg would stop there—and as we know, it was also Passepartout's conviction—which would give the warrant of arrest the time to arrive.

But after the last orders which his master had given him on leaving the *Mongolia*, Passepartout had understood very well that it would be the same with Bombay as with Suez and Paris, that the journey would not stop here, that it would be continued at least as far as Calcutta, and perhaps farther. And he began to ask himself if, after all, this bet of Mr. Fogg was not really serious, and if fatality was not dragging him, he who wished to live at rest, to accomplish the tour of the world in eighty days! Whilst waiting, and after having obtained some shirts and shoes, he took a walk through the streets of Bombay. There was a great crowd of people there, and among them Europeans of all nationalities. Persians with pointed caps, Bunyas with round turbans, Sindes, with square caps, Armenians in long robes, Parsees in black mitres. A festival was just being held by the Parsees, the direct descendants of the followers of Zoroaster, who are the most industrious, the most civilised, the most intelligent, the most austere of the Hindus—a race to which now belong the rich native merchants of Bombay. Upon this day they were celebrating a sort of

47

religious carnival, with processions and amusements, in which figured dancing girls dressed in rosecoloured gauze embroidered with gold and silver, who danced wonderfully and with perfect decency to the sound of viols and tamtams.

It is superfluous to insist here whether Passepartout looked at these curious ceremonies, whether his eyes and ears were stretched wide open to see and hear, whether his entire appearance was that of the freshest greenhorn that can be imagined. Unfortunately for himself and his master, whose journey he ran the risk of interrupting, his curiosity dragged him farther than was proper.

In fact, after having looked at this Parsee carnival, Passepartout turned towards the station, when passing the splendid pagoda on Malebar Hill, he took the unfortunate notion to visit its interior. He was ignorant of two things: First, that the entrance into certain Hindu pagodas is formally forbidden to Christians, and next, that the believers themselves cannot enter there without having left their shoes at the door. It must be remarked here that the British Government, for sound political reasons, respecting and causing to be respected in its most insignificant details the religion of the country, punishes severely whoever violates its practices. Passepartout having gone in, without thinking of doing wrong, like a simple traveller, was admiring in the interior the dazzling glare of the Brahmim ornamentation, when he was suddenly thrown down on the sacred floor. Three priests, with furious looks, rushed upon him, tore off his shoes and stockings, and commenced to beat him, uttering savage cries. The Frenchman, vigorous and agile, rose again quickly. With a blow of his fist and a kick he upset two of his adversaries, very much hampered by their long robes, and rushing out of the pagoda with all the quickness of his legs, he had soon distanced the third Hindu, who had followed him closely, by mingling with the crowd.

At five minutes of eight, just a few minutes before the leaving of the train, hatless and barefoot, having lost in the scuffle the bundle containing his purchases, Passepartout arrived at the railway station. Fix was on the wharf. Having followed Mr. Fogg to the station, he understood that the rogue was going to leave Bombay. His mind was immediately made up to accompany him to Calcutta, and farther, if it was necessary. Passepartout did not see Fix, who was standing in a dark place, but Fix heard him tell his adventures in a few words to his master.

"I hope it will not happen to you again," was all Phileas Fogg replied, taking a seat in one of the cars of the train. The poor fellow, barefoot and quite discomfited, followed his master without saying a word.

Fix was going to get in another car, when a thought stopped him, and suddenly modified his plan of departure. "No, I will remain," he said to himself "A transgression committed upon Indian territory. I have my man."

At this moment the locomotive gave a vigorous whistle, and the train disappeared in the darkness.

CHAPTER 11

In which Phileas Fogg buys a Conveyance at a Fabulous Price

The train had started to time. It carried a certain number of travellers, some officers, civil officials, and opium and indigo merchants, whose business called them to the eastern part of the peninsula.

Passepartout occupied the same compartment as his master. A third traveller was in the opposite corner.

It was the brigadier-general, Sir Francis Cromarty, one of the partners of Mr. Fogg during the trip from Suez to Bombay, who was rejoining his troops, stationed near Benares.

Sir Francis Cromarty, tall, fair, about fifty years old, who had distinguished himself highly during the last revolt of the

Sepoys, had truly deserved to be called a native. From his youth he had lived in India, and had only been occasionally in the country of his birth. He was a well-posted man, who would have been glad to give information as to the manners, the history, the organisation of this Indian country, if Phileas Fogg had been the man to ask for such things. But this gentleman was not asking anything. He was not travelling, he was describing a circumference. He was a heavy body, traversing an orbit around the terrestrial globe, according to the laws of rational mechanics. At this moment he was going over in his mind the calculations of the hours consumed since his departure from London, and he would have rubbed his hands, if it had been in his nature to make a useless movement.

Sir Francis Cromarty had recognised the originality of his travelling companion, although he had only studied him with his cards in his hand, and between two rubbers. He was ready to ask whether a human heart beat beneath this cold exterior, whether Phileas Fogg had a soul alive to the beauties of nature and to moral aspirations. That was the question for him. Of all the oddities the general had met, none were to be compared to this product of the exact sciences. Phileas Fogg had not kept secret from Sir Francis Cromarty his plan for a tour around the world, nor the conditions under which he was carrying it out. The general saw in this bet only an eccentricity without a useful aim, and which was wanting necessarily in the *transire benefaciendo* which ought to guide every reasonable man. In the manner in which this singular gentleman was moving on, he would evidently be doing nothing, either for himself or for others.

An hour after having left Bombay, the train, crossing the viaducts, had left behind the Island of Salcette and reached the main-land. At the station Callyan, it left to the right the branch which, via Kandallah and Pounah descends towards the south-east of India, and reaches the station Panwell. At this point, it became entangled in the defiles of the Western Ghaut mountains, with bases of trappe and basalt, whose highest summits are covered with thick woods.

From time to time, Sir Francis Cromarty and Phileas Fogg

exchanged a few words, and at this moment the general, recommencing a conversation which frequently lagged, said:

"A few years ago, Mr. Fogg, you would have experienced at this point a delay which would have probably interrupted your journey."

"Why so, Sir Francis?"

"Because the railway stopped at the base of these mountains, which had to be crossed in a palanquin or on a pony's back as r as the station of Kandallah, on the opposite slope."

"That delay would not have deranged my programme," replied Mr. Fogg. "I would have foreseen the probability of certain obstacles."

"But, Mr. Fogg," replied the general, "you are in danger of having a bad business on your hands with this young man's adventure."

Passepartout, with his feet wrapped up in his cloak, was sleeping soundly, and did not dream that they were talking about him.

"The British Government is extremely severe, and rightly, for this kind of trespass," replied Sir Francis Cromarty. "It insists, above all things, that the religious customs of the Hindus shall be respected, and if your servant had been taken—"

"Yes, if he had been taken, Sir Francis," replied Mr. Fogg, "he would have been sentenced, he would have undergone his punishment, and then he would have quietly returned to Europe. I do not see how this matter could have delayed his master!"

And, thereupon, the conversation stopped again. During the night, the train crossed the Ghauts, passed on to Nassik, and the next day, the 21st of October, it was hurrying across a comparatively flat country, formed by the Khandeish territory. The country, well cultivated, was strewn with small villages, above which the minaret of the pagoda took the place of the steeple of the European church. Numerous small streams, principally tributaries of the Godavery, irrigated this fertile country.

Passepartout having waked up, looked around, and could not believe that he was crossing the country of the Hindus in a train of the Great Peninsular Railway. It appeared improbable to him. And yet there was nothing more real! The locomotive, guided by the arm of an English engineer and heated with English coal, was puffing out its smoke over plantations of cotton trees, coffee, nutmeg, clove, and red pepper. The steam twisted itself into spirals about groups of palms, between which appeared picturesque bungalows, a few viharis (a sort of abandoned monasteries), and wonderful temples enriched by the inexhaustible ornament of Indian architecture. Then immense reaches of country stretched out of sight, jungles, in which were not wanting snakes and tigers whom the noise of the train did not frighten, and finally forests cut through by the route of the road, still the haunt of elephants, which, with a pensive eye, looked at the train as it passed so rapidly.

During the morning, beyond the station of Malligaum, the travellers traversed that fatal territory, which was so frequently drenched with blood by the sectaries of the goddess Kali. Not far off rose Ellora and its splendid pagodas, and the celebrated Aurungabad, the capital of the ferocious Aureng-Zeb, now simply the principal place of one of the provinces detached from the kingdom of Nizam. It was over this country that Feringhea, the chief of the Thugs, the king of stranglers, exercised his dominion. These assassins, united in the association that could not be reached, strangled in honour of the goddess of death, victims of every age, without ever shedding blood, and there was a time when the ground could not be dug up anywhere in this neighbourhood without finding a corpse. The British Government has been able, in great part, to prevent these murders, but the horrible organisation exists yet, and carries on its operations.

At half-past twelve, the train stopped at the station at Burhampour, and Passepartout was able to obtain for gold a pair of Indian slippers, ornamented with false pearls, which he put on with an evident show of vanity. The travellers took a hasty breakfast, and started again for Assurghur, after having for a moment stopped upon the shore of the Tapty, a small river emptying into the Gulf of Cambay, near Surat.

It is opportune to mention the thoughts with which

Passepartout was busied. Until his arrival at Bombay, he had thought that matters would go no farther. But now that he was hurrying at full speed across India. his mind had undergone a change. His natural feelings came back to him with a rush. He felt again the fancied ideas of youth, he took seriously his master's plans, he believed in the reality of the bet, and consequently in this tour of the world, and in this maximum of time which could not be exceeded. Already he was disturbed at the possible delays, the accidents which might occur upon the route. He felt interested in the wager, and trembled at the thought that he might have compromised it the evening before by his unpardonable foolishness, so that, much less phlegmatic than Mr. Fogg, he was much more uneasy. He counted and recounted the days that had passed, cursed the stopping of the train, accused it of slowness, and blamed Mr. Fogg *in petto* for not having promised a reward to the engineer. The good fellow did not know that what was possible upon a steamer was not on a railway train, whose speed is regulated.

Towards evening they entered the defiles of the mountains of Sutpour, which separate the territory of Khandeish from that of Bundelcund.

The next day, the 22nd of October, Passepartout, having consulted his watch, replied to a question of Sir Francis Cromarty that it was three o'clock in the morning. In fact, this famous watch, always regulated by the meridian of Greenwich, which is nearly seventy-seven degrees west, ought to be and was four hours slow.

Sir Francis then corrected the hour given by Passepartout, and added the same remark that the latter had already heard from Fix. He tried to make him understand that he ought to regulate his watch on each new meridian, and that since he was constantly going towards the east, that is, in the face of the sun, the days were shorter by as many times four minutes as he had crossed degrees. It was useless. Whether the stubborn fellow had understood the remarks of the general or not, he persisted in not putting his watch ahead, which he kept always at London time. An innocent madness at any rate, which could hurt no one.

At eight o'clock in the morning, and fifteen miles before they reached Rothal, the train stopped in the midst of an immense opening, on the edge of which were some bungalows and workmen's huts. The conductor of the train passed along the cars calling out, "The passengers will get out here!"

Phileas Fogg looked at Sir Francis Cromarty, who appeared not to understand this stop in the midst of a forest of tamarinds and acacias. Passepartout, not less| surprised? rushed on to the track and returned almost immediately, crying, "Monsieur, no more railway!"

"What do you mean?" asked Sir Francis Cromarty.

"I mean that the train goes no farther."

The brigadier-general immediately got out of the car. Phileas Fogg, in no hurry, followed him. Both spoke to the conductor.

"Where are we?" asked Sir Francis Cromarty.

"At the hamlet of Kholby," replied the conductor.

"We stop here?"

"Without doubt. The railway is not finished—"

"How! It is not finished?"

"No! There is still a section of fifty miles to construct between this point and Allahabad, where the track commences again."

"But the papers have announced the opening of the entire line."

"But, generally, the papers were mistaken."

"And you give tickets from Bombay to Calcutta!" replied Sir Francis Cromarty, who was beginning to be excited.

"Of course," replied the conductor; "but travellers know very well that they have to be otherwise transported from Kholby to Allahabad."

Sir Francis Cromarty was furious. Passepartout would have willingly knocked the conductor down, who could not help himself He did not dare look at his master.

"Sir Francis," said Mr. Fogg simply, "we will go, if you will be kind enough to see about some way of reaching Allahabad."

"Mr. Fogg, this is a delay absolutely prejudicial to your interests!"

"No, Sir Francis, it was provided for."

"What, did you know that the railway—"

"By no means, but I knew that some obstacle or other would occur sooner or later upon my route. Now, nothing is interfered with. I have gained two days which I can afford to lose. A steamer leaves Calcutta for Hong-Kong at noon on the 25th. This is only the 23rd, and we shall arrive at Calcutta in time."

Nothing could be said in reply to such complete certainty.

It was only too true that the finished portion of the railway stopped at this point. The newspapers are like certain watches which have a mania of getting ahead of time, and they had announced the finishing of the line prematurely. The most of the passengers knew of this break in the line, and descending from the train, they examined the vehicles of all sorts in the village, four-wheeled palkigharis, carts drawn by zebus, a sort of ox with humps, travelling cars resembling walking pagodas, palanquins, ponies, etc. Mr. Fogg and Sir Francis Cromarty, after having hunted through the entire village, returned without having found anything.

"I shall go on foot," said Mr. Fogg.

Passepartout, who had then rejoined his master, made a significant grimace, looking down at his magnificent but delicate slippers. Very fortunate, he had also been hunting for something, and hesitating a little, he said:

"Monsieur, I believe I have found a means of conveyance."

"What?"

"An elephant belonging to an Indian living a hundred steps from here."

"Let us go to see the elephant," replied Mr. Fogg. Five minutes later, Phileas Fogg, Sir Francis Cromarty, and Passepartout arrived at a hut which was against an enclosure of high palisades. In the hut there was an Indian, and in the enclosure an elephant. Upon their demand, the Indian took Mr. Fogg and his two companions into the enclosure.

They found there a half-tamed animal, which his owner was raising, not to hire out, but as a beast of combat. To this end he had commenced to modify the naturally mild character of the animal in a manner to lead him gradually to that paroxysm of rage called "mutsh" in the Hindu language, and that by feeding him for three months with sugar and butter. This treatment may not seem the proper one to obtain such a result, but it is none the less employed with success by their keepers.

Kiouni, the animal's name, could, like all his fellows, go rapidly on a long march, and in default of other conveyance, Phileas Fogg determined to employ him. But elephants are very expensive in India, where they are beginning to get scarce. The males, which alone are fit for circus feats, are very much sought for. These animals are rarely reproduced when they are reduced to the tame state, so that they can be obtained only by hunting. So they are the object of extreme care, and when Mr. Fogg asked the Indian if he would hire him his elephant he flatly refused.

Fogg persisted, and offered an excessive price for the animal, ten pounds per hour. Refused. Twenty pounds. Still refused. Forty pounds. Refused again. Passepartout jumped at every advance in price. But the Indian would not be tempted. The sum was a handsome one, however. Admitting the elephant to be employed fifteen hours to reach Allahabad, it was six hundred pounds earned for his owner.

Phileas Fogg, without being at all excited, proposed then to the Indian to buy his animal, and offered him at first one thousand pounds. The Indian would not sell! Perhaps the rogue scented a large transaction.

Sir Francis Cromarty took Mr. Fogg aside and begged him to reflect before going further. Phileas Fogg replied to his companion that he was not in the habit of acting without reflection, that a bet of twenty thousand pounds was at stake, that this elephant was necessary to him, and that, should he pay twenty times his value, he would have this elephant.

Mr. Fogg went again for the Indian, whose small eyes, lit up with greed, showed that with him it was only a question of price. Phileas Fogg offered successively twelve hundred, fifteen hundred, eighteen hundred, and finally two thousand pounds. Passepartout, so rosy ordinarily, was pale with emotion.

At two thousand pounds the Indian gave up.

"By my slippers," cried Passepartout, "here is a magnificent price for elephant meat!"

The business concluded, all that was necessary was to find a guide. That was easier. A young Parsee, with an intelligent face, offered his services. Mr. Fogg accepted him, and offered him a large reward to sharpen his wits. The elephant was brought out and equipped without delay. The Parsee understood perfectly the business of "mahout," or elephant-driver. He covered with a sort of saddle cloth the back of the elephant, and put on each flank two kinds of rather uncomfortable howdahs.

Phileas Fogg paid the Indian in bank-notes taken from the famous carpet bag. It seemed as if they were taken from Passepartout's very vitals. Then Mr. Fogg offered to Sir Francis Cromarty to convey him to Allahabad. The general accepted; one passenger more was not enough to tire this enormous animal. Some provisions were bought at Kholby. Sir Francis Cromarty took a seat in one of the howdahs, Phileas Fogg in the other. Passepartout got astride the animal, between his master and the brigadier-general. The Parsee perched upon the elephant's neck, and at nine o'clock the animal, leaving the village, penetrated the thick forest of palm trees.

CHAPTER 12

In which Phileas Fogg and his Companions venture through the Forests of India, and what follows

The guide, in order to shorten the distance to be gone over, left to his right the line of the road, the construction of which was still in process. This line, very crooked, owing to the capricious ramifications of the Vindhia mountains, did not follow the shortest route, which it was Phileas Foggs interest to take. The Parsee, very familiar with the roads and paths of the country, thought to gain twenty miles by cutting through the forest, and they submitted to him.

Phileas Fogg and Sir Francis Cromarty, plunged to their necks in their howdahs, were much shaken up by the rough trot of the elephant, whom his mahout urged into a rapid gait. But they bore it with the peculiar British apathy, talking very little, and scarcely seeing each other.

As for Passepartout, perched upon the animal's back, and directly subjected to the swaying from side to side, he took care, upon his master's recommendation, not to keep his tongue between his teeth, as it would have been cut short off. The good fellow, at one time thrown forward on the elephant's neck, at another thrown back upon his rump, was making leaps like a clown on a spring-board But he joked and laughed in the midst of his somersaults, and from time to time he would take from his bag a lump of sugar, which the intelligent Kiouni took with the end of his trunk, without interrupting for an instant his regular trot.

After two hours' march the guide stopped the elephant, and gave him an hour's rest. The animal devoured branches of trees and shrubs, first having quenched his thirst at a neighbouring pond. Sir Francis Cromarty did not complain of this halt. He was worn out. Mr. Fogg appeared as if he had just got out of bed.

"But he is made of iron!" said the brigadier-general, looking at him with admiration.

"Of wrought iron," replied Passepartout, who was busy preparing a hasty breakfast.

At noon the guide gave the signal for starting. The country soon assumed a very wild aspect. To the large forests there succeeded copses of tamarinds and dwarf palms, then vast, arid plains, bristling with scanty shrubs, and strewn with large blocks of syenites. All this part of upper Bundelcund, very little visited by travellers, is inhabited by a fanatical population, hardened in the most terrible practices of the Hindu religion. The government of the British could not have been regularly established over a territory subject to the influence of the rajahs, whom it would have been difficult to reach in their inaccessible retreats in the Vindhias.

They were descending the last declivities of the Vindhias. Kiouni had resumed his rapid gait. Towards noon, the guide went round the village of Kallenger, situated on the Cani, one of the tributaries of the Ganges. He always avoided inhabited places, feeling himself safer, in those desert open stretches of country which mark the first depressions of the basin of the great river. Allahabad was not twelve miles to the north-east. Halt was made under a clump of banana trees, whose fruit, as healthy as bread, "as succulent as cream," travellers say, was very much appreciated.

At two o'clock, the guide entered the shelter of a thick forest, which he had to traverse for a space of several miles. He preferred to travel thus under cover of the woods. At all events, up to this moment there had been no unpleasant meeting, and it seemed a if the journey would be accomplished without accident, when the elephant, showing some signs of uneasiness, suddenly stopped.

It was then four o'clock.

"What is the matter?" asked Sir Francis Cromarty, raising his head above his howdah.

"I do not know, officer," replied the Parsee, listening to a confused murmur which came through the thick branches.

A few moments after, this murmur became more defined. It might have been called a concert, still very distant, of human voices and brass instruments.

Passepartout was all eyes, all ears. Mr. Fogg waited patiently, without uttering a word.

The Parsee jumped down, fastened the elephant to a tree, and plunged into the thickest of the undergrowth. A few minutes later he returned, saying:

"A Brahmin procession coming this way. If it is possible, let us avoid being seen."

The guide unfastened the elephant, and led him into a thicket, recommending the travellers not to descend. He held himself ready to mount the elephant quickly, should flight become necessary. But he thought that the troop of the faithful would pass without noticing him, for the thickness of the foliage entirely concealed him.

The discordant noise of voices and instruments approached. Monotonous chants were mingled with the sound of the drums and cymbals. Soon the head of the procession appeared from under the trees, at fifty paces from the spot occupied by Mr. Fogg and his companions. Through the branches they readily distinguished the curious personnel of this religious ceremony.

In the first line were the priests, with mitres upon their heads and attired in long robes adorned with gold and silver lace. They were surrounded by men, women, and children, who were singing a sort of funeral psalmody, interrupted at regular intervals by the beating of tom-toms and cymbals. Behind them on a car with large wheels, whose spokes and felloes represented serpents intertwined, appeared a hideous statue, drawn by two pairs of richly caparisoned zebus. This statue had four arms, its body coloured with dark red, its eyes haggard, its hair tangled, its tongue hanging out, its lips coloured with henna and betel. Its neck was encircled by a collar of skulls, around its waist a girdle of human hands. It was erect upon a prostrate giant, whose head was missing.

Sir Francis Cromarty recognised this statue.

"The goddess Kali," he murmured; "the goddess of love."

"Of death, I grant, but of love, never!" said Passepartout. The ugly old woman."

The Parsee made him a sign to keep quiet.

Around the statue there was a group of old fakirs, jumping and tossing themselves about convulsively. Smeared with bands of ochre, covered with cross-like cuts, whence their blood escaped drop by drop—stupid fanatics, who, in the great Hindu ceremonies, precipitated themselves under the wheels of the car of Juggernaut.

Behind them, some Brahmins in all the magnificence of their Oriental costume, were dragging a woman who could hardly hold herself erect.

This woman was young, and as fair as a European. Her head, her neck, her shoulders, her ears, her arms, her hands, and her toes were loaded down with jewels, necklaces, bracelets, ear-rings and finger-rings. A tunic, embroidered with gold, covered with a light muslin, displayed the outlines of her form.

Behind this young woman—a violent contrast for the eyes—were guards, armed with naked sabres fastened to their girdles and long damascened pistols, carrying a corpse upon a palanquin.

It was the body of an old man, dressed in the rich garments of a rajah, having, as in life, his turban embroidered with pearls, his robe woven of silk and gold, his sash of cashmere ornamented with diamonds, and his magnificent arms as an Indian prince.

Then, musicians and a rearguard of fanatics, whose cries sometimes drowned the deafening noise of the instruments, closed up the *cortège*.

Sir Francis Cromarty looked at all this pomp with a singularly sad air, and turning to the guide, he said:

"A suttee!"

The Parsee made an affirmative sign and put his fingers on his lips. The long procession came out from the trees, and soon the last of it disappeared in the depths of the forest.

Little by little the chanting died out. There were still the sounds of distant cries, and finally a profound silence succeeded all this tumult.

Phileas Fogg had heard the word uttered by Sir Francis Cromarty, and as soon as the procession had disappeared, he asked:

"What is a suttee?"

"A suttee, Mr. Fogg," replied the brigadier-general, "is a human sacrifice, but a voluntary sacrifice. The woman that you have just seen will be burned to-morrow in the early part of the day."

Oh, the villains!" cried Passepartout, who could not prevent this cry of indignation.

"And this corpse?" asked Mr. Fogg.

"It is that of the prince, her husband," replied the guide, "an independent rajah of Bundelcund."

61

"How," replied Phileas Fogg, without his voice betraying the least emotion, "do these barbarous customs still exist in India, and have not the British been able to extirpate them?"

"In the largest part of India," replied Sir Francis Cromarty, "these sacrifices do not come to pass; but we have no influence over these wild countries, and particularly over this territory of Bundelcund. All the northern slope of the Vindhias is the scene of murders and incessant robberies."

"The unfortunate woman," murmured Passepartout, "burned alive!"

"Yes," replied the general, "burned, and if she was not, you would not believe to what a miserable condition she would be reduced by her near relatives. They would shave her hair; they would scarcely feed her with a few handfuls of rice; they would repulse her; she would be considered as an unclean creature, and would die in some corner like a sick dog. So that the prospect of this frightful existence frequently drives these unfortunates to the sacrifice much more than love or religious fanaticism. Sometimes, however, the sacrifice is really voluntary, and the energetic intervention of the government is necessary to prevent it. Some years ago, I was living at Bombay, when a young widow came to the Governor to ask his authority for her to be burned with the body of her husband. As you may think, the Governor refused. Then the widow left the city, took refuge with an independent rajah, and there she accomplished the sacrifice."

During the narrative of the general, the guide shook his head, and when he was through, said:

"The sacrifice which takes place to-morrow is not voluntary."

"How do you know?"

"It is a story which everybody in Bundelcund knows," replied the guide.

"But this unfortunate did not seem to make any resistance," remarked Sir Francis Cromarty.

"Because she was intoxicated with the fumes of hemp and opium."

"But where are they taking her?"

"To the pagoda of Pillaji, two miles from here. There she will pass the night in waiting for the sacrifice."

"And this sacrifice will take place—?"

"At the first appearance of day."

After this answer, the guide brought the elephant out of the dense thicket, and jumped on his neck. But at the moment that he was going to start him off by a peculiar whistle, Mr. Fogg stopped him and addressing Sir Francis Cromarty, said, "If we could save this woman!"

"Save this woman, Mr. Fogg." cried the brigadier-general.

"I have still twelve hours to spare. I can devote them to her."

"Why, you are a man of heart!" said Sir Francis Cromarty.

"Sometimes," replied Phileas Fogg simply, "when I have time."

CHAPTER 13

In which Passepartout proves again that Fortune smiles upon the Bold

The design was bold, full of difficulties, perhaps impracticable. Mr. Fogg was going to risk his life, or at least his liberty, and consequently the success of his plans, but he did not hesitate. He found, besides, a decided ally in Sir Francis Cromarty.

As to Passepartout, he was ready and could be depended upon. His master's idea excited him. He felt that there was a heart and soul under this icy covering. He almost loved Phileas Fogg.

Then there was the guide. What part would he take in the matter? Would he not be with the Indians? In default of his aid, it was at least necessary to be sure of his neutrality.

Sir Francis Cromarty put the question to him frankly.

"Officer," replied the guide, "I am a Parsee, and that woman is a Parsee. Make use of me."

"Very well, guide," replied Mr. Fogg.

"However, do you know," replied the Parsee, "that we not only risk our lives, but horrible punishments if we are taken. So see."

"That is seen," replied Mr. Fogg. "I think that we shall have to wait for night to act?"

"I think so too," replied the guide.

The brave Hindu then gave some details as to the victim. She was an Indian of celebrated beauty, of the Parsee race, the daughter of a rich merchant of Bombay. She had received in that city an absolutely English education, and from her manners and cultivation she would have been thought an European. Her name was Aouda.

An orphan, she was married against her will to this old rajah of Bundelcund. Three months after she was a widow. Knowing the fate that awaited her, she fled, was retaken immediately, and the relatives of the rajah, who had an interest in her death, devoted her to this sacrifice from which it seemed that she could not escape.

This narrative could only strengthen Mr. Fogg and his companions in their generous resolution. It was decided that the guide should turn the elephant towards the pagoda of Pillaji, which he should approach as near as possible.

A half-hour afterwards a halt was made under a thick clump of trees, five hundred paces from the pagoda, which they could not see, but they heard distinctly the yellings of the fanatics.

The means of reaching the victim were then discussed. The guide was acquainted with the pagoda, in which he asserted that the young woman was imprisoned. Could they enter by one of the doors, when the whole band was plunged in the sleep of drunkenness, or would they have to make a hole through the wall? This could be decided only at the moment and the place. But there could be no doubt hat the abduction must be accomplished this very night, and not when, daylight arrived, the victim would be led to the sacrifice. Then no human intervention could save her.

Mr. Fogg and his companions awaited for night. As soon as the shadows fell, towards six o'clock in the evening, they determined to make a reconnaissance around the pagoda. The last cries of the fakirs had died out. According to their customs, these Indians were plunged in the heavy intoxication of "bang," liquid opium mixed with an infusion of hemp, and it would perhaps be possible to slip in between them to the temple.

The Parsee guiding, Mr. Fogg, Sir Francis Cromarty, and Passepartout advanced noiselessly through the forest. After ten minutes' creeping under the branches, they arrived on the edge of a small river, and there by the light of iron torches at the end of which was burning pitch, they saw a pile of wood. It was the funeral pile, made of costly sandal wood, and already saturated with perfumed oil. On its upper part the embalmed body of the rajah was resting, which was to be burned at the same time as his widow. At one hundred paces from this pile rose the pagoda, whose minarets in the darkness pierced the tops of the trees.

"Come!" said the guide in a low voice.

Soon the guide stopped at the end of a clearing, lit up by a few torches. The ground was covered with groups of sleepers, heavy with drunkenness.

In the background, among the trees, the temple of Pillaji stood out indistinctly. But to the great disappointment of the guide, the guards of the rajah, lighted by smoky torches, were watching at the doors, and pacing up and down with drawn sabres. Phileas Fogg and Sir Francis Cromarty understood as well as himself that they could attempt nothing on this side. They stopped and talked in a low tone.

"Let us wait," said the brigadier-general, "it is not eight o'clock yet, and it is possible that these guards may succumb to sleep."

"That is possible, indeed," replied the Parsee.

Phileas Fogg and his companions stretched themselves out at the foot of a tree and waited.

They waited thus until midnight. The situation did not change. The same watching outside. It was evident that they could not count on the drowsiness of the guards.

After a final conversation, the guide said he was ready to start. Mr. Fogg, Sir Francis, and Passepartout followed him. They made a pretty long detour, so as to reach the pagoda by the rear.

About a half-hour past midnight they arrived at the foot of the walls, without having met anyone. No watch had been established on this side, but windows and doors were entirely wanting.

But it was not sufficient to reach the foot of the walls, it was necessary to make an opening there. For this operation Phileas Fogg and his companions had nothing at all but their pocket-knives. Fortunately, the temple walls were composed of a mixture of bricks and wood, which could not be difficult to make a hole through. The first brick once taken out, the others would easily follow.

They went at it, making as little noise as possible. The Parsee, from one side, and Passepartout, from the other, worked to unfasten the bricks, so as to get an opening two feet wide.

The work was progressing, but—unfortunate mischance—some guards showed themselves at the rear of the pagoda, and established themselves there so as to hinder an approach.

It would be difficult to describe the disappointment of these four men, stopped in their work.

"What can we do but leave?" asked the general in a low voice.

"We can only leave," replied the guide.

"Wait," said Fogg. "It will do if I-reach Allahabad to-morrow before noon."

"But what hope have you?" replied Sir Francis Cromarty. "It will soon be daylight, and—"

"The chance which escapes us now may return at the last moment."

The general would have liked to read Phileas Fogg's eyes.

What was this cold-blooded Englishman counting on? Would he, at the moment of the sacrifice, rush towards the young woman, and openly tear her from her murderers?

That would have been madness, and how could it be admitted

that this man was mad to this degree? Nevertheless, Sir Francis Cromarty consented to wait until the *dénouement* of this terrible scene. However, the guide did not leave his companions at the spot where they had hid, and he took them back to the foreground of the clearing. There, sheltered by a clump of trees, they could watch the sleeping groups.

In the meantime Passepartout, perched upon the lower branches of a tree, was meditating an idea which had first crossed his mind like a flash, and which finally embedded itself in his brain.

He had commenced by saying to himself, "What madness!" and now he repeated, "Why not, after all? It is a chance, perhaps the only one, and with such brutes—"

At all events, Passepartout did not put his thought into any other shape, but he was not slow in sliding down, with the ease of a snake, on the lower branches of the tree, the end of which bent towards the ground.

The hours were passing, and soon a few less sombre shades announced the approach of day. But the darkness was still great.

It was the time fixed. It was like a resurrection in this slumbering crowd. The groups wakened up. The beating of tom-toms sounded, songs and cries burst out anew. The hour had come in which the unfortunate was to die.

The doors of the pagoda were now opened. A more intense light came from the interior. Mr. Fogg and Sir Francis could see the victim, all lighted up, whom two priests were dragging to the outside. It seemed to them that, shaking off the drowsiness of intoxication by the highest instinct of self-preservation, the unfortunate woman was trying to escape from her executioners. Sir Francis's heart throbbed violently and with a convulsive movement seizing Phileas Fogg's hand, he felt that it held an open knife.

At this moment the crowd was agitated. The young woman had fallen again into the stupor produced by the fumes of the hemp. She passed between the fakirs, who escorted her with their religious cries.

Phileas Fogg and his companions followed her, mingling with the rear ranks of the crowd.

Two minutes after they arrived at the edge of the river, and stopped less than fifty paces from the funeral pile, upon which was lying the rajah's body. In the semi-obscurity they saw the victim, motionless, stretched near her husband's corpse.

Then a torch was brought, and the wood, impregnated with oil soon took fire.

At this moment, Sir Francis Cromarty and the guide held back Phileas Fogg, who in a impulse of generous madness, was going to rush towards the pile.

But Phileas Fogg had already pushed them back, when the scene changed suddenly. A cry of terror arose. The whole crowd, frightened, cast themselves upon the ground.

The old rajah was not dead, then; he was seen suddenly rising upright, like a phantom, raising the young woman in his arms, descending from the pile in the midst of the clouds of smoke which gave him a spectral appearance.

The fakirs, the priests, overwhelmed with a sudden fear, were prostrate, their faces to the ground, not daring to raise their eyes, and look at such a miracle!

The inanimate victim was held by the vigorous arms carrying her, without seeming to be much of a weight. Mr. Fogg and Sir Francis had remained standing. The Parsee had bowed his head, and Passepartout, without doubt, was not less stupefied.

The resuscitated man came near the spot where Mr. Fogg and Sir Francis Cromarty were, and said shortly:

"Let us be off!"

It was Passepartout himself who had slipped to the pile in the midst of the thick smoke! It was Passepartout who, profiting by the great darkness still prevailing, had rescued the young woman from death! It was Passepartout who, playing his part with the boldest good luck, passed out in the midst of the general fright.

An instant after the four disappeared in the woods, and the elephant took them onwards with a rapid trot. But cries, shouts, and even a ball, piercing Phileas Fogg's hat, apprised them that the stratagem had been discovered.

Indeed, on the burning pile still lay the body of the old rajah.

The priests, recovered from their fright, learned that the abduction had taken place.

They immediately rushed into the forest. The guards followed them. Shots were fired; but the abductors fled rapidly, and, in a few moments, they were out of range of balls or arrows.

CHAPTER 14

In which Phileas Fogg descends the entire splendid Valley of the Ganges without ever thinking of looking at it

The bold abduction had succeeded. An hour after Passepartout was still laughing at his success. Sir Francis Cromarty grasped the hand of the brave fellow. His master said to him, "Good," which in that gentleman's mouth was equivalent to high praise. To which Passepartout replied that all the honour of the affair belonged to his master. As for himself he had only had a "droll" idea, and he laughed in thinking that for a few moments he, Passepartout, the former gymnast, the ex-sergeant of firemen, had been the widower of a charming woman, and old embalmed rajah!

As for the young Indian widow, she had no knowledge of what had passed. Wrapped up in travelling cloaks, she was resting in one of the howdahs.

Meanwhile the elephant, guided with the greatest certainty by the Parsee, moved on rapidly through the still dark forest. One hour after having left the pagoda of Pillaji, he shot across an immense plain. At seven o'clock they halted. The young woman was still in a state of complete prostration. The guide made her drink a few swallows of water and brandy, but the stupefying influence which overwhelmed her continued for some time longer. Sir Francis Cromarty, who knew the effects of intoxication produced by inhalation of the fumes of hemp, had no uneasiness on her account.

But if the restoration of the young woman was not a question in the general's mind, he was not less assured for the future. He did not hesitate to say to Phileas Fogg that if Mrs. Aouda remained in India, she would inevitably fall again into 'the hands of her executioners. These fanatics were scattered throughout the entire peninsula, and notwithstanding the English police, they would certainly be able to recapture their victim, whether at Madras, at Bombay, or at Calcutta. And in support of this remark, Sir Francis quoted a fact of the same nature which had recently transpired. According to his view, the young woman would really not be safe until after leaving India.

Phileas Fogg replied that he would note these remarks and think them over.

Towards ten o'clock the guide announced the station of Allahabad. The interrupted line of the railway recommenced there, whence trains traverse, in less than a day and a night, the distance separating Allahabad from Calcutta.

Phileas Fogg ought then to arrive in time to take a steamer which would not leave until the next day, October 25, at noon, for Honk-Kong.

The young woman was placed in a waiting-room of the station. Passepartout was directed to purchase for her various articles of dress, such as a robe, shawl, furs, etc., whatever he would find. His master opened an unlimited credit for him.

Passepartout went out immediately and ran through the streets of the city. Allahabad, that is, the "City of God," is one of the most venerated of India, on account of its being built at the junction of two sacred rivers, the Ganges and the Jumna, whose waters attract pilgrims from the whole peninsula It is said also that, according to the legends of the Ramayana, the Ganges takes its source in heaven, whence, thanks to Brahma, it descends upon the earth.

In making his purchases, Passepartout had soon seen the city, at one time defended by a magnificent fort, which had become a State prison. There are no more commerce and no more manufactures in this city, formerly a manufacturing and commercial point. Passepartout, who vainly sought a variety shop, such as there was in Regent Street, a few steps off from Farmer & Co., found only at a second-hand dealer's, an old whimsical Jew, the objects which he needed—a dress of Scotch stuff, a large mantle, and a magnificent otter-skin, pelisse, for which he did not hesitate to pay seventy-five pounds. Then, quite triumphant, he returned to the station.

Mrs. Aouda commenced to revive. The influence to which the priests of Pillaji had subjected her, disappeared by degrees, and her beautiful eyes resumed all their Indian softness.

When the poet-king, Ucaf Uddaul celebrates the charms of the Queen of Ahemhnagara, he thus expressed himself:

"Her shining tresses, regularly divided into two parts, encircle the harmonious outlines of her delicate and white cheeks, brilliant with their flow and freshness. Her ebony eyebrows have the form and strength of the bow of Kama, god of love; and under her long silken lashes, in the black pupil of her large limpid eyes, there float, as in the sacred lakes of the Himalaya, the purest reflections of the celestial light. Fine, regular, and white, her teeth shine out between her smiling lips, like dewdrops in the half-closed bosom of the pomegranate blossom. Her ears, types of the symmetric curves, her rosy hands, her little feet, curved and tender as lotus buds, shine with the splendour of the finest pearls of Ceylon, the most beautiful diamonds of Golconda Her delicate and supple waist, which a hand can clasp, heightens the elegant outline of her rounded figure, and the wealth of her bosom, where youth in its prime displays its most perfect treasures and under the silken folds of her tunic she seems to have been modelled in pure silver by the divine hand of Vicvarcarma, the immortal sculptor."

But, without all this poetic amplification, it is sufficient to say that Mrs. Aouda, the widow of the Rajah of Bundelcund, was a charming woman in the entire European acceptation of the phrase. She spoke English with great purity, and the guide had not exaggerated in asserting that this young Parsee woman had been transformed by education.

Meanwhile the train was about to leave Allahabad. The Parsee was waiting. Mr. Fogg paid him the compensation agreed upon, without exceeding it a farthing. This astonished Passepartout a little, who knew everything that his master owed to the devotion of the guide. The Parsee, in fact, had risked his life voluntarily in the affair at Pillaji; and if, later, the Hindus should learn it, he would hardly escape their vengeance.

The question of Kiouni also remained. What would be done with an elephant bought so dearly?

But Phileas Fogg had already taken a resolution upon this point.

"Parsee," he said to the guide, "you have been serviceable and devoted. I have paid for your service, but not for your devotion. Do you wish this elephant? It is yours."

The eyes of the guide sparkled.

"Your honour is giving me a fortune!" he cried.

"Accept, guide," replied Mr. Fogg, "and I will be yet your debtor."

"Good!" cried Passepartout. "Take him, friend! Kiouni is a brave and courageous animal."

And going to the brave, he gave him some lumps of sugar, saying:

"Here, Kiouni, here, here."

The elephant uttered some grunts of satisfaction. Then taking Passepartout by the waist, and encircling him with his trunk, he raised him as high as his head. Passepartout, not at all frightened, caressed the animal, who replaced him gently on the ground, and to the shaking of the honest Kiouni's trunk there answered a vigorous shaking of the good fellow's hand.

A few moments after, Phileas Fogg, Sir Francis Cromarty, and Passepartout, seated in a comfortable car, the best seat in which Mrs. Aouda occupied, were running at full speed towards Benares.

Eighty miles at the most separate this place from Allahabad, and they were passed over in two hours.

During this passage the young woman completely revived; the drowsy fumes of the "bang" disappeared.

What was her astonishment to find herself on this railway, in this compartment, clothed in European habiliments, in the midst of travellers entirely unknown to her.

At first, her companions gave her the greatest care, and revived her with a few drops of liquor; then the brigadier-general told the story. He dwelt upon the devotion of Phileas Fogg, who had not hesitated to stake his life to save her, and upon the *dénouement* of the adventure, due to the bold imagination of Passepartout.

Mr. Fogg let him go on without saying a word.

Passepartout, quite ashamed, repeated that "it was not worth while."

Mrs. Aouda thanked her deliverers profusely, by her tears more than by her words. Her beautiful eyes, rather than her lips, were the interpreters of her gratitude. Then, her thoughts carrying her back to the scenes of the suttee, seeing again the Indian country where so many dangers still awaited her, she shuddered with terror.

Phileas Fogg understood what was passing in Mrs. Aouda's mind, and, to reassure her, offered, very coolly, to take her to Hong-Kong, where she might remain until this affair had died out.

Mrs. Aouda accepted the offer gratefully. At Hong-Kong there resided one of her relatives, a Parsee like herself, and one of the principal merchants of that city, which is entirely English, though occupying a point on the Chinese coast

At half-past twelve noon the train stopped at the Benares station. The Brahmin legends assert that this place occupies the site of the ancient Casi, which was formerly suspended in space, between the zenith and the nadir, like Mohammed's tomb. But at this more material period, Benares, the Athens of India, in the saying of the Orientals, was prosaically resting on the earth, and Passepartout could for an instant see its brick houses, its clay huts, which gave it a very desolate appearance, without any local colour.

Here was where Sir Francis Cromarty was going to stop. The troops which he was rejoining were camping a few miles to the north of the city. The brigadier-general then made his adieux to Phileas Fogg, wishing him all possible success, and expressing the wish that he would recommence the journey in a less original but more profitable manner. Mr. Fogg pressed lightly his companion's fingers. The parting greetings of Mrs. Aouda were more demonstrative. She would never forget what she owed Sir Francis Cromarty. As for Passepartout, he was honoured with a hearty shake of the hand by the general. Quite affected, he asked where and when he could be of service to him. Then they parted.

Leaving Benares, the railway followed in part the Valley of the Ganges. Through the windows of the car, the weather being quite clear, appeared the varied country of Behar, mountains covered with verdure, fields of barley, corn, and wheat, jungles full of green alligators, villages well kept, forests yet green. A few elephants, and zebus with large humps, came to bathe in the waters of the sacred river, and also, notwithstanding the advanced season, and the already cold temperature, bands of Hindus of both sexes, who were piously performing their holy ablutions. These faithful ones, the bitter enemies of Buddhism, are fervent sectaries of the Brahmin religion, which is incarnate in these three persons: Vishnu, the solar deity; Shiva, the divine personification of the natural forces; and Brahma, the supreme master of priests and legislators. But in what light would Brahma, Shiva, and Vishnu regard this India, now "Britonised," when some steamboat passes, puffing and disturbing the consecrated waters of the Ganges, frightening the gulls flying over its surface, the turtles swarming on its banks, and the faithful stretched along its shores.

All this panorama passed like a flash, and frequently a cloud of steam concealed its details from them. The travellers could scarcely see the fort of Chunar, twenty miles to the south-east of Benares, the old stronghold of the rajahs of Behar, Ghazepour, and its large rose-water manufactories; the tomb of Lord Cornwallis rising on the left bank of the Ganges; the fortified town of Buxar; Patna the great manufacturing and commercial city, where the principal opium market in India is held; Monghir, a more than European town, as English as Manchester or Birmingham, famous for its iron foundries, its manufactories of cutlery, and whose high chimneys cover with a black smoke the heavens of Brahma—a real fist-blow in the country of dreams!

Then night came, and in the midst of the howlings of the tigers, the bears, and the wolves, which fled before the locomotive, the train passed on at full speed, and they saw nothing of the wonders of Bengal, or Golconda, or Gour in ruins, or Mourshedabad, the former capital, or Burdwan, or Hougly, or Chandernager, that French point in the Indian territory, on which Passepartout would have been proud to see his native flag floating.

Finally, at seven o'clock a.m., Calcutta was reached. The steamer to leave for Hong-Kong did not weigh anchor until noon. Phileas Fogg had then five hours before him.

According to his journal, this gentleman should arrive in the capital of India, October 25, twenty-three days after leaving London, and he arrived there on the stipulated day. He was neither behind nor ahead of time. Unfortunately, the two days gained by him between London and Bombay had been lost, we know how, in this trip across the Indian peninsula, but it is to be supposed that Phileas Fogg did not regret them.

CHAPTER 15

In which the Bag with the Bank-notes is relieved of a few Thousand Pounds more

The train had stopped at the station. Passepartout first got out of the car, and was followed by Mr. Fogg, who aided his young companion to descend. Phileas Fogg counted on going directly to the Hong-Kong steamer, in order to fix Mrs. Aouda there comfortably, whom he did not wish to leave as long as she was in this country, so dangerous for her.

At the moment that Mr. Fogg was going out of the station a policeman approached him and said:

"Mr. Phileas Fogg?"

"I am he."

"Is this man your servant?" added the policeman, pointing to Passepartout.

"Yes."

"You will both be so kind as to follow me."

Mr. Fogg made no movement indicating any surprise. This agent was a representative of the law, and for every Englishman the law is sacred. Passepartout, with his French habits, wanted to discuss the matter, but the policeman touched him with his stick, and Phileas Fogg made him a sign to obey.

"This young lady can accompany us?" asked Mr. Fogg.

"She can," replied the policeman.

The policeman conducted Mr. Fogg, Mrs. Aouda, and Passepartout to a palkighari, a sort of four-wheeled vehicle with four seats, drawn by two horses. They started. No one spoke during the twenty minutes' ride.

The vehicle first crossed the "black town," with its narrow streets, its huts in which grovelled a miscellaneous population, dirty and ragged; then they passed through the European town, adorned with brick houses, shaded by coconut trees, bristling with masts, through which, notwithstanding the early hour, were driving handsomely-dressed gentlemen, in elegant turn-outs.

The palkighari stopped before a dwelling of plain appearance, but which was not used for private purposes. The policeman let his prisoners out, for they could, indeed, be called thus, and he led them into a room with grated windows, saying to them:

"At half-past eight you will appear before Judge Obadiah."

Then he left, and dosed the door.

"See! we are prisoners!" cried Passepartout, dropping into a chair.

Mrs. Aouda, addressing Mr. Fogg immediately, said in a voice whose emotion she sought in vain to disguise:

"Sir, you must leave me! It is on my account that you are pursued! It is because you have rescued me!"

Phileas Fogg contented himself with saying that that would not be possible. Pursued on account of this suttee affair. Inadmissible! How would the complainants dare present themselves? There was a mistake. Mr. Fogg added that, in any event he would not abandon the young woman, and that he would take her to Hong-Kong.

"But the steamer leaves at noon!" remarked Passepartout.

"Before noon we will be on board," was the simple reply of the impassible gentleman.

This was so flatly asserted that Passepartout could not help saying to himself:

"*Parbleu!* that is certain! before noon we will be on board!" But he was not at all reassured.

At half-past eight the door of the room was opened. The policeman reappeared, and he led the prisoners into the next room. It was a court-room, and quite a large crowd, composed of Europeans and natives, already occupied the rear of the room.

Mr. Fogg, Mrs. Aouda, and Passepartout were seated on a bench in front of the seats reserved for the magistrate and the clerk.

This magistrate, Judge Obadiah, entered almost immediately, followed by the clerk. He was a large, fat man. He took down a wig hung on a nail and hastily put it on his head.

"The first case," he said.

But putting his hand to his head, he said:

"Humph! this is not my wig!"

"That's a fact, Mr. Obadiah, it is mine," replied the clerk.

"My dear Mr. Oysterpuff, how do you think that a judge can give a wise sentence with a clerk's wig?"

An exchange of wigs had been made. During these preliminaries Passepartout was boiling over with impatience, for the hands appeared to him to move terribly fast over the face of the large clock in the court-room.

"The first case,' said Judge Obadiah again.

"Phileas Fogg?" said Clerk Oysterpuff.

"Here I am," replied Mr. Fogg.

"Passepartout?"

"Present!" replied Passepartout.

"Good!" said Judge Obadiah. "For two days, prisoners, you have been looked for upon the arrival of all the trains from Bombay."

"But of what are we accused?" cried Passepartout impatiently.

"You shall know now," replied the judge.

"Sir," said Mr. Fogg then, "I am an English citizen, and have the right—"

"Have you been treated disrespectfully?" asked Mr. Obadiah.

"Not at all."

"Very well, let the complainants come in."

Upon the order of the judge a door was opened, and three Hindu priests were led in by a tip-staff.

"Well, well!" murmured Passepartout, "they are the rascals who were going to burn our young lady!"

The priest stood up before the judge, and the clerk read in a loud voice a complaint of sacrilege, preferred against Mr. Fogg and his servant, accused of having violated a place consecrated by the Brahmin religion.

"You have heard the charge?" the judge asked Phileas Fogg.

"Yes, sir," replied Mr. Fogg, consulting his watch, "and I confess it."

"Ah! You confess?"

"I confess and expect these three priests to confess in their turn what they were going to do at the pagoda of Pillaji."

The priests looked at each other. They did not seem to understand the words of the accused.

"Truly!" cried Passepartout impetuously, "at the pagoda of Pillaji, where they were going to burn their victim!"

78

More stupefaction of the priests, and profound astonishment of Judge Obadiah.

"What victim!" he answered. "Burn whom? In the heart of the city of Bombay?"

"Bombay?" cried Passepartout.

"Certainly. We are not speaking of the pagoda of Pillaji, but of the pagoda of Malebar in Bombay."

"And as a proof here are the desecrator's shoes," added the clerk, putting a pair on his desk.

"My shoes!" cried Passepartout, who, surprised at the last charge, could not prevent this involuntary exclamation.

The confusion in the minds of the master and servant may be imagined. They had forgotten the incident of the pagoda of Bombay, and that was the very thing which had brought them before the magistrate in Calcutta.

In fact, Fix understood the advantage that he might get from this unfortunate affair. Delaying his departure twelve hours, he had taken counsel with the priests of Malebar Hill, and had promised them large damages, knowing very well that the British Government was very severe upon this kind of trespass; then by the following train he had sent them forward on the track of the perpetrator. But in consequence of the time employed in the deliverance of the young widow, Fix and the Hindus arrived at Calcutta before Phileas Fogg and his servant, whom the authorities, warned by telegraph, were to arrest as they got out of the train. The disappointment of Fix may be judged of, when he learned that Phileas Fogg had not yet arrived in the capital of India. He was compelled to think that his robber, stopping at one of the stations of the Peninsular Railway, had taken refuge in the northern provinces. For twenty-four hours, in the greatest uneasiness, Fix watched for him at the station. What was his joy then when, this very morning, he saw him get out of the car accompanied, it is true, by a young woman whose presence he could not explain. He immediately sent a policeman after him; and this is how Mr. Fogg, Passepartout, and the widow of the rajah of Bundelcund were taken before Judge Obadiah.

And if Passepartout had been less preoccupied with his

affair, he would have perceived in a corner of the room the detective, who followed the discussion with an interest easy to understand, for at Calcutta, as at Bombay, and as at Suez, the warrant of arrest, was still not at hand!

But Judge Obadiah had taken a note of the confession escaped from Passepartout who would have given all he possessed to recall his imprudent words.

"The facts are admitted?" said the judge.

"Admitted," replied Mr. Fogg coldly.

"Inasmuch," continued the judge, "as the English law intends to protect equally and rigorously all the religions of the people of India, the trespass being admitted by this man Passepartout, convicted of having violated with sacrilegious feet the pavement of the pagoda of Malebar Hill in Bombay, on the 20th day of October, I sentence the said Passepartout to fifteen days' imprisonment, and a fine of three hundred pounds."

"Three hundred pounds!" cried Passepartout, who was really only alive to the fine.

"Silence!" said the tip-staff in a shrill voice.

"And," added Judge Obadiah, "inasmuch as it is not materially proved that there was not a connivance between the servant and the master, the latter of whom ought to be held responsible for the acts and gestures of a servant in his employ, I detain the said Phileas Fogg and sentence him to eight days' imprisonment and one hundred and fifty pounds fine. Clerk, call another case!"

Fix, in his corner, experienced an unspeakable satisfaction. Phileas Fogg, detained eight days in Calcutta! It would be more than time enough for the warrant to arrive.

Passepartout was crushed. This sentence would ruin his master. A wager of twenty thousand pounds lost, and all because, in the height of folly, he had gone into that cursed pagoda!

Phileas Fogg, as much master of himself as if this sentence did not concern him, did not even knit his eyebrows. But at the moment that the clerk was calling another case, he rose, and said:

"I offer bail."

"It is your right," replied the judge.

Fix felt a cold shudder down his back, but he recovered himself again, when he heard the judge, "in consideration of the fact of Phileas Fogg and his servant both being strangers," fix the bail for each at the enormous sum of one thousand pounds.

It would cost Mr. Fogg two thousand pounds, unless he would be cleared from his sentence.

"I will pay it," said that gentleman.

And he took from the bag which Passepartout carried a bundle of bank-notes, which he placed on the clerk's desk.

"This sum will be returned to you on coming out of prison," said the judge. "In the meantime, you are free under bail."

"Come," said Phileas Fogg to his servant.

"But they should at least return me my shoes," cried Passepartout, with an angry movement.

They returned him his shoes.

"These are dear!" he murmured; "more than a thousand pounds apiece! Without counting that they pinch me!"

Passepartout, with a very pitiful look, followed Mr. Fogg, who had offered his arm to the young woman. Fix still hoped that his robber would not decide to surrender this sum of two thousand pounds, and that he would serve out his eight days in prison. He put himself, then, on Fogg's tracks.

Mr. Fogg took a carriage, into which Mrs. Aouda, Passepartout, and he got immediately. Fix ran behind the carriage, which soon stopped on one of the wharves of the city.

Half a mile out in the harbour the *Rangoon* was anchored, her sailing flag hoisted-to the top of the mast. Eleven o'clock struck. Mr. Fogg was one hour ahead. Fix saw him get out of the carriage, and embark in a boat with Mrs. Aouda and his servant. The detective stamped his foot.

"The rascal!" he cried. "He is going off! Two thousand pounds sacrificed! Prodigal as a robber! Ah! I will follow him to the end of the world, if it is necessary; but, at the rate at which he is going, all the stolen money will be gone!"

The detective had good reason for making this remark. In

fact, since he left London, what with travelling expenses, rewards, the elephant purchase, bail, and fines, Phileas Fogg had already scattered more than five thousand pounds on his route, and the percentage of the sum recovered, promised to the detectives, was constantly diminishing.

CHAPTER 16

In which Fix has not the Appearance of knowing anything about the Matters concerning which They talk to Him

The *Rangoon*, one of the vessels employed by the Peninsular and Oriental Company in the Chinese and Japanese seas, was an iron screw steamer, of seventeen hundred and seventy tons, and nominally of four hundred horse-power. She was equally swift, but not so comfortable as the *Mongolia* Mrs. Aouda was not as well fixed in her as Phileas Fogg would have desired. But, after all, it was only a distance of three thousand five hundred miles, and the young woman did not show herself a troublesome passenger.

During the first few days of the passage Mrs. Aouda became better acquainted with Phileas Fogg. On every occasion she showed him the liveliest gratitude. The phlegmatic gentleman listened to her, at least in appearance, with the most extreme indifference, not one tone of his voice or gesture betraying in him the slightest emotion. He saw that she was wanting in nothing. At certain hours he came regularly, if not to talk with her, at least to listen to her. He fulfilled towards her the duties of the strictest politeness, but with the grace and startling effects of an automaton whose movements have been put together for that purpose. Mrs. Aouda did not know what to think of him, but Passepartout had explained to her a little the eccentric character of his master. He had told her what sort of a wager was taking him round the world. Mrs. Aouda had smiled! but, after all, she owed her life to him, and her deliverer could not lose, because she saw him through her gratitude.

Mrs. Aouda confirmed the narrative of the guide in reference to her affecting history. She belonged, in fact, to the race which occupies the first rank among the natives. Several Parsee merchants have made large fortunes in India in the cotton trade. One of them, Sir James Jejeebhoy, was raised to the nobility by the British Government, and Mrs. Aouda was a relative of this rich person, who lived in Bombay. It was indeed a cousin of Sir Jejeebhoy, the honourable Jejeeh, whom she counted on joining at Hong-Kong. Would she find a refuge with him and assistance? She could not say so positively. To which Mr. Fogg replied that she should not be uneasy, and everything would be mathematically arranged. That was the phrase he used.

Did the young woman understand this horrible adverb? We do not know. However, her large eyes were fixed upon those of Mr. Fogg—her large eyes "clear as the sacred lakes of the Himalaya!" But the intractable Fogg, as reserved as ever, did not seem to be the man to throw himself into this lake.

The first part of the *Rangoon's* voyage was accomplished under excellent conditions. The weather was moderate. All the lower portion of the immense Bay of Bengal was favourable to the steamer's progress. The *Rangoon* soon sighted the great Andaman, the principal one of the group of islands, which is distinguished by navigators at a great distance by the picturesque Saddle Peak mountain, two thousand four hundred feet high.

They kept pretty close to the coast. The savage Papuans of the island did not show themselves. They are beings in the lowest grade of humanity, but they have been wrongfully called cannibals.

The panoramic development of this island was superb.

Immense forests of palm-trees, arecas, bamboo, nutmeg-trees, teak-wood, giant mimosas, and tree-like ferns covered the country in the fore-ground, and in the background there stood out in relief the graceful outline of the mountains. Along the shore there swarmed by thousands those precious swallows whose edible nests form a dish much sought for in the Celestial Empire. But all this varied spectacle offered to the eyes by the Andaman group passed quickly, and the *Rangoon* swiftly pursued her way towards the Straits of Malacca, which were to give her access to the Chinese seas.

During this trip what was detective Fix doing, so unluckily dragged into a voyage round the world? On leaving Calcutta, after-having left instructions to forward the warrant to him at Hong-Kong, if it should arrive, he succeeded in getting aboard the *Rangoon* without being perceived by Passepartout, and he hoped that he might conceal his presence until the arrival of the steamer. In fact, it would have been difficult for him to explain how he was on board, without awaking the suspicions of Passepartout, who thought he was in Bombay. But he was led to renew his acquaintance with the good fellow by the very logic of circumstances. How? We will see.

All the hopes, all the desires of the detective were now concentrated on a single point in the world, Hong-Kong—for the steamer would stop too short a time in Singapore for him to operate in that city. The arrest of the robber must then be made in Hong-Kong, or he would escape irrecoverably.

In fact, Hong-Kong was still English soil, but the last he would find on the road. Beyond China and Japan, America would offer a pretty certain refuge to Mr. Fogg. At Hong-Kong, if he should finally find there the warrant of arrest, which was evidently running after him, Fix would arrest Fogg, and put him in the hands of the local police. No difficulty there. But after Hong-Kong a simple warrant of arrest would not be sufficient. An extradition order would be necessary. Thence delays and obstacles of every kind, of which the rogue would take advantage to escape finally. If he failed at Hong-Kong, it would be, if not impossible, at least very difficult to attempt it again with any chance of success.

"Then," repeated Fix during the long hours that he passed in his cabin, "then, either the warrant will be at Hong-Kong and I will arrest my man, or it will not be there, and this time I must, at all hazards, delay his departure! I have failed at Bombay, I have failed at Calcutta! If I miss at Hong-Kong, I shall lose my reputation! Cost what it may, I *must* succeed. But what means shall I employ to delay, if it is necessary, the departure of this accursed Fogg?"

As a last resort, Fix had decided to tell everything to Passepartout; to let him know who the master was that he was serving, and whose accomplice he certainly was not. Passepartout, enlightened by this revelation, fearing to be compromised, would without doubt take sides with him, Fix But it was a very hazardous means, which could only be employed in default of any other. One word from Passepartout to his master would have been sufficient to compromise the affair irrevocably.

The detective was then extremely embarrassed when the presence of Mrs. Aouda on board of the *Rangoon,* in company with Phileas Fogg, opened new perspectives to him.

Who was this woman? What combination of circumstances had made her Fogg's companion? The meeting had evidently taken place between Bombay and Calcutta. But at what point of the peninsula? Was it chance which had brought together Phileas Fogg and the young traveller? Had not his journey across India, on the contrary, been undertaken by this gentleman with the aim of joining this charming person? For she was charming! Fix had had a good view of-her in the audience-hall of the Calcutta tribunal.

It may be comprehended to what a point the detective would be entangled. He asked himself if there was not a criminal abduction in this affair. Yes! that must be it! This idea once fastened in the mind of Fix, and he recognised all the advantage that he could get from this circumstance. Whether this young woman was married or not, there was an abduction, and it was possible to put the ravisher in such embarrassment in Hong-Kong that he could not extricate himself by paying money.

But it was not necessary to await the arrival of the *Rangoon* at Hong-Kong. This Fogg had the detestable habit of jumping from one vessel into another, and before the affair was entered upon he might be far enough off.

The important thing was to warn the English authorities, and to signal the *Rangoon* before her arrival. Now, nothing would be easier to accomplish, as the steamer would put in at Singapore, which is connected with the Chinese coast by a telegraph line.

But, before acting, and to be more certain, Fix determined to question Passepartout. He knew it was not very difficult to start the young man talking, and he decided to throw off the incognito that he had maintained until that time. Now there was no time to lose. It was October 30, and the next day the *Rangoon* would drop anchor at Singapore.

This very day, October 30, Fix, leaving his cabin, went upon deck, with the intention of meeting Passepartout first, with signs of the greatest surprise. Passepartout was walking in the forward part of the vessel, when the detective rushed towards him, exclaiming:

"Is this you, on the *Rangoon*?"

"Monsieur Fix aboard!" replied Passepartout, very much surprised, recognised his old acquaintance of the *Mongolia*.

"What! I left you at Bombay, and I meet you again on the route to Hong-Kong! Are you making also the tour of the world?"

"No, no," replied Fix. "I expect to stop at Hong-Kong at least for a few days."

"Ah!" said Passepartout, who seemed astonished for a moment. "But why have I not seen you aboard since we left Calcutta?"

"Indeed, I was sick—a little sea-sickness—I remained lying down in my cabin—I did not get along as well in the Bay of Bengal as in the Indian Ocean. And your master, Phileas Fogg?"

"Is in perfect health, and as punctual as his diary! Not one day behind! Ah! Monsieur Fix, you do not know it, but we have a young lady with us also."

"A young lady!" replied the detective, who acted exactly as if he did not understand what his companion was saying.

But Passepartout soon gave him the thread of the whole story. He related the incident of the pagoda in Bombay, the purchase of the elephant at the cost of two thousand pounds, the suttee affair, the abduction of Aouda, the sentence of the Calcutta court, and their freedom under bail. Fix, who knew the last portion of these incidents, seemed not to know any of them, and Passepartout gave himself up to the pleasure of telling his adventures to a hearer who showed so much interest.

"But," asked Fix, at the end of the story, "does your master intend to take this young woman to Europe?"

"Not at all, Monsieur Fix; not at all! We are simply going to put her in charge of one of her relatives, a rich merchant of Hong-Kong."

"Nothing to be done there," said the detective to himself, concealing his disappointment. "Take a glass of gin, Mr. Passepartout."

"With pleasure, Monsieur Fix. It is the least that we should drink to our meeting aboard the *Rangoon*."

CHAPTER 17

In which one thing and another is talked about during the Trip from Singapore to Hong-Kong

After this day, Passepartout and the detective met frequently, but the latter maintained a very great reserve towards his companion, and he did not try to make him talk. Once or twice only he had a glimpse of Mr. Fogg, who was glad to remain in the grand saloon of the Rangoon, either keeping company with Mrs. Aouda, or playing at whist, according to his invariable habit.

As for Passepartout, he thought very seriously over the singular chance which had once more put Fix on his master's route. And, in fact, it was a little surprising. This gentleman, very amiable and very complacent, certainly, whom they met first at Suez, who embarked upon the *Mongolia*, who landed at Bombay, where he said that he would stop, whom they meet again on the *Rangoon, en route* for Hong-Kong—in a word, followng step by step the route marked out by Mr. Fogg—he was worth the trouble of being thought about. There was at least a singular coincidence in it all. What interest had Fix in it? Passepartout was ready to bet his slippers—he had carefully preserved them—that Fix would leave Hong-Kong at the same time as they, and probably on the same steamer.

If Passepartout had thought for a century, he would never have guessed the detective's mission. He would never have imagined that Phileas Fogg was being "followed," after the fashion of a robber, around the terrestrial globe. But as it is in human nature to give an explanation for everything, Passepartout, suddenly enlightened, interpreted in this way the permanent presence of Fix, and, indeed, his interpretation was very plausible. According to him Fix was, and could be, only a detective sent upon Mr. Fogg's tracks by his colleagues of the Reform Club, to prove that this tour around the world was accomplished regularly, according to the time agreed upon.

"That is plain! that is plain!" repeated the honest fellow to himself, quite proud of his clear sightedness. "He is a spy whom these gentlemen have put upon our heels. This is undignified! To have Mr. Fogg, a man so honourable and just, tracked by a detective! Ah! gentlemen of the Reform Club, this will cost you dearly!"

Passepartout delighted with his discovery, resolved, however, to say nothing of it to his master, feeling that he would be justly wounded at this mistrust which his opponents showed. But he promised himself to banter Fix, as opportunity offered, with covert allusions, and without committing himself.

On Wednesday, October 30, in the afternoon, the *Rangoon* entered the Straits of Malacca, separating the peninsula of that name from Sumatra Mountainous, craggy, and very picturesque islets concealed from the passenger the view of this large island.

At four o'clock the next morning, the *Rangoon*, having gained a half-day on its timetable, put in at Singapore, to take in a new supply of coal.

Phileas Fogg noted this gain in the proper column, and this time he landed, accompanying Mrs. Aouda, who had expressed a desire to walk about for a few hours.

Fix, to whom every act of Fogg seemed suspicious, followed him without letting himself be noticed. Passepartout, who was going to make his ordinary purchases, laughed *in petto* seeing Fix's manoeuvre.

The Island of Singapore is neither large nor of an imposing aspect. It is wanting in mountains, that is to say, in profiles. However, it is charming, even in its meagreness. It is a park laid out with fine roads. An elegant carriage, drawn by handsome horses, such as have been imported from New Holland, took Mrs. Aouda and Phileas Fogg into the midst of massive groups of palm trees, the brilliant foliage, and close trees, the cloves of which are formed from the very bud of the half-opened flower. There pepper plants replaced the thorny hedges of European countries; sage-trees, and large ferns with their superb branches, varied the aspect of this tropical region; and nutmeg-trees with shining leaves impregnated the air with a penetrating odour. Bands of monkeys, lively and grimacing, were not wanting in the woods, nor perhaps tigers in the jungles. Should anyone be astonished to learn that in this island, comparatively so small, these terrible carnivorous animals were not destroyed to the very last one, we may reply that they come from Malacca, swimming across the straits.

After having driven about the country for two hours, Mrs.

Aouda and her companion—who looked a little without seeing anything—returned into the town, a vast collection of heavy, flat-looking houses, surrounded by delightful gardens, in which grow mangoes, pineapples, and all the best fruits in the world.

At ten o'clock they returned to the steamer, having been followed, without suspecting it, by the detective, who had also gone to the expense of a carriage.

Passepartout was waiting for them on the deck of the *Rangoon*. The good fellow had bought a few dozen of mangoes, as large as ordinary apples—dark brown outside, brilliant red inside—and whose white pulp, melting in the mouth, gives the true gourmand an unexcelled enjoyment. Passepartout was only too happy to offer them to Mrs. Aouda, who thanked him very gracefully.

At eleven o'clock the *Rangoon*, having obtained a full supply of coal, slipped from her moorings, and a few hours later the passengers lost sight of the high mountains of Malacca, whose forests shelter the most beautiful tigers in the world.

About thirteen hundred miles separate Singapore from the Island of Hong-Kong, a small British territory, detached from the Chinese coast. It was Phileas Fogg's interest to accomplish this in six days at the most, in order to take at Hong-Kong the steamer leaving on the 6th of November for Yokohama, one of the principal ports of Japan.

The *Rangoon* was heavily laden. Many passengers had come aboard at Singapore—Hindus, Ceylonese, Chinamen, Malays, and Portuguese—mostly second class.

The weather, which had been quite fine until this time, changed with the last quarter of the moon. The sea was high. The wind sometimes blew a gale, but fortunately from the south-east, which favoured the movement of the steamer. When it was practicable, the captain had the sails unfurled. The *Rangoon*, brig-rigged, sailed frequently with its two topsails and foresail, and its speed increased under the double impetus of steam and sail. The vessel thus made her way over a short and sometimes fatiguing sea, along the shores of Anam and Cochin China.

But the passengers would have to blame the *Rangoon* rather than the ocean for their sickness and fatigue.

In fact, the ships of the Peninsular Company, in the China service, are seriously defective in their construction. The proportion of their draught, when loaded, to their depth of hold, has been badly calculated, and consequently they stand the sea but poorly. Their bulk, closed, impenetrable to the water, is insufficient. They are "drowned," to use a maritime expression, and, in consequence, it does not take many waves thrown upon the deck to slacken their speed. These ships are then very inferior—if not in motive power and steam escapes—to the models of the French mail steamers, such as the *Imperattice* and *Cambodge*. Whilst, according to the calculations of the engineers, the latter can take on a weight of water equal to their own before sinking, the vessels of the Peninsular Company, the *Golcanda*, the *Corea*, and finally the *Rangoon*, could not take on the sixth of their weight without going to the bottom.

Great precautions had to be taken then in bad weather. It was sometimes necessary to sail under a small head of steam. This loss of time did not seem to affect Phileas Fogg at all, but Passepartout was much put out about it. He blamed the captain, the engineer, and the company, and set to old Nick all those who had anything to do with the transportation of the passengers. Perhaps, also, the thought of the gas-burner still burning at his expense in the house in Saville Row had a large share in his impatience.

"Are you in a very great hurry to arrive at Hong-Kong?" the detective asked him one day.

"In a very great hurry!" replied Passepartout.

"You think that Mr. Fogg is in a hurry to take the Yokohama steamer?"

"In a dreadful hurry."

"Then you believe now in this singular voyage around the world?"

"Absolutely. And you, Monsieur Fix?"

"I? I don't believe in it."

"You're a sly fellow," replied Passepartout, winking at him.

This expression left the detective in a reverie. The epithet disturbed him without his knowing very well why. Had the Frenchman guessed his purpose? He did not know what to think. But how had Passepartout been able to discover his capacity as a detective, the secret of which he alone knew. And yet, in speaking thus to him Passepartout certainly had an afterthought.

It happened another day that the good fellow went further. It was too much for him; he could no longer hold his tongue.

"Let us see, Monsieur Fix," he asked his companion, in a roguish tone, "when we have arrived at Hong-Kong, shall we be so unfortunate as to leave you there?"

"Oh!" replied Fix, quite embarrassed, "I do not know! Perhaps—"

"Ah!" said Passepartout, "if you accompany us, I would be so happy! Let us see! An agent of the Peninsular Company could not stop on the route! You were only going to Bombay, and now you will soon be in China. America is not far off, and from America to Europe is only a step!"

Fix looked attentively at his companion, who showed the pleasantest face in the world, and he decided to laugh with him. But the latter who was in humour, asked him if his business brought him in much?

"Yes and no," replied Fix without frowning. "There are fortunate and unfortunate business enterprises. But you understand of course that I don't travel at my own expense!"

"Oh! I am very sure of that," replied Passepartout, laughing still louder.

The conversation finished, Fix returned to his cabin, and sat down to think. He was evidently suspected. In one way or another the Frenchman had recognised his capacity as a detective. But had he warned his master? What role would he play in all this? Was he an accomplice or not? Had they got wind of the matter, and was it consequently all up? The detective passed some perplexing hours there, at one time believing everything lost; at one time hoping that Fogg was ignorant of the situation; and, finally, not knowing what course to pursue.

Meanwhile his brain became calmer, and he resolved to act

frankly with Passepartout. If matters were not in the proper shape to arrest Fogg at Hong-Kong, and if Fogg was then prepared to leave finally the English territory, he (Fix) would tell Passepartout everything. Either the servant was the accomplice of his master, and the latter knew everything, and in this case the affair was definitely compromised, or the servant had no part in the robbery, and then his interest would be to abandon the robber.

Such was the respective situation of these two men, and above them Phileas Fogg was hovering in his majestic indifference. he was accomplishing rationally his orbit around the world, without being troubled by the asteroids gravitating around him.

And yet, in the vicinity, there was—according to the expression of astronomers—a disturbing star which ought to have produced a certain agitation in this gentleman's heart. But no! The charm of Mrs. Aouda did not act, to the great surprise of Passepartout, and the disturbances, if they existed, would have been more difficult to calculate that those of Uranus, which led to the discovery of Neptune.

Yes ! it was a surprise every day for Passepartout, who read in the eyes of the young woman so much gratitude to his master. Phileas Fogg had decidedly heart enough for heroic actions, but for love, none at all! As for the thoughts which the chances of the journey might have produced in him, there was not a trace. But Passepartout was living in a continual trance. One day, leaning on the railing of the engine-room, he was looking at the powerful engine which sometimes moved very violently, when, with the pitching of the vessel the screw would fly out of the water. The steam then escaped from the valves, which provoked the anger of the worthy fellow.

"These valves are not charged enough!" he cried. "We are not going! Oh, these Englishmen! If we were only in an American vessel, we would blow up, perhaps, but we would go more swiftly!"

CHAPTER 18

In which Phileas Fogg, Passepartout, and Fix each goes about His own business

During the last few days of the voyage the weather was pretty bad. The wind became very boisterous. Remaining in the north-west quarter, it impeded the progress of the steamer. The *Rangoon*, too unsteady already, rolled heavily, and the passengers quite lost their temper over the long, tiresome waves which the wind raised at a distance.

During the days of the 3rd and 4th of November it was a sort of tempest. The squall struck the sea with violence. The *Rangoon* had to go slowly for half a day, keeping herself in motion with only ten revolutions of the screw, so as to lean with the waves. All the sails had been reefed, and there was still too much rigging whistling in the squall.

The rapidity of the steamer, it may be imagined, was very much diminished, and it was estimated that she would arrive at Hong-Kong twenty hours behind time, and perhaps more, if the tempest did not cease.

Phileas Fogg looked intently at this spectacle of a raging sea, which seemed to struggle directly against him, with his customary impassibility. His brow did not darken an instant, and yet a delay of twenty hours might seriously interfere with his voyage, by making him miss the departure of the Yokohama steamer. But this man without nerves felt neither impatience nor annoyance. It seemed truly as if this tempest formed a part of his programme, and was foreseen. Mrs. Aouda, who talked with her companion about this mishap, found him as calm as in the past.

Fix did not look at these things in the same light. On the contrary, this tempest pleased him very much. His satisfaction would have known no bounds, if the *Rangoon* had been obliged to fly before the violent storm. All these delays suited him, for they would oblige this man Fogg to remain some days at Hong-Kong. Finally the skies with their squalls and tempests became his ally. He was a little sick, it is true, but what did that matter? He did not count his nausea, and when his body was writhing under the sea-sickness, his spirit was merry with the height of its satisfaction.

As for Passepartout, it may be guessed how ill concealed his anger was during this time of trial. Until then everything had moved on so well! Land and sea seemed to be devoted to his master. Steamers and railways obeyed him. Wind and steam combined to favour his journey. Had the hour of mistakes finally sounded? Passepartout, as if the twenty thousand pounds of the wager had to come out of his purse, was no longer happy. This tempest exasperated him, this squall put him in a rage, and he would have gladly whipped the disobedient sea! Poor fellow! Fix carefully concealed from him, his personal satisfaction, and it was well, for if Passepartout had guessed the secret delight of Fix, Fix would have been roughly used.

Passepartout remained on the *Rangoon's* deck during the entire continuance of the blow. He could not remain below; he climbed up in the masts; he astonished the crew, and helped at everything with the agility of a monkey. A hundred times he questioned the captain, the officers, the sailors, who could not help laughing at seeing him so much out of countenance. Passepartout wanted to know positively how long the storm would last. They sent him to the barometer, which would not decide to ascend. Passepartout shook the barometer, but nothing came of it, neither the shaking nor the insults that he heaped upon that irresponsible instrument.

Finally the tempest subsided. The sea became calmer on the 4th of November. The wind veered two points to the south and again became favourable.

Passepartout cleared up with the weather. The top-sails and lower sails could be unfurled, and the *Rangoon* resumed her route with marvellous swiftness.

But all the time lost could not be regained. They could only submit, and land was not signalled until the 6th at five o'clock a.m. The diary of Phileas Fogg put down the arrival of the steamer on the 5th, and she did not arrive until the 6th, which was a loss of twenty-four hours, and of course they would miss the Yokohama steamer.

At six o'clock the pilot came aboard the *Rangoon* and took his place on the bridge to guide the vessel through the channels into the port of Hong-Kong.

Passepartout was dying to ask this man whether the Yokohama steamer had left Hong-Kong. But he did not dare, preferring to preserve a little hope until the last moment. He had confided his anxiety to Fix, who—the cunning fox—tried to console him by saying that Mr. Fogg would be in time to take the next boat. This put Passepartout in a towering rage.

But if Passepartout did not venture to ask the pilot, Mr. Fogg, after consulting his *Bradshaw*, asked in his quiet manner of the said pilot if he knew when a vessel would leave Hong-Kong for Yokohama.

"To-morrow morning, at high tide," replied the pilot.

"Ah," said Mr. Fogg, without showing any astonishment.

Passepartout, who was present, would have liked to hug the pilot, whose neck Fix would have wrung with pleasure.

"What is the name of the steamer?" asked Fogg.

"The *Carnatic*," replied the pilot.

"Was she not to leave yesterday?"

"Yes, sir, but they had to repair one of her boilers, and her departure has been put off until to-morrow."

"Thank you," replied Mr. Fogg, who, with his automatic step, went down again into the saloon of the *Rangoon*.

Passepartout caught the pilot's hand, and, pressing it warmly, said:

"Pilot, you are a good fellow!"

The pilot doubtless never knew why his answers had procured him this friendly expression. A whistle blew, and he went again upon the bridge of the steamer and guided her through the flotilla of junks, tankas, fishing-boats, and vessels of all kinds which crowded the channels of Hong-Kong.

In an hour the *Rangoon* was at the wharf, and the passengers landed.

It must be confessed that in this circumstance chance had singularly served Phileas Fogg. Without the necessity of repairing the boilers, the *Carnatic* would have left on the 5th of November, and the passengers for Japan would have had to wait a week for the departure of the next steamer. Mr. Fogg, it is true, was twenty-four hours behind time, but this delay could not have any evil consequences for the rest of the journey.

In fact, the steamer which crosses the Pacific from Yokohama to San Francisco was in direct connection with the Hong-Kong steamer, and the former could not leave before the latter had arrived. Evidently they would be twenty-four hours behind time at Yokohama, but it would be easy to make them up during the voyage across the Pacific, lasting twenty-two days. Phileas Fogg found himself, then, within about twenty-four hours of the conditions of his programme thirty-five days after leaving London.

The *Carnatic* not leaving until five o'clock the next morning, Mr. Fogg had sixteen hours to attend to his business—that is, that which concerned Mrs. Aouda. On landing from the vessel, he offered his arm to the young woman and led her to a palanquin. He asked the men who carried it to point him out a hotel, and they named the Club Hotel. The palanquin started, followed by Passepartout, and twenty minutes after they arrived at their destination.

An apartment was secured for the young woman, and Phileas Fogg saw that she was made comfortable. Then he told Mrs. Aouda that he was going immediately to look for the relative in whose care he was to leave her at Hong-Kong. At the same time he ordered Passepartout to remain at the hotel until his return, so that the young woman should not be left alone.

The gentleman was shown the way to the Exchange. There, they would unquestionably know the personage, such as the honourable Jejeeh, who was reckoned among the richest merchants of the city.

The broker whom Mr. Fogg addressed did indeed know the Parsee merchant. But for two years he had not lived in China. Having made his fortune, he had gone to live in Europe—in Holland, it was believed, which was explained by the extensive correspondence which he had had with that country during his life as a merchant.

Phileas Fogg returned to the Club Hotel. He immediately asked permission to see Mrs. Aouda, and without any other preamble, told her that the honourable Jejeeh was no longer living in Hong-Kong, but probably was living in Holland.

Mrs. Aouda did not reply at first. Passing her hand over her forehead, she thought for a few moments, and then said in her sweet voice:

"What ought I to do, Mr. Fogg?"

"It is very simple," replied the gentleman. "Go on to Europe."

"But I cannot abuse—"

"You do not abuse, and your presence does not at all embarrass my programme. Passepartout!"

"Monsieur," replied Passepartout.

"Go to the *Carnatic* and engage three cabins."

Passepartout, delighted with continuing his voyage in the company of the young woman, who was very gracious to him, immediately left the Club Hotel.

CHAPTER 19

In which Passepartout takes a little too lively interest in his Master, and what follows

Hong-Kong is only a small island secured to England by the treaty of Nanking, after the war of 1842. In a few years, the colonising genius of Great Britain had established there an important city, and created the port Victoria. This island is situated at the mouth of the Canton River, and sixty miles only separate it from the Portuguese city of Macao, built on the other shore. Hong-Kong must necessarily vanquish Macao in a commercial struggle, and now the greatest part of the Chinese transportation is done through the English city. Docks, hospitals, wharves, warehouses, a Gothic cathedral, a Government House, macadamised streets, all would lead one to believe that one of the commercial cities of the counties of Kent or Surrey, traversing the terrestrial sphere, had found a place at this point in China nearly at its antipodes.

Passepartout, with his hands in his pockets, sauntered towards the port Victoria, looking at the palanquins, the curtained carriages still in favour in the Celestial Empire, and all the crowd of Chinese, Japanese, and Europeans hurrying along in the streets. In some things, it was like Bombay, Calcutta, or Singapore that the worthy fellow was finding again on his route. There is thus a track of English towns all around the world.

Passepartout arrived at Victoria port. There, at the mouth of Canton River, was a perfect swarm of the ships of all nations, English, French, American, Dutch, war and merchant vessels, Japanese or Chinese craft, junks, sempas, tankas, and even flower-boats, which formed so many parterres floating on the waters. Walking along, Passepartout noticed a certain number of natives dressed in yellow, all of quite advanced age. Having gone into a Chinese barber's to be shaved "à la Chinese," he learned from Figaro in the shop, who spoke pretty good English, that these ancient men were at least eighty years old, and that at this age they had the privilege of wearing yellow, the Imperial colour. Passepartout found this very funny, without knowing exactly why.

His beard shaved, he repaired to the wharf from which the *Carnatic* would leave, and there he perceived Fix walking up and down, at which he was not at all astonished. But the detective showed upon his face the marks of great disappointment.

"Good!" said Passepartout to himself; "that will be bad for the gentlemen of the Reform Club!"

And he accosted Fix with his merry smile, without seeming to notice the vexed air of his companion.

Now, the detective had good reason to fret about the infernal luck which was pursuing him. No warrant! It was evident that the warrant was running after him, and that it could reach him only if he stopped some days in this city. Now, Hong-Kong being the last British territory on the route, this Mr. Fogg would escape him finally, if he did not succeed in detaining him there.

"Well, Monsieur Fix, have you decided to come with us as far as America?" asked Passepartout.

"Yes," replied Fix between his closed teeth.

"Well then!" cried Passepartout, shouting with laughter. "I knew very well that you could not separate yourself from us. Come and engage your berth, come!"

And both entered the ticket office and engaged cabins for four persons. But the clerk told them that the repairs of the *Carnatic* being completed, the steamer would leave at eight o'clock in the evening, and not the next morning, as had been announced.

"Very good!" replied Passepartout, "that will suit my master. I am going to inform him."

At this moment Fix took an extreme step. He determined to tell Passepartout everything. It was the only means, perhaps, that he had of retaining Phileas Fogg for a few days in Hong-Kong.

Leaving the office, Fix offered to treat his companion in a tavern. Passepartout had the time. He accepted Fix's invitation.

A tavern opened on the quay. It had an inviting appearance. Both entered. It was a large room, finely decorated, at the back of which was stretched a camp-bed, furnished with cushions. Upon this bed were lying a number of sleepers.

Some thirty customers in the large room occupied small tables of plaited rushes. Some emptied pints of English beer, ale, or porter, others jugs of alcoholic liquors, gin, or brandy. Besides, the most of them were smoking long, red-clay pipes, stuffed with little balls of opium mixed with essence of rose. Then, from time to time, some smoker, overcome, would fall down under the table, and the waiters of the establishment, taking him by the head and feet, carried him on to the camp-bed, alongside of another. Twenty of these sots were thus laid side by side, in the last stage of brutishness.

Fix and Passepartout understood that they had entered a smoking-house haunted by those wretched, stupefied, lean, idiotic creatures, to whom mercantile England sells annually ten millions four hundred thousand pounds' worth of the fatal drug called opium. Sad millions are these, levied on one of the most destructive vices of human nature.

The Chinese Government has tried hard to remedy such an abuse by severe laws, but in vain. From the rich class, to whom the use of opium was at first formally reserved, it has descended to the lower classes, and its ravages can no longer be arrested. Opium is smoked everywhere and always in the Middle Empire. Men and women give themselves up to this deplorable passion, and when they are accustomed to inhaling the fumes they can no longer do without it, except by suffering terrible cramps in the stomach. A great smoker can smoke as many as eight pipes a day, but he dies in five years.

Now, it was in one of the numerous smoking-houses of this kind, which swarm even in Hong-Kong, that Fix and Passepartout had entered with the intention of refreshing themselves. Passepartout had no money, but he accepted willingly the "politeness" of his companion, ready to return it to him at the proper time and place.

They called for two bottles of port, to which the Frenchman did full justice, whilst Fix, more reserved, observed his companion with the closest attention. They talked of one thing and another, and especially of the excellent idea that Fix had of taking passage on the *Carnatic*. The bottles now being empty, Passepartout rose to inform his master that the steamer would leave several hours in advance of the time announced.

Fix detained him.

"One moment," he said.

"What do you wish, Monsieur Fix?"

"I have some serious matters to talk to you about."

"Serious matters?" cried Passepartout, emptying the few drops of wine remaining in the bottom of his glass. "Very well, we will talk about them to-morrow. I have not the time to-day."

"Remain," replied Fix. "It concerns your master."

Passepartout, at this phrase, looked attentively at his questioner.

The expression of Fix's face seemed singular to him. He took a seat again.

"What have you to say to me?" he asked.

Fix placed his hand upon his companion's arm, and lowering his voice, he asked him:

"You have guessed who I was."

"*Parbleu*?" said Passepartout, smiling.

"Then I am going to tell you everything."

"Now that I know everything, my friend. Ah! that's pretty tough! But go on. But first let me tell you that these gentlemen have put themselves to very useless expense."

"Useless," said Fix. "You speak confidently! It may be seen that you do not know the size of the sum!"

"But I do know it," said Passepartout. "Twenty thousand pounds!"

"Fifty-five thousand!" replied Fix, grasping the Frenchman's hand.

"What!" cried Passepartout, "Monsieur Fogg would have dared—fifty-five thousand pounds! Well, well! All the more reason that I should not lose an instant," he added, rising again.

"Fifty-five thousand pounds!" replied Fix, who forced Passepartout to sit down again, after having ordered a decanter of brandy— "and if I succeed, I get a reward of two thousand pounds. Do you wish five hundred of them on condition that you help me?"

"Help you!" cried Passepartout, whose eyes were opened very wide.

"Yes, help me to detain Mr. Fogg in Hong-Kong for a few days!"

102

"Phew!" said Passepartout, "what are you saying? How, not satisfied with having my master followed, with suspecting his faithfulness, do these gentlemen wish to throw new obstacles in his way. I am ashamed for them."

"Ah! what do you mean by that?" asked Fix.

"I mean that it is simple indelicacy. It is about the same as stripping Monsieur Fogg and putting his money in their pockets."

"Ah! that is the very thing we are coming to!"

"But it is a trap!" cried Passepartout—who was getting lively under the influence of the brandy with which Fix was plying him, and which he drank without noticing it—"a real trap! Gentlemen! Colleagues!"

Fix began to be puzzled.

"Colleagues!" cried Passepartout, "members of the Reform Club! You must know, Monsieur Fix, that my master is an honest man, and that, when he has made a bet, he intends to win it fairly."

"But who do you think I am?" asked Fix, fastening his look upon Passepartout.

"*Parbleu*! an agent of the members of the Reform Club with the mission to interfere with my master's journey, which is singularly humiliating. So, although it has been some time already since I guessed your business, I have taken good care not to disclose it to Monsieur Fogg."

"He knows nothing?" asked Fix quickly.

"Nothing," answered Passepartout, emptying his glass once more.

The agent passed his hand over his forehead. He hesitated before continuing the conversation. What ought he to do? The error of Passepartout seemed sincere, but it rendered his plan more difficult. It was evident that this young man was speaking with perfect good faith, and that he was not his master's accomplice—which Fix had feared.

"Well," he said to himself, "since he is not his accomplice, he will aid me."

The detective had the advantage a second time. Besides, he had no more time to wait At any cost Fogg must be arrested at Hong-Kong.

"Listen," said Fix, in an abrupt tone, "listen carefully to me. I am not what you think, that is, an agent of the members of the Reform Club—"

"Bah!" said Passepartout, looking at him in a jocose way.

"I am a police detective, charged with a mission by the Metropolitan Government."

"You—a detective!"

"Yes, and I will prove it," replied Fix. "Here is my commission."

And the agent, taking a paper from his pocket-book, showed his companion a commission signed by the Commissioner of the Central Police. Passepartout stunned, unable to articulate a word, looked at Fix.

"The bet of Mr. Fogg," continued Fix, "is only a pretext of which you are the dupes, you and his colleagues of the Reform Club, for he had an interest in assuring himself of your unconscious complicity."

"But why?" cried Passepartout.

"Listen. The 28th of September, ultimo, a robbery of fifty-five thousand pounds was committed at the Bank of England, by an individual whose description they were able to obtain. Now, look at this description, and it is feature for feature that of Mr. Fogg."

"Humbug!" cried Passepartout, striking the table with his clenched fist. "My master is the most honest man in the world!"

"How do you know?" replied Fix. "You are not even acquainted with him. You entered his service the day of his departure, and he left precipitately under a senseless pretext, without trunks, and carrying with him a large sum in banknotes! And you dare to maintain that he is an honest man?"

"Yes, yes!" repeated the poor fellow mechanically.

"Do you wish, then, to be arrested as his accomplice?"

Passepartout dropped his head in his hands. He could no longer be recognised. He did not look at the detective. Phileas Fogg, the deliverer of Aouda, the brave and generous man, a robber! And yet how many presumptions there were against him. Passepartout tried to force back the suspicions which would slip into his mind. He would never believe in his master's guilt.

"To conclude, what do you want of me?" said he to the detective by a strong effort.

"See here," replied Fix, "I have tracked Mr. Fogg to this point, but I have not yet received the warrant of arrest, for which I asked, from London. You must help me, then, to keep him in Hong-Kong—"

"I! Help you!"

"And I will share with you the reward of two thousand pounds promised by the Bank of England!"

"Never!" replied Passepartout, who wanted to rise, and fell back, feeling his reason and his strength at once escaping him.

"Monsieur Fix," he said, stammering, "even if everything you have told me should be true—if my master should be the robber whom you seek—which I deny—I have been—I am in his service—I have seen him kind and generous—betray him—never—no, not for all the gold in the world—I am from a village where they don't eat that kind of bread!"

"You refuse?"

"I refuse."

"Treat it as if I had said nothing," replied Fix, "and let's take a drink."

"All right, let's take a drink!"

Passepartout felt himself more and more overcome by intoxication. Fix, understanding that he must at all hazards separate him from his master, wanted to finish him. On the table were a few pipes filled with opium. Fix slipped one into Passepartout's hand, who took it, lifted it to his lips, lighted it, took a few puffs, and fell over, his head stupefied under the influence of the narcotic.

"At least," said Fix, seeing Passepartout out of the way, "Mr. Fogg will not be informed in time of the departure of the *Carnatic*, and if he leaves, he will be at least without this Frenchman !"

Then he left, after paying his bill.

Chapter 20

In which Fix comes in direct contact with Phileas Fogg

During this scene, which might perhaps seriously interfere with his future, Mr. Fogg, accompanying Mrs. Aouda, was taking a walk through the streets of the English town. Since Mrs. Aouda accepted his offer to take her to Europe, he had to think of all the details necessary for so long a journey. That an Englishman like him should make the tour of the world with a carpet-bag in his hand, might pass; but a lady could not undertake such a journey under the same conditions. Hence, the necessity of buying clothing and articles necessary for the voyage. Mr. Fogg acquitted himself of his task with the quiet characteristic of him, and he invariably replied to all the excuses and objections of the young woman, confused by so much kindness:

"It is in the interest of my journey; it is in my programme."

The purchases made, Mr. Fogg and the young woman returned to the hotel, and dined at the table d'hote which was sumptuously served. Then Mrs. Aouda, a little tired, went up into her room, after having shaken hands, English fashion, with her imperturbable deliverer.

He, Fogg, was absorbed all the evening in reading *The Times* and the *Illustrated London News*.

If he had been a man to be astonished at anything it would have been not to have seen his servant at the hour for retiring. But knowing that the Yokohama steamer was not to leave Hong-Kong before the next morning, he did not otherwise bother himself about it. The next morning Passepartout did not come at Mr. Fogg's ring.

What the honourable gentleman thought on learning that his servant had not returned to the hotel, no one could have said.

Mr. Fogg contented himself with taking his carpet-bag, calling for Mrs. Aouda, and sending for a palanquin.

It was then eight o'clock, and high tide, of which the *Carnatic* was to take advantage to go out through the passes, was put down at half-past nine.

When the palanquin arrived at the door of the hotel, Mr. Fogg and Mrs. Aouda got into the comfortable vehicle, and their baggage followed them on a wheelbarrow.

Half an hour later the travellers dismounted on the wharf, and there Mr. Fogg learned that the *Carnatic* had left the evening before.

Mr. Fogg, who counted on finding at the same time both the steamer and his servant, was compelled to do without both. But not a sign of disappointment appeared upon his face; and, when Mrs. Aouda looked at him with uneasiness, he contented himself with replying:

"It is an incident, madame, nothing more."

At this moment a person who had been watching him closely came up to him. It was the detective, Fix, who turned to him and said:

"Are you not like myself, sir, one of the passengers of the *Rangoon* who arrived yesterday"

"Yes, sir," replied Mr. Fogg coldly, "but I have not the honour "

"Pardon me, but I thought I would find your servant here."

"Do you know where he is, sir?" asked the young woman quickly.

"What!" replied Fix, feigning surprise," is he not with you?"

"No," replied Mrs. Aouda. "He has not returned since yesterday. Has be perhaps embarked without us aboard the *Carnatic*?"

"Without you, madame?" replied Fix. "But, excuse my question, you expected then to leave by that steamer?"

"Yes, sir."

"I too, madame, and I am much disappointed. The *Carnatic*, having completed her repairs, left Hong-Kong twelve hours sooner without warning anyone, and we must now wait a week for another steamer!"

Fix felt his heart jump for joy in pronouncing these words, "a week." A week! Fogg detained a week at Hong-Kong! There would be time to receive the warrant of arrest. Chance would at last declare for the representative of the law.

It may be judged then what a stunning blow he received, when he heard Phileas Fogg say in his calm voice:

"But there are other vessels than the *Carnatic*, it seems to me, in the port of Hong-Kong."

And Mr. Fogg, offering his arm to Mrs. Aouda, turned towards the docks in search of a vessel leaving.

Fix, stupefied, followed. It might have been said that a thread attached him to this man.

However, chance seemed really to abandon him whom it had served so well up to that time. Phileas Fogg, for three hours, traversed the port in every direction, decided, if it was necessary, to charter a vessel to take him to Yokohama; but he saw only vessels loading or unloading, and which consequently could not set sail. Fix began to hope again.

But Mr. Fogg was not disconcerted, and he was going to continue his search if he had to go as far as Macao, when he was accosted by a sailor on the end of the pier.

"Your honour is looking for a boat.?" said the sailor to him taking off his hat.

"You have a boat ready to sail?" asked Mr. Fogg.

"Yes, your honour, a pilot-boat, No. 43, the best in the flotilla."

"She goes fast?"

"Between eight and nine knots an hour, nearly the latter. Will you look at her?"

"Yes."

"Your honour will be satisfied. Is it for an excursion?"

"No; for a voyage."

"A voyage?"

"You will undertake to convey me to Yokohama?"

The sailor, at these words, stood with arms extended and eyes starting from his head.

"Your honour is joking?" he said.

"No, I have missed the sailing of the *Carnatic*, and I must be at Yokohama on the 14th, at the latest, to take the steamer for San Francisco."

"I regret it," replied the pilot, abut it is impossible."

"I offer you one hundred pounds per day, and a reward of two hundred pounds if I arrive in time."

"You are in earnest?" asked the pilot.

"Very much in earnest," replied Mr. Fogg.

The pilot withdrew to one side. He looked at the sea, evidently struggling between the desire to gain an enormous sum and the fear of venturing so far. Fix was in mortal suspense.

During this time, Mr. Fogg had returned to Mrs. Aouda.

"You will not be afraid, madame?" he asked.

"With you—no; Mr. Fogg," replied the young woman.

The pilot had come toward the gentleman again, and was twisting his hat in his hands.

"Well, pilot.?" said Mr. Fogg.

"Well, your honour," replied the pilot, "I can risk neither my men, nor myself, nor yourself in so long a voyage on a boat of scarcely twenty tons at this time of the year. Besides, we would not arrive in time, for it is sixteen hundred and fifty miles from Hong-Kong to Yokohama."

"Only sixteen hundred," said Mr. Fogg.

"It is the same thing."

Fix took a good long breath.

"But," added the pilot, "there might perhaps be a means to arrange it otherwise."

Fix did not breathe any more.

"How?" asked Phileas Fogg.

"By going to Nagasaki, the southern extremity of Japan, eleven hundred miles, or only to Shanghai, eight hundred miles from Hong-Kong. In this last journey, we would not be at any distance from the Chinese coast, which would be a great advantage, all the more so that the currents run to the north."

"Pilot," replied Phileas Fogg, "I must take the American mail steamer at Yokohama, and not at Shanghai or Nagasaki."

"Why not?" replied the pilot. "The San Francisco steamer

does not start from Yokohama She stops there and at Nagasaki, but her port of departure is Shanghai."

"You are certain of what you are saying?"

"Certain."

"And when does the steamer leave Shanghai?"

"On the 11th, at seven o'clock in the evening. We have then four days before us. Four days, that is ninety-six hours, and with an average of eight knots, if we have good luck, if the wind keeps to the south-east, if the sea is calm, we can make the eight hundred miles which separate us from Shanghai."

"And you can leave—"

"In an hour, time enough to buy my provisions and hoist sail."

"It is a bargain—you are the master of the boat?"

"Yes, John Bunsby, master of the *Tankadere*."

"Do you wish some earnest money?"

"If it does not inconvenience your honour."

"Here are two hundred pounds on account—sir," added Phileas Fogg, turning toward Fix, "if you wish to take advantage—"

"Sir," answered Fix resolutely, "I was going to ask this favour of you."

"Well, in half an hour we will be on board."

"But this poor fellow—" said Mrs. Aouda, whom Passepartout's disappearance worried very much.

"I am going to do all I can to find him," replied Phileas Fogg.

And while Fix, nervous, feverish, angry, repaired to the pilot boat, the two others went to the police station at Hong-Kong. Phileas Fogg gave there Passepartout's description, and left a sufficient sum to find him. The same formality was carried out at the French consular agent's, and the palanquin having stopped at the hotel where the baggage had been taken, took the travellers back to the outer pier.

Three o'clock struck. The pilot-boat, No. 43, her crew on board, and her provisions stowed away, was ready to set sail.

She was a charming little schooner of twenty tons—this *Tankadere*—with a sharp cut-water, very graceful shape, and long water lines. She might have been called a racing yacht.

Her shining copper sheathing, her galvanised iron work, her deck white as ivory, showed that Master John Bunsby knew how to keep her in good condition. Her two masts leaned a little to the rear. She carried brigantine-foresail, storm jib, and standing jib, and could rig up splendidly for a rear wind. She ought to sail wonderfully well, and in fact she had won several prizes in pilot-boat matches.

The crew of the *Tankadere* were composed of the master, John Bunsby, and four men. They were of that class of hardy sailors who, in all weathers, ventured out in search of vessels, and are thoroughly acquainted with these seasons. John Bunsby, a man about forty-five years, vigorous, well sunburnt, of a lively expression, of an energetic face, self-reliant, well posted in his business, would have inspired confidence in the most timorous.

Phileas Fogg and Mrs. Aouda went on board. Fix was already there. They went down by steps in the rear of the schooner into a square cabin, whose walls bulged out in the form of cots, above a circular divan. In the middle there was a table lighted by a hanging lamp. It was small, but neat.

"I regret having nothing better to offer you," said Mr. Fogg to Fix, who bowed without replying.

The detective felt somewhat humiliated by thus taking advantage of Mr. Fogg's kindnesses.

"Surely," he thought, "he is a very polite rogue, but he is a rogue!"

At ten minutes after three the sails were hoisted. The English flag was flying at the gaff of the schooner. The passengers were seated on deck. Mr. Fogg and Mrs. Aouda cast a last look at the wharf, in hopes of seeing Passepartout.

Fix was not without apprehension, for chance might have brought to this place the unfortunate young man whom he had treated with such indignity, and then an explanation would have taken place, from which the detective would not have got out to advantage. But the Frenchman did not show himself, and doubtless the stupefying narcotic still held him under its influence.

Finally, Master John Bunsby gave the order to start, and the *Tankadere*, taking the wind under her brigantine-foresail and standing jib, flew out in the sea bounding.

CHAPTER 21

In which the Master of the "Tankadere" runs great risk of losing a Reward of Two Hundred Pounds

This voyage of eight hundred miles, undertaken in a craft of twenty tons, and especially in that season of the year, was venturesome. The Chinese seas are generally rough, exposed to terrible blows, principally during the equinoxes, and this was in the first days of November.

It would have very evidently been to the advantage of the pilot to take his passengers so far as Yokohama, as he was paid so much per day. But it would have been great imprudence on his part to attempt such a voyage under such conditions, and it was a bold act, if not a rash one, to go as far as Shanghai. But John Bunsby had confidence in his *Tankadere*, which rode the waves he a gull, and perhaps he was not wrong.

During the latter hours of this day the *Tankadere* sailed through the capricious channels of Hong-Kong, and, in all her movements, from whatever quarter the wind came, she behaved handsomely.

"I do not need, pilot," said Phileas Fogg, the moment the schooner touched the open sea, "to recommend to you all possible diligence."

"Your honour may depend upon me," replied John Bunsby. "In the matter of sails, we are carrying all that the wind will allow us to carry. Our poles would add nothing, and would only interfere with the sailing of our craft."

"It is your trade, and not mine, pilot, and I trust to you."

Phileas Fogg, his body erect and legs wide apart, standing straight as a sailor, looked at the surging sea without staggering. The young woman seated aft, felt quite affected looking at the ocean, already darkened by the twilight, which she was

112

braving upon so frail a craft. Above her head were unfurled the white sails, looking in space like immense wings. The schooner, impelled by the wind, seemed to fly through the air.

Night set in. The moon was entering her first quarter, and her scanty light was soon extinguished in the haze of the horizon. Clouds were rising from the east, and already covered a portion of the heavens.

The pilot had put his lights in position—an indispensable precaution to take in these seas, so much frequented by vessels bound landward. Collisions were not rare, and at the rate she was going, the schooner would be shattered by the least shock.

Fix was dreaming forward on the vessel. He kept himself apart, knowing Fogg naturally to be not much of a talker. Besides, he hated to speak to this man, whose accommodations he had accepted. He was thinking thus of the future. It appeared certain to him that Mr. Fogg would not stop at Yokohama, that he would immediately take the San Francisco steamer to reach America, whose vast extent would assure him impunity with security. It seemed to him that Phileas Fogg's plan could not be simpler.

Instead of embarking in England for the United States, like a common rogue, this Fogg had made the grand rounds, and traversed three-quarters of the globe, in order to gain more surely the American continent, where he would quietly consume the large sum stolen from the bank, after having thrown the police off his track. But, once upon the soil of the United States, what would Fix do? Abandon this man? No, a hundred times no! And until he had obtained an extradition order he would not leave him for an instant. It was his duty, and he would fulfil it to the end. In any event, one happy result had been obtained. Passepartout was no longer with his master; and, especially after the confidence Fix had reposed in him, it was important that the master and servant should never see each other again.

Phileas Fogg was constantly thinking of his servant, who had disappeared so singularly. After having thought over everything, it seemed not impossible to him that, in consequence of a misunderstanding, the poor fellow had set sail

113

upon the *Carnatic* at the last moment. It was the opinion of Mrs. Aouda also, who regretted very much this good servant, to whom she owed so much. It might be that they would find him again at Yokohama, and if the *Carnatic* had taken him thither, it would be easy to find it out.

Towards ten o'clock the breeze began to freshen. Perhaps it would have been prudent to take in a reef, but the pilot, having carefully examined the state of the heavens, left the rigging as it was. Besides the *Tankadere* carried sail admirably, having a deep draft of water, and everything was prepared to go rapidly, in case of a gale.

At midnight Phileas Fogg and Mrs. Aouda descended into the cabin. Fix had preceded them, and was stretched on one of the cots. As for the pilot and his men, they remained on deck all night.

The next day, the 8th of November, at sunrise, the schooner had made more than one hundred miles. Her course, frequently checked, showed that her average speed was between eight and nine knots. The *Tankadere* carried full sail, and in this rig she obtained the maximum of speed. If the wind kept the same, the chances were in her favour.

The *Tankadere*, during the whole day, did not go far from the coast, whose currents were favourable to her, and which was five miles off at the most from her starboard quarter, and irregularly outlined appeared sometimes across the clearings. The wind coming from the land was, on that account, not quite so strong, a fortunate circumstance for the schooner, for vessels of a small tonnage suffer above all from the roll of the sea which interferes with their speed, "killing" them, to use the sailors' expression.

Towards noon the breeze abated a little and set in from the south-east. The pilot put up his poles; but at the end of two hours it was necessary to take them down, as the wind freshened up again.

Mr. Fogg and the young woman, very fortunately unaffected by sea-sickness, ate with a good appetite the preserves and the ship biscuit. Fix was invited to share their repast, and was compelled to accept, knowing very well that it is as necessary to ballast stomachs as vessels, but it vexed him! To travel at this man's expense, to be fed from his provisions, was rather against his grain. He ate, daintily, it is true, but finally he ate.

However, this repast finished, he took Mr. Fogg aside and said to him:

"Sir—"

This "sir" scorched his lips, and he controlled himself so as not to collar this "gentleman!"

"Sir, you have been very kind to offer me a passage on your vessel. But, although my resources do not permit me to expend as freely as you, I intend to pay my share—"

"Let us not speak of that, sir," replied Mr. Fogg.

"But, if I insist—"

"No, sir," repeated Fogg, in a tone which did not admit of reply. "That will enter into the general expenses."

Fix bowed; he had a stifling feeling, and going forward, he lay down, and did not say a word more during the day.

In the meantime they were moving on rapidly. John Bunsby had high hopes. He said to Mr. Fogg several times that they would arrive at Shanghai at the desired time. Mr. Fogg simply replied that he counted on it. The whole crew went to work in earnest. The reward enticed these good people. So there was not a sheet which was not conscientiously tightened! Not a sail which was not vigorously hoisted! Not a lurch for which the man at the helm could be blamed! They would not have manoeuvred more vigorously in a regatta of the Royal Yacht Club.

In the evening, the pilot marked on the log a distance of two hundred and twenty miles from Hong-Kong, and Phileas Fogg might hope that on arriving at Yokohama he would not have to note any delay in his journal. Thus, the first serious mischance that he had suffered since his departure from London would probably not affect his journey worth mentioning.

During the night, towards the early morning hours, the *Tankadere* entered, without difficulty the Straits of Fo Kien, which separate the large Island of Formosa from the Chinese coast, and she crossed the Tropic of Cancer. The sea was very rough in these straits, full of eddies formed by counter-currents. The schooner laboured heavily. The short waves broke her course. It became very difficult to stand up on the deck.

With daybreak the wind became fresher. There was the appearance of a squall in the heavens. Besides, the barometer announced a speedy change of the atmosphere; its daily movement was irregular, and the mercury oscillated capriciously. The sea was seen rising towards the south-east in long swells betokening a tempest. The evening before the sun had set in a red haze, amid the phosphorescent scintillations of the ocean.

The pilot examined the threatening aspect of the sky for a long time, and muttered between his teeth indistinctly. At a certain moment, finding himself near his passenger, he said in a low voice:

"Can I speak freely to your honour?"

"You can," replied Phileas Fogg.

"Well, we are going to have a squall."

"Will it come from the north or the south?" asked Mr. Fogg simply-

"From the south. See. A typhoon is coming up."

"Good for the typhoon from the south, since it will send us in the right direction," replied Mr. Fogg.

"If you take it so," replied the pilot, "I have nothing more to say."

John Bunsby's presentiments did not deceive him. At a less advanced season of the year, the typhoon, according to the expression of a celebrated meteorologist, would have passed off like a luminous cascade of electric flames, but in the winter equinox it was to be feared that it would burst with violence.

The pilot took his precautions in advance. He had all the schooner's sails reefed, and the yards brought on deck. The polemasts were dispensed with. All hands went forward. The hatches were carefully fastened. Not a drop of water could then enter the hull of the vessel. A single triangular sail, a foresail of strong canvas, was hoisted as a storm-jib, so as to hold the schooner to the wind behind. And they waited.

John Bunsby had begged his passengers to go down into the cabin; but in the narrow space, almost deprived of air, and knocked about by the waves, this imprisonment had in it nothing agreeable. Neither Mr. Fogg, nor Mrs. Aouda, nor even Fix was contented to leave the deck.

Towards eight o'clock the storm of rain and wind struck the deck. With nothing but her little bit of sail, the *Tankadere* was raised like a feather by the wind, the violence of which could not well be described in words. Compare her speed to quadruple that of a locomotive rushing along under full head of steam, and it would still be below the truth.

During the whole day the vessel ran on thus towards the north, carried by the tremendous waves, preserving, fortunately, a rapidity equal to theirs. Twenty times she was almost submerged by these mountains of water which rose upon her from the rear, but an adroit turn of the helm by the pilot warded off the catastrophe. The passengers were sometimes covered over by the showers of spray, which they received philosophically. Fix did not like it, doubtless, but the intrepid Aouda, with her eyes fixed upon her companion, whose coolness she could only admire, showed herself worthy of him, and braved the storm at his side. As for Phileas Fogg, it seemed as if this typhoon formed a part of his programme.

Up to this time the *Tankadere* had always held her course towards the north: but, towards evening, as might have been feared, the wind, shifting three-quarters, blew from the north-west. The schooner, now having her side to the waves, was terribly shaken. The sea struck her with a violence well calculated to terrify anyone who does not know how solidly every part of a vessel is fastened together.

With nightfall the tempest grew wilder. Seeing darkness come on, and with it the increase of the storm, John Bunsby felt great uneasiness. He asked himself if it would not be time to put in somewhere, and he consulted his crew.

His men consulted, John Bunsby approached Mr. Fogg, and said to him:

"I believe, your honour, that we would do well to make one of the ports of the coast."

"I believe so, also," replied Phileas Fogg.

"Ah!" said the pilot, "but which one?"

"I only know one," replied Mr. Fogg quietly.

"And that is—?"

"Shanghai!"

The pilot could not at first comprehend for a few moments what this answer meant; how much obstinacy and tenacity it comprised. Then he cried:

"Ah well, yes! your honour is right. On to Shanghai!"

And the direction of the *Tankadere* was unwaveringly kept to the north.

It was truly a terrible night! It was a miracle that the little craft did not capsize. Twice she was submerged, and everything would have been carried off the deck, if the fastening of the ropes had given way. Mrs. Aouda was worn out, but she did not utter a complaint. More than once Mr. Fogg had to rush towards her to protect her from the violence of the waves.

Daylight reappeared. The tempest was still raging with the greatest fury. However, the wind fell again into the south-east. It was a favourable change, and the *Tankadere* resumed her way on this high sea, whose waves then struck those produced by the new direction of the wind. Thence a shock of counter-rolling waves, which would have crushed a less solidly-built barque.

From time to time through the broken mist the coast could be perceived, but not a ship in sight. The *Tankadere* was the only one keeping the sea.

At noon there were some signs of a calm, which, with the sinking of the sun towards the horizon, were more distinct.

The short duration of the tempest was owing to its very violence. The passengers, completely worn out, could eat a little and take some rest.

The night was comparatively quiet. The pilot had the sails again hoisted at a low reef. The speed of the vessel was considerable. The next day, the 11th, at daydawn, the coast being sighted,John Bunsby was able to assert that they were not one hundred miles from Shanghai.

One hundred miles, and only this day left to make the

distance! That very evening Mr. Fogg ought to arrive at Shanghai, if he did not wish to miss the departure of the Yokohama steamer. Without this storm, during which he lost several hours, he would not, at this moment, have been thirty miles from port.

The breeze sensibly slackened, but fortunately the sea fell with it. The schooner was covered with canvas. Poles, stay-sails, counter-jibs, all were carried, and the sea foamed under her keel.

At noon, the *Tankadere* was not more than forty-five miles from Shanghai. She had six hours more to make that port before the departure of the steamer for Yokohama.

The fears of all were great; they wanted to arrive at any cost. All felt their hearts impatiently beating—Phileas Fogg doubt-less excepted. The little schooner must keep up an average of nine knots, and the wind was constantly going down! It was an irregular breeze, with capricious puffs coming from the coast. They passed, and the sea became more smooth immedi-ately after.

But the vessel was so light, and her high sails, of a fine material, caught the capricious breeze so well that, with the current in their favour, at six o'clock John Bunsby counted only ten miles to Shanghai River, for the city itself is situated at a distance of twelve miles at least above the mouth.

At seven o'clock they were still three miles from Shanghai. A formidable oath escaped from the pilot's lips. It was evident that the reward of two hundred pounds was going to slip from him. He looked at Mr. Fogg. Mr. Fogg was impassible, and yet his whole fortune was at stake at this moment.

At this moment, too, a long, black funnel, crowned with a wreath of smoke, appeared on the edge of the water. It was the American steamer going at the regular hour.

"Maledictions on her!" cried John Bunsby, who pushed back the rudder desperately.

"Signal her!" said Phileas Fogg simply.

A small brass cannon stood on the forward deck of the *Tankadere*. It served to make signals in hazy weather.

The cannon was loaded to the muzzle, but at the moment

that the pilot was going to apply a red-hot coal to the touch-hole, Mr. Fogg said:

"Hoist your flag."

The flag was hoisted half-mast. It was a signal of distress, and it was to be hoped that the American steamer, perceiving it, would change her course for a moment to assist the little craft.

"Fire!" said Mr. Fogg.

And the booming of the little cannon sounded through the air.

CHAPTER 22

In which Passepartout sees very well that, even at the Antipodes, it is Prudent to have some Money in One's pocket

The *Carnatic* having left Hong-Kong on the 6th of November, at half-past six p.m., turned under full head of steam towards the Japanese shores. She carried a full load of freight and passengers. Two cabins aft were unoccupied. They were the ones retained for Mr. Phileas Fogg.

The next morning the men in the forward part of the vessel saw, not without some surprise, a passenger, with half-stupe-fied eyes and disordered head, coming out of the second cabin, and with tottering steps taking a seat on deck.

This passenger was Passepartout himself. This is what happened:

Some minutes after Fix left the smoking-house two waiters raised Passepartout, who was in a deep sleep, and laid him on the bed reserved for the smokers. But, three hours later,

Passepartout, pursued even in his bad dreams by a fixed idea, woke again and struggled against the stupefing action of the narcotic. The thought of unaccomplished duty shook off his torpor. He left this drunkard's bed, reeling, supporting himself by the wall, falling and rising, but always and irresistibly urged on by a sort of instinct. He finally went out of the smoking-house, crying in a dream, "the *Carnatic!* the *Carnatic!*"

The steamer was there, steam up, ready to leave. Passepartout had only a few steps to go. He rushed upon the plank, crossed it, and fell unconscious on the forward deck at the moment that the *Carnatic* was slipping her moorings.

Some of the sailors, as men accustomed to these kind of scenes, took the poor fellow down into a second cabin, and Passepartout only waked the next morning, one hundred and fifty miles from the Chinese coast.

This is then why Passepartout found himself this morning on the *Carnatic's* deck, taking full draughts of the fresh sea-breezes. The pure air sobered him. He commenced to collect his idea, but he did not succeed without difficulty. But, finally, he recalled the scenes of the day before, the confidences of Fix, the smoking-house, etc.

"It is evident," he said to himself, "that I have been abominably drunk! What will Mr. Fogg say. In any event I have not missed the steamer, and this is the principal thing."

Then, thinking of Fix, he said to himself:

"As for him, I hope we are now rid of him, and that he has not dared, after what he proposed to me, to follow us on the *Carnatic*. A police detective on my master's heels, accused of the robbery committed upon the Bank of England! Pshaw! Mr. Fogg is as much a robber as I am a murderer!"

Ought Passepartout to tell these things to his master? Would it be proper to inform him of the part played by Fix in this affair? Would it not be better to wait until his return to London, to tell him that an agent of the Metropolitan police had followed him, and then have a laugh with him? Yes, doubtless. In any event, it was a matter to be looked into. The most pressing thing was to rejoin Mr. Fogg and beg him to pardon him for his inexcusable conduct.

Passepartout then rose. The sea was rough, and the ship rolled heavily. The worthy fellow—his legs not very steady yet—reached as well as he could the after-deck of the ship.

He saw no one on the deck that resembled either his master or Mrs. Aouda.

"Good," said he, "Mrs. Aouda is still abed at this hour. As for Mr. Fogg, he has probably found some whist-player, and according to his habit—"

So saying, Passepartout descended to the saloon. Mr. Fogg was not there. Passepartout had but one thing to do; to ask the purser which cabin Mr. Fogg occupied. The purser replied that he did not know any passenger of that name.

"Pardon me," said Passepartout, persisting. "The gentleman in question is tall, cold, non-communicative, accompanied by a young lady—"

"We have no young lady on board," replied the purser. "To convince you, here is the list of passengers. You can examine it n Passepartout looked over the list. His master's name did not appear. He felt bewildered. Then an idea struck him.

"Ah! but see! I am on the *Carnatic*?" he cried.

"Yes," replied the purser.

"*En route* for Yokohama?"

"Exactly so."

Passepartout had for a moment feared that he had mistaken the vessel! But though he was on the *Carnatic*, he was certain that his master was not there.

Passepartout dropped into an armchair. It was a thunder-stroke for him. And suddenly there was a gleam of light. He recollected that the hour of departure for the *Carnatic* had been anticipated, that he was to notify his master, and that he had not done it! It was his fault, then, if Mr. Fogg and Mrs. Aouda had missed this steamer!

His fault, yes, but still more that of the traitor who, to separate him from his master, to keep the latter in Hong-Kong, had made him drunk! For at last he understood the detective's manoeuvre. And now Mr. Fogg, surely ruined, his bet lost, arrested, perhaps imprisoned! Passepartout at this thought tore his hair. Ah! if Fix ever fell into his hands, what a settlement of accounts there would be!

Finally, after the first moment of bewilderment, Passepartout recovered his coolness and studied the situation. It was not enviable. The Frenchman was on the road to Japan. Certain of arriving there, how was he to get away? His pocket was empty. Not a shilling, not a penny in it! However, his passage and meals on board were paid in advance. He had then five or six days to come to a decision. It could not be described how he ate and drank during the voyage. He ate for his master, for Mrs. Aouda, and for himself. He ate as if Japan, where he was going to land, was a desert country, bare of every eatable substance.

At high tide on the morning of the 13th, the *Carnatic* entered the port of Yokohama.

This place is an important stopping point in the Pacific, where all the mail and passenger steamers between North America, China, Japan, and the Malay Islands put in. Yokohama is situated on the bay of Jeddo, at a short distance from that immense city, the second capital of the Japanese Empire, formerly the residence of the Tycoon, at the time that civil emperor existed, and the rival of Miako, the large city in which the Mikado, the ecclesiastical emperor, the descendant of the gods, lives.

The *Carnatic* came alongside the wharf at Yokohama near the jetties of the port and the Custom House, in the midst of the numerous vessels belonging to all nations.

Passepartout set foot, without any enthusiasm, on this so curious soil of the Sons of the Sun. He had nothing better to do than to take chance for his guide, and to go at a venture through the streets of the city.

Passepartout found himself at first in an absolutely European city, with its low front houses, ornamented with verandas, under which showed elegant peristyles, and which covered with its streets, its squares, its docks, its warehouses, the entire space comprised between "Treaty Promontory" and the river. There, as at Hong-Kong, and as at Calcutta, there was a confused swarm of people of all races, Americans, English,

Chinese, Dutch, merchants ready to sell everything and to buy everything, in the midst of whom the Frenchman found himself as strange as if he had been cast into the Hottentot country.

Passepartout had, it is true, one resource; it was to make himself known at the French or English consular agents established at Yokohama; but he hated to tell his story, so intimately connected with that of his master, and before coming to that, he wished to exhaust all other chances.

Then, having gone through the European quarter of the city without chance having served him in anything, he entered the Japanese quarter, decided, if it was necessary, to push on to Jeddo.

This native portion of Yokohama is called Benten, from the name of the goddess of the sea, worshipped in the neighbouring islands. There were to be seen splendid avenues of firs and cedars; the sacred gates of a strange architecture; bridges half-hid in the midst of bamboos and reeds; temples sheltered under the immense and melancholy shade of aged cedars, retreats in the depths of which vegetated the priest of Buddhism and the sectaries of the religion of Confucius; interminable streets in which could have been gathered a whole crop of children, rose-tinted and red-cheeked, good little people that might have been cut out of some native screen, and which were playing in the midst of short-legged poodles, and yellowish, tailless cats, very indolent, and very affectionate.

In the streets there was a constant swarm, going and coming incessantly; priests passing in procession, beating their monotonous tambourines; patrolmen, Custom House or police officers, with pointed hats encrusted with lace, and carrying two sabres in their belts; soldiers dressed in blue cottonade, with white stripes, and armed with percussion muskets; guards of the Mikado, enveloped in their silken doublets, with hauberk and coat-of-mail, and a number of other military men of all ranks—for in Japan the profession of a soldier is as much esteemed as it is despised in China. Then, mendicant friars, pilgrims in long robes, simple civilians, with their glossy and jet-black hair, large heads, long bust, slender legs, short stature, and complexions from the dark shades of copper to dead white, but never yellow like that of the Chinese, from whom the Japanese differ essentially. Finally, between the carriages, the palanquins, the horses, the porters, the curtained wheelbarrows, the "norimons" with lace-covered sides, and the substantial "cangos," genuine bamboo litters, were seen moving some homely women, with tightly-drawn eyes, sunken chests, and teeth blackened according to the fashion of the time, taking short steps with their little feet, upon which were canvas shoes, straw sandals, or clogs of worked wood. They also wore with elegance the national garment, the "kiri mon," a sort of dressing-gown, crossed with a silk scarf, whose broad girdle expanded behind into an extravagant knot, which the modern Parisian ladies seem to have borrowed from the Japanese.

Passepartout walked for some hours in the midst of this checkered crowd, looking at the curious and rich shops; the bazaars, where are heaped up all the display of Japanese jewellery; the restaurants, adorned with streamers and banners, into which he was interdicted from entering; and those tea-houses in which are drank full cups of the warm, fragrant tea, with "saki"—a liquor extracted from fermented rice—and those comfortable smoking-houses, where very fine tobacco is smoked, and not opium, whose use is almost unknown in Japan.

Then Passepartout found himself in the fields, in the midst of immense rice fields. There were expanding, with flowers which threw out their last perfumes, dazzling camelias, not borne upon shrubs, but upon trees; and in the bamboo enclosures, cherry, plum, and apple trees, which the natives cultivate rather for their blossoms than for their fruit, and which grinning scarecrows protect from the peak of the sparrows, the pigeons, the crows, and other voracious birds. There was not a majestic cedar which did not shelter some large eagle; not a weeping willow which did not cover with its foliage some heron, sadly perched on one foot; while, finally, in all directions there were rooks, ducks, hawks, wild geese, and a large number of those cranes which the Japanese treat as "lords," and which symbolise for them long life and good fortune.

Wandering thus, Passepartout saw some violets among the grass, and said: "food! there is my supper."

But having smelt them, he found no odour in them.

The good fellow had certainly had the foresight to breakfast as heartily as possible before he left the *Carnatic;* but after walking around for a day he felt that his stomach was very empty. He had noticed that sheep, goats, or pigs were entirely wanting at the stalls of the native butchers; and as he knew that it is a sacrilege to kill beeves, kept only for the needs of agriculture, he concluded that meat was scarce in Japan. He was not mistaken; but in default of butcher's meat, his stomach would have accommodated itself well to quarters of deer or wild boar, some partridges or quails, some poultry or fish, with which the Japanese feed themselves almost exclusively, with the product of the rice fields. But he had to put a brave heart against ill luck, and postponed to the next day the care of providing for his nourishment.

Night came on. Passepartout returned to the native quarter, and wandered in the streets in the midst of the many-coloured lanterns, looking at the groups of dancers, executing their feats of agility, and the astrologers in the open air gathering the crowd around their telescopes. Then he saw again the harbour, relieved by the fires of the fishermen who were catching fish by the light of their torches.

Finally, the streets became empty. To the crowd succeeded the rounds of the patrolmen. These officers, in their magnificent costumes and in the midst of their suite, resembled ambassadors, and Passepartout repeated pleasantly, each time that he met some dazzling patrol:

"Good, good! Another Japanese embassy starting for Europe!"

CHAPTER 23

In which Passepartout's nose is lengthened enormously

The next day Passepartout, tired out and hungry, said to himself that he must eat at any cost, and the sooner the better. He had this resource, to sell his watch, but he would rather die of hunger. Now was the time, or never, for this good fellow to utilise the strong, if not melodious voice, with which nature had favoured him.

He knew a few French and English airs, and he determined to try them. The Japanese ought certainly to be lovers of music, since everything with them was done to the sound of the cymbals, the tom-tom, and drums, and they could not but appreciate the talents of a European amateur.

But, perhaps, he was a little early to organise a concert, and the dilettanti, unexpectedly wakened, would, perhaps, not have paid the singer in money with the Mikado's likeness.

Passepartout decided, then, to wait a few hours; but in sauntering along the thought came to him that he would look too well dressed for a wandering artist, and the idea struck him to exchange his clothing for A suit more in harmony with his position. This exchange would besides produce a sum which he could immediately apply to satisfying his appetite.

This resolution taken, it only remained to execute it. It was only after a long search that Passepartout found a native clothes dealer, to whom he told his want. The European garments pleased the man, and soon Passepartout came out wrapped in an old Japanese robe, and on his head a sort of one-sided turban, discoloured by the action of the weather. But in return, a few small pieces of money jingled in his pocket.

"Good," he thought. "I will fancy that we are in the carnival!"

Passepartout's first care, thus, "Japanesed," was to enter a teahouse of modest appearance, and there, with some remains of poultry and a few handfuls of rice, he breakfasted like a man for whom dinner would be still a problem to be solved. "Now," he said to himself, when he had taken hearty refreshment, "the question is not to lose my head. I have no longer the resource of selling this garment for another still more Japanese. I must then consider the means of getting away as promptly as possible from this country of the Sun, of which I will preserve but a sorry recollection."

Passepartout then thought of visiting the steamers about to set sail for America. He counted on offering himself in the capacity of cook or servant, asking only his passage and his meals as his entire compensation. Once at San Francisco, he would see how he would get out of his scrape. The important thing was to traverse these four thousand seven hundred miles of the Pacific stretching between Japan and the New World.

Passepartout, not being a man to let an idea languish, turned towards the port of Yokohama. But as he approached the docks, his plans, which had appeared so simple to him at the moment when he had the idea, seemed more and more difficult of execution. Why should they need a cook or servant aboard an American steamer, and what confidence would he inspire, muffled up in this manner? What recommendations would be of any service? What references could he give?

As he was thus reflecting, his eyes fell upon an immense placard which a sort of clown was carrying through the streets of Yokohama. This programme was thus worded in English:

ACROBATIC JAPANESE TROUPE
OF THE
HONOURABLE WILLIAM BATULCAR.
LAST REPRESENTATIONS,
BEFORE THEIR DEPARTURE FOR THE
UNITED STATES OF AMERICA,
OF THE
LONG NOSES! LONG NOSES!
UNDER THE DIRECT PROTECTION OF THE
GOD TINGOU!
GREAT ATTRACTION!

"The United States of America," cried Passepartout, "that's just what I want!"

He followed the man with his placard, and thus soon he reentered the Japanese quarters. A quarter of an hour later, he stopped before a large house surrounded by clusters of streamers, and whose exterior walls represented, without perspective, but in violent colours, a whole company of jugglers.

It was the Honorable Batulcar's establishment, who was a sort of American Barnum, director of a troupe of montebanks, jugglers, clowns, acrobats, equilibrists, gymnasts, which, according to the placard, was giving its last performance before leaving the empire of the Sun for the States of the Union.

Passepartout entered under the porch in front of the house, and asked for Mr. Batulcar. He appeared in person.

"What do you wish?" he said to Passepartout, taking him at first for a native.

"Do you need a servant?" asked Passepartout.

"A servant," cried the Barnum, stroking his thick grey beard hanging heavily under his chin. "I have two, obedient and faithful, who have never left me, and who serve me for nothing, on condition that I feed them. And here they are," he added, showing his two robust arms, furrowed with veins as large as the strings of a bass viol.

"So I can be of no good to you?"

"None."

"The devil! It would have suited me so well to leave with you."

"Ah, I see!" said the Honourable Batulcar. "You are as much a Japanese as I am a monkey! Why are your dressed in this way?"

"One dresses as one can."

"Very true. You are a Frenchman.?"

"Yes, a Parisian from Paris."

"Then you ought to know how to make grimaces?"

"Indeed," replied Passepartout, vexed at seeing his nationality call forth this question, "we Frenchmen know how to make grimaces, it is true, but not better than the Americans."

"Just so. Well, if I do not take you as a servant I can take you as a clown. You understand, my good fellow. In France they exhibit foreign clowns, and abroad, French clowns."

"Ah!"

"You are strong, are you not?"

"Particularly when I have been at the table."

"And you know how to sing?"

"Yes," replied Passepartout, who had formerly taken part in street concerts.

"But do you know how to sing on your head, with a top spinning on the sole of your left foot, and a sabre balanced on the sole of your right?"

"*Parbleu*?"replied Passepartout, who recalled the first exercises of his youth.

"Then, you see, all is right!" replied the Honourable Batulcar.

The engagement was concluded there and then.

At last Passepartout had found a position. He was engaged to do everything in the celebrated Japanese troupe. It was not very flattering, but within a week he would be on his way to San Francisco.

The performance, so noisily announced by the Honourable Batulcar, was to commence at three o'clock, and soon the formidable instruments of a Japanese orchestra, drums and tam-tams, sounded at the door. We understand very well that Passepartout could not have studied a part, but he was to give the support of his solid shoulders in the grand feat of the "human pyramid," executed by the Long Noses of the god Tingou. This great attraction of the performance was to close the series.

Before three o'clock the spectators had crowded the large building. Europeans and natives, Chinese and Japanese, men, woman, and children, rushed upon the narrow benches and into the boxes opposite the stage. The musicians had entered, and the full orchestra, with gongs, tam-tams, bones, flutes, tambourines, and large drums went to work furiously.

The performance was what all these acrobatic exhibitions are. But it must be confessed that the Japanese are the best equilibrists in the world. One, with his fan and small bits of paper, executed the graceful trick of the butterflies and flowers. Another, with the odorous smoke of his pipe, traced rapidly in the air a series of bluish words, which formed a compliment addressed to the audience. The latter juggled with lit candles, which he blew out in succession as they passed before his lips, and which he lit again, one after the other, without interrupting for a single moment his wonderful jugglery. The former produced, by means of spinning-tops, the most improbable combinations. Under his hand these humming machines seemed to be gifted with a life of their own in their interminable whirling; they ran over pipe stems, over the edges of sabres, over wires as thin as hair, stretched from one side of the stage to the other; they went round large glass vases, they went up and down bamboo ladders, and scattered into all the corners, and produced harmonic effects of a strange character by combining their various tones. The jugglers tossed them up, and they turned in the air; they threw them like shuttlecocks with wooden battledores, and they kept on turning; they thrust them into their pockets, and when they brought them out they were still spinning—until the moment when a relaxed spring made them bud out into a Chinese tree!

It is useless to describe here the wonderful feats of the acrobats and gymnasts of the troupe. The turning on ladders, poles, balls barrels, etc., was executed with remarkable precision. But the principal attraction of the performance was the exhibition of the Long Noses, astonishing equilibrists, with whom Europe is not yet acquainted.

These Long Noses form a special company placed under the direct patronage of the god Tingou. Dressed like heroes of the Middle Ages, they bore a splendid pair of wings on their shoulders. But what distinguished them more particularly was a long nose with which their faces were ornamented, and, above all, the use they made of them. These noses were nothing less than bamboos, five, six, ten feet long; some straight, others curved; the latter smooth, the former with warts on them. It was on these appendages, fastened firmly, that all their balancing feats were performed. A dozen of these sectaries of the god Tingou lay upon their backs, and their comrades came, dressed like lightning rods, to make sport on their noses, jumping, leaping from one to the other, executing the most incredible somersaults.

To close, they had specially announced to the public the "human pyramid," in which fifty Long Noses were to represent,the Car of Juggernaut. But instead of forming this pyramid by taking their shoulders for a point of support, the artists of the Honourable Batulcar made it with their noses. Now, the one of them who usually formed the base of the car had left the troupe, and as all that was necessary was to be strong and agile, Passepartout was chosen to take his place.

The good fellow felt quite melancholy, when—sad recollection of his youth—he had put on this costume of the Middle Ages, adorned with parti-coloured wings, and when a nose six feet long had been put on his face. But this nose was to earn his bread for him, and he took his part.

Passepartout went upon the stage and took his place with those of his colleagues who were to form the base of the Car of Juggernaut. All stretched themselves on the floor, their noses turned towards the ceiling. A second section of equilibrists placed themselves upon these long appendages, a third formed a story above, then a fourth, and on these noses which only touched at the point, a human monument soon rose to the height of the cornices of the theatre.

Now, the applause was redoubled, and the instruments in the orchestra crashed like so much thunder, when the pyramid shook, the equilibrium was broken, one of the noses of the base was missing, and the monument fell like a house of cards.

It was Passepartout's fault, who, leaving his post, clearing the footlights, without the aid of his wings, and climbing up to the right-hand gallery, fell at the feet of a spectator, crying:

"Ah! my master! my master!"

"You here?"

"Myself!"

"Well, then, in that case, to the steamer, young man!"

Mr. Fogg, Mrs. Aouda, who accompanied him, and Passepartout rushed through the lobbies to the outside of the building. But there they found the Honourable Batulcar, furious, claiming damages for the "breakage." Phileas Fogg appeased his anger by throwing him a handful of bank-notes. Mr. Fogg and Mrs. Aouda set foot on the American steamer, followed by Passepartout with his wings on his back, and on his face the nose six feet long which he had not yet been able to tear off!

CHAPTER 24

During which is Accomplished the Voyage across the Pacific Ocean

What had happened in sight of Shanghai is understood. The signals made by the *Tankadere* had been observed by the Yokohama steamer. The captain, seeing a flag at halfmast, had turned his vessel towards the little schooner. A few minutes after, Phileas Fogg, paying for his passage at the price agreed upon, put in the pocket of John Bunsby, master, five hundred and fifty pounds. Then the honourable gentleman, Mrs. Aouda, and Fix ascended to the deck of the steamer, which immediately took its course for Nagasaki and Yokohama

Having arrived on the morning of the 14th of November, on time, Phileas Fogg, letting Fix go about his business, had gone aboard the *Carnatic*, and there he learned, to the great joy of Mrs. Aouda—and perhaps to his own, but he did not let it appear— that the Frenchman, Passepartout, had really arrived the day before at Yokohama.

Phileas Fogg, who was to start again the same evening for San Francisco, set immediately in search of his servant. He inquired in vain of the French and English consular agents, and after uselessly running through the streets of Yokohama, he despaired of finding Passepartout again, when chance, or perhaps a sort of presentiment, made him enter the theatre of the Honourable Batulcar. He would certainly not have recognised his servant under this eccentric mountebank dress; but the latter, lying on his back, saw his master in the gallery. He could not restrain a movement of his nose. Thence a breaking of the equilibrium and what followed.

This is what Passepartout learned from Mrs. Aouda's mouth, who told him then how the voyage had been made from Hong-Kong to Yokohama in company of a Mr. Fix, on the schooner *Tankadere*.

At the name of Fix, Passepartout did not change countenance. He thought that the time had not come to tell his master what had passed between the detective and himself£ Thus, in the story which Passepartout told of his adventures, he only accused and excused himself of having been overcome by the intoxication of opium in a smoking-house in Hong-Kong.

Mr. Fogg listened coldly to this narrative, without replying; then he opened for his servant a credit sufficient for him to procure on board more suitable garments. And, indeed, an hour had not passed, when the good fellow, having cut off his nose and shed his wings, had nothing more about him which recalled the sectary of the god Tingou.

The steamer making the voyage from Yokohama to San Francisco belonged to the Pacific Mail Steamship Company, and was named the *General Grant*. She was a large side-wheel steamer of two thousand five hundred tons, well equipped, and of great speed. An enormous walking-beam rose and fell successively above the deck; at one of its ends moved the piston-rod, and at the other the connecting-rod which, changing the movement in a straight line to a circular one, was applied directly to the shaft of the wheels. The General Grant was rigged as a three-masted schooner, and she had a large surface of sails, which aided her steam power materially. By making twelve knots the steamer would only need twenty-one days to cross the Pacific. Phileas Fogg then had good reasons for believing that, landed at San Francisco on the 2nd of December, he would be in New York on the 11th, and in

London on the 20th, thus gaining some hours on the fatal date of the 21st of December.

The passengers aboard the steamer were quite numerous— some Englishmen, many Americans, a genuine emigration of coolies to America, and a certain number of officers of the Indian army, who made use of their leave of absence by making the tour of the world.

During this voyage there was no nautical incident. The steamer, borne up on its large wheels, supported by its large amount of canvas, rolled but little. The Pacific Ocean justified its name sufficiently. Mr. Fogg was as calm and non-communicative as usual. His young companion felt herself more and more attached to this man by other ties than those of gratitude. This silent nature, so generous in short, made a greater impression upon her than she thought, and almost unknown to herself she allowed herself to have feelings which did not seem to affect in any way the enigmatic Fogg.

Besides, Mrs. Aouda was very much interested in the gentleman's plans. She was uneasy at the retarding circumstances which might prevent the success of the tour. She frequently talked with Passepartout, who readily detected the feelings of Mrs. Aouda's heart. This good fellow had the most implicit faith with regard to his master; he did not exhaust his praises of the honesty, the generosity, the devotion of Phileas Fogg; then he reassured MTS. Aouda as to the issue of the voyage, repeating that the most difficult part was done, that they had left the fantastic countries of China and Japan, that they were returning to civilised countries, and finally, that a train from San Francisco to New York, and a transatlantic steamer from New York to Liverpool, would be sufficient, doubtless, to finish this impossible tour of the world in the time agreed upon.

Nine days after leaving Yokohama, Phileas Fogg had traversed exactly the half of the terrestrial globe.

In fact, the *General Grant*, on the 23rd of November, passed the one hundred and eightieth meridian, upon which in the southern hemisphere are to be found the antipodes of London. It is true that of the eighty days at his disposal he had used fifty-two, and there only remained to him twenty-eight to be consumed. But we must notice that if the gentleman only found himself half-way round by the difference of meridians, he had really accomplished more than two-thirds of its entire course. Indeed, what forced detours from London to Aden, from Aden to Bombay, from Calcutta to Singapore, from Singapore to Yokohama! By following around the fiftieth parallel, which is that of London, the distance would have been but about twelve thousand miles, while Phileas Fogg was compelled, by the caprices of the means of locomotion, to travel over twenty-six thousand, of which he had already made about seventeen thousand five hundred, at this date, the 23rd of November. But now the route was a straight one, and Fix was no longer there to accumulate obstacles.

It happened also that on this 23rd of November, Passepartout made quite a joyful discovery. It will be recollected that the obstinate fellow had insisted on keeping London time with his famous family watch, deeming incorrect the time of the various countries that he traversed. Now this day, although he had neither put his watch forward or back, it agreed with the ship's chronometers.

The triumph of Passepartout may be comprehended. He would have liked to know what Fix would have said if he had been present.

"The rogue who told me a heap of stories about the meridians, the sun and the moon!" said Passepartout. "Pshaw! if one listened to that sort of people, we should have a nice sort of clocks and watches! I was very sure that one day or another, the sun would decide to regulate itself by my watch!"

Passepartout was ignorant of this: that if the face of his watch had been divided into twenty-four hours like the Italian clocks, he would have had no reason for triumph, for the hands of his watch, when it was nine o'clock in the morning on the vessel, would have indicated nine o'clock in the evening, that is, the twenty-first hour after midnight—a difference precisely equal to that which exists between London and the one hundred and eightieth meridian.

But if Fix had been capable of explaining this purely

physical effect, Passepartout, doubtless, would have been incapable, if not of understanding it, at least of admitting it. And in any event, if the impossible thing should occur that the detective would unexpectedly show himself aboard at this moment, it is probable that Passepartout would have spitefully talked with him on quite a different subject, and in quite a different manner.

Now, where was Fix at this moment?

He was actually on board the *General Grant*.

In fact, on arriving at Yokohama the detective, leaving Mr. Fogg, whom he thought he would see again during the day, had immediately gone to the English Consul's. There he finally found the warrant of arrest, which, running after him from Bombay, was already forty days old, which had been sent to him from Hong-Kong on the very *Carnatic* on board of which he was supposed to be. The detective's disappointment may be imagined! The warrant was useless! Mr. Fogg had left the English possessions! An order of extradition was now necessary to arrest him!

"Let it be so!" said Fix to himself, after the first moment of anger. "My warrant is no longer good here; it will be in England. This rogue has the appearance of returning to his native country believing that he has thrown the police off their guard. Well, I will follow him there. As for the money, Heaven grant there may be some left! But what with travelling, rewards, trials, fines, elephants, expenses of every kind, my man has already left more than five thousand pounds on his route. After all, the Bank is rich!"

His decision taken, he immediately went on board the *General Grant*, and was there when Mr. Fogg and Mrs. Aouda arrived. To his extreme surprise, he recognised Passepartout under his fantastic costume. He concealed himself immediately in his cabin, to avoid an explanation which might damage everything—and, thanks to the number of the passengers, he counted on not being seen by his enemy, when this very day he found himself face to face with him on the forward part of the ship.

Passepartout jumped at Fix's throat, without any other

137

explanation, and to the great delight of certain Americans who immediately bet for him, he gave the unfortunate detective a superb volley of blows, showing the great superiority of French over English boxing.

When Passepartout had finished he found himself calmer and comforted. Fix rose in pretty bad condition, and, looking at his adversary, he said to him coldly:

"Is it finished.?"

"Yes, for the moment."

"Then I want a word with you."

"But I—"

"In your master's interest."

Passepartout, as if conquered by this coolness, followed the detective, and they both sat down in the forward part of the steamer.

"You have thrashed me," said Fix. "Good; I expected it. Now, listen to me. Until the present I have been Mr. Fogg's adversary, but now I am with him."

"At last!" cried Passepartout, "you believe him to be an honest man?"

"No," replied Fix coldly. "I believe him to be a rogue. Sh! Don't stir, and let me talk. As long as Mr. Fogg was in the English possessions, I had an interest in retaining him whilst waiting for a warrant of arrest. I did everything I could for that. I sent against him the priests of Bombay, I made you drunk at Hong-Kong, I separated you from your master, I made him miss the Yokohama steamer."

Passepartout listened with clenched fists.

"No," continued Fix, "Mr. Fogg seems to be returning to England? Well, I will follow him there. But henceforth it shall be my aim to clear the obstacles from his path as zealously and carefully as before I took pains to accumulate them. You see my game is changed, and it is changed because my interest desires it. I add, that your interest is similar to mine, for you will only know in England whether you are in the service of a criminal or an honest man!"

Passepartout listened to Fix very attentively, and he was convinced that the latter spoke with entire good faith.

"Are we friends?" asked Fix.

"Friends, no," replied Passepartout; "allies, yes; and under this condition that, at the least appearance of treason, I will twist your neck."

"Agreed," said the detective quietly.

Eleven days after, on the 3rd of December, the *General Grant* entered the Bay of the Golden Gate, and arrived at San Francisco.

Mr. Fogg had neither gained nor lost a single day.

CHAPTER 25

In which a slight glimpse of San Francisco is had—a Political Meeting

It was seven o'clock in the morning, when Phileas Fogg, Mrs. Aouda, and Passepartout set foot on the American continent, if this name can be given to the floating wharf on which they landed. These wharves, rising and falling with the tide facilitate the loading and unloading of vessels. Clippers of all sizes were moored there, steamers of all nationalities, and those steamboats with several decks, which ply on the Sacramento and its tributaries. There were accumulated also the products of a commerce which extends to Mexico, Peru, Chile, Brazil, Europe, Asia, and all the islands of the Pacific Ocean.

Passepartout, in his joy at finally touching American soil, thought in landing he would execute a perilous leap in his finest style. But when he fell upon the wharf, the planks of which were worm-eaten, he almost fell through. Quite put out by the manner in which he had "set foot" on the new continent, the good fellow uttered a terrible cry, which sent flying an innumerable flock of cormorants and pelicans, the customary inhabitants of the movable wharves.

Mr. Fogg, as soon as he landed, ascertained the hour at which the first train left for New York. It was six o'clock in the evening. He had, then, an entire day to spend in the California capital. He ordered a carriage for Mrs. Aouda and himself Passepartout mounted the box, and the vehicle, at three dollars for the trip, turned towards the International Hotel.

From the elevated position that he occupied, Passepartout observed with curiosity the great American city, the broad streets, low, evenly-ranged houses, the Anglo-Saxon Gothic churches and temples, the immense docks, the palatial warehouses, some of wood and some of brick; the numerous vehicles in the streets, omnibuses and horse-cars, and on the crowded sidewalks not only Americans and Europeans, but also Chinese and Indians—the component parts of the population of more than two hundred thousand inhabitants.

Passepartout was quite surprised at all he saw. He was yet in the city of 1849, in the city of bandits, incendiaries, and assassins, running after the native gold, an immense concourse of all the outlaws, who gambled with gold-dust, a revolver in one hand and a knife in the other. But this "good time" had passed away. San Francisco presented the aspect of a large commercial city. The high tower of the City Hall overlooked all these streets and avenues, crossing each other at right angles, between which were spread out verdant squares, then a Chinese quarter, which seemed to have been imported from the Celestial Empire, in a toybox. No more sombreros, or red shirts after the fashion of the miners, or Indians with feathers; but silk hats and black clothes, worn by a large number of gentlemen of absorbing activity. Certain streets, among others Montgomery Street, The Regent Street of London, the Boulevard des Italiens of Paris, the Broadway of New York, the State Street of Chicago were lined with splendid stores, in whose windows were displayed the products of the entire world.

When Passepartout arrived at the International Hotel, it seemed to him that he had not left England.

The ground floor of the hotel was occupied by an immense bar, a sort of sideboard opened gratis to every passer-by. Dried beef, oyster soup, biscuit, and cheese were dealt out without the customer having to take out his purse. He only paid for his drink—ale, porter, or sherry, if he fancied refreshment. That appeared "very American" to Passepartout.

The hotel restaurant was comfortable. Mr. Fogg and Mrs. Aouda took seats at a table and were abundantly served in very small dishes by negroes of darkest hue.

After breakfast, Phileas Fogg, accompanied by Mrs. Aouda, left the hotel to go to the office of the English Consul to have his passport *viséd* there. On the pavement he found his servant, who asked him if it would not be prudent, before starting on the Pacific railroad, to buy a few dozen Enfield rifles or Colt's revolvers. Passepartout had heard so much talk of the Sioux and Pawnees stopping trains like ordinary Spanish brigands. Mr. Fogg replied that it was a useless precaution, but he left him free to act as he thought best. Then he went to the office of the Consul.

Phileas Fogg had not gone two hundred steps, when, "by the greatest accident," he met Fix, who manifested very great surprise. How! Mr. Fogg and he had taken together the voyage across the Pacific, and they had not met on board the vessel! At all events, Fix could only be honoured by seeing again the gentleman to whom he owed so much; and his business calling him to Europe, he would be delighted to continue his journey in such agreeable company.

Mr. Fogg replied that the honour would be his, and Fix— who made it a point not to lose sight of him—asked his permission to visit with him this curious city of San Francisco, which was granted.

Mrs. Aouda, Phileas Fogg, and Fix sauntered through the streets. They soon found themselves in Montgomery Street, where the crowd of people was enormous. On the sidewalks, in the middle of the street, on the horse-car rails, notwithstanding the incessant passage of the coaches and omnibuses, on the steps of the stores, in the windows of all the houses, and even up to the roofs, there was an innumerable crowd.

141

Men with placards circulated among the groups. Banners and streamers floated in the wind. There were shouts in every direction.

"Hurrah for Camerfield!"

"Hurrah for Mandiboy!"

It was a political meeting. At least so Fix thought, and he communicated his ideas to Mr. Fogg, adding:

"We will perhaps do well, sir, not to mingle in this crowd. Only hard blows will be got here."

"In fact," replied Phileas Fogg, "blows, if they are political, are not less blows."

Fix could not help smiling at this remark, and in order to see, without being caught in the crowd, Mrs. Aouda, Phileas Fogg, and he secured a place upon the upper landing of a flight of steps reaching to the top of a terrace, situated in the upper end of Montgomery Street. Before them, on the other side of the street, between the wharf of a coal merchant and the warehouse of a petroleum dealer, there was a large platform in the open air, towards which the various currents of the crowd seemed to be tending.

And now, why this meeting? What was the occasion of its being held? Phileas Fogg did not know at all. Was it for the nomination of some high military or civil official, a State Governor, or a Member of Congress? It might be supposed so, seeing the great excitement agitating the city.

At this moment there was quite a movement in the crowd. Every hand was thrown in the air. Some, tightly closed, seemed to rise and fall rapidly in the midst of the cries—an energetic manner, no doubt, of casting a vote. The crowd fell back. The banners wavered, disappeared for an instant, and reappeared in tatters. The surging of the crowd extended to the steps, whilst every head moved up and down on the surface like a sea suddenly agitated by a squall. The number of black hats diminished perceptibly, and the most of them seemed to have lost their normal height.

"It is evidently a meeting," said Fix; "and the question which has excited it must be a stirring one. I would not be astonished if they were still discussing the Alabama affair, although it has been settled."

"Perhaps," simply replied Mr. Fogg.

"In any event," replied Fix, "two champions are in each other's presence, the Hon. Mr. Camerfield and the Hon. Mr. Mandiboy."

Mrs. Aouda, leaning on Phileas Fogg's arm, looked with surprise at this noisy scene, and Fix was going to ask one of his neighbours the reason of this popular effervescence, when a more violent movement broke out. The hurrahs, interspersed with insults, redoubled. The staffs of the banners were transformed into offensive arms. Instead of hands, there were fists everywhere. From the top of carriages and omnibuses, blocked in their course, formidable blows were exchanged. Everything was made use of as projectiles. Boots and shoes described extended curves in the air, and it seemed even as if some revolvers mingled their national sounds with the loud cries of the crowd.

The crowd approached the night of stairs, and swept over on to the lower steps. One of the parties had evidently been repulsed without disinterested spectators knowing whether the advantage was with Mandiboy or Camerfield.

"I believe that it is prudent for us to retire," said Fix, who did not want his "man" to get hurt or mixed up in a bad business. "If this is an English question, and we are recognised, we will be treated roughly in this mixed crowd."

"An English citizen—" replied Phileas Fogg.

But the gentleman could not finish his sentence. Behind him, on the terrace above the stairs, there were frightful yells. They cried "Hip! hip! hurrah for Mandiboy!" It was a party of voters coming to the rescue, flanking the Camerfield party.

Mr. Fogg, Mrs. Aouda, and Fix found themselves between two-fires. It was too late to escape. This torrent of men, armed with loaded canes and bludgeons, was irresistible. Phileas Fogg and Fix, in protecting the young woman, were very roughly treated. Mr. Fogg, not less phlegmatic than usual, tried to defend himself with the natural weapons placed at the end of the arms of every Englishman, but in vain. A large rough fellow, with a red beard, flushed face, and broad shoulders, who seemed to be the chief of the band, raised his formidable fist to strike r. Fogg, and he would have damaged that gentleman very much, if Fix, throwing himself in the way, had not received the blow in his place. An enormous bump rose at once under the detective's silk hat, transformed into a simple cap.

"Yankee!" said Mr. Fogg, casting at his adversary a look of deep scorn.

Englishman!" replied the other. "We will see each other again."

"When you please."

"Your name?"

"Phileas Fogg. And yours?"

"Colonel Stamp Proctor."

Then the crowd passed on, throwing Fix down. He rose with his clothes torn, but without serious hurt. His travelling overcoat was torn in two unequal parts, and his pantaloons resembled those of certain Indians. But to sum up, Mrs. Aouda had been spared, and Fix alone had been harmed by the fist-blow.

"Thanks," said Mr. Fogg to the detective, as soon as they were out of the crowd.

"No thanks necessary;" replied Fix, "but come with me."

"Where?"

"To a tailor's."

In fact, this visit was opportune. The garments of Phileas Fogg and Fix were in tatters, as if these two gentlemen had fought for the Hon. Messrs. Camerfield and Mandiboy.

An hour afterwards they had respectable clothes and hats. Then they returned to the International Hotel.

Passepartout was waiting there for his master, armed with a half-dozen sharp-shooting, six-barrelled, breech-loading revolvers. When he perceived Fix in company with Mr. Fogg, his brow darkened. Mrs. Aouda, however, having told in a few words what had happened, Passepartout became calm again. Fix was evidently no longer an enemy but an ally. He was keeping his word.

144

Dinner over, a coach drove up to take the passengers and their baggage to the station. As they were getting into the coach Mr. Fogg said to Fix:

"Did you see Colonel Proctor again?"

"No," replied Fix.

"I shall return to America to find him again," said Mr. Fogg coldly. "It would not be proper for an English citizen to allow himself to be treated in this way."

The detective smiled and did not answer him. But it is seen that Mr. Fogg was one of those Englishmen, who, while they do not tolerate duelling at home, will fight abroad, when it is necessary to maintain their honour.

At a quarter before six the travellers reached the station and found the train ready to start.

At the moment that Mr. Fogg was going to get into the car, he called a porter and asked him:

"Was there not some disturbance in San Francisco today?"

"It was a political meeting, sir," replied the porter.

"But I thought I noticed a certain excitement in the streets."

"It was simply a meeting organised for an election."

"The election of a general-in-chief, doubtless?" asked Mr. Fogg.

"No, sir, of a Justice of the Peace."

Upon this reply, Phileas Fogg jumped aboard the car, and the train started at full speed.

CHAPTER 26

In which our Party takes the Express Train on the Pacific Railroad

"From Ocean to Ocean"—so say the Americans, and these four words ought to be the general name of the "Grand Trunk," which traverses the United States in their greatest breadth. But in reality, the Pacific Railroad is divided into two distinct parts; the Central Pacific from San Francisco to Ogden, and the Union Pacific from Ogden to Omaha At that point five distinct lines meet, which place Omaha in frequent communications with New York.

New York and San Francisco are therefore now united by an uninterrupted metal ribbon, measuring not less than three thousand seven hundred and eighty-six miles. Between Omaha and the Pacific, the railroad traverses a country still frequented by the Indians and wild animals—a vast extent of territory which the Mormons commenced to colonise about 1845, after they were driven out of Illinois.

Formerly, under the most favourable circumstances, it took six months to go from New York to San Francisco. Now it is done in seven days.

It was in 1862, notwithstanding the opposition of the Southern Congressmen, who wished a more southerly line, that the route of the railroad was fixed between the forty-first and the forty-second parallel. President Lincoln, of so lamented memory, himself fixed in the State of Nebraska, at the city of Omaha, the beginning of the new network. Work was commenced immediately, and prosecuted with that American activity, which is neither slow nor routine-like. The rapidity of the construction did not in any way injure its thoroughness. On the prairies the road progressed at the rate of a mile and a half per day. A locomotive, moving over the rails laid yesterday, carried the rails for the next day, and ran upon them in proportion as they were laid.

The Pacific Railroad throws off several branches on its route in the States of Iowa, Kansas, Colorado, and Oregon. Leaving Omaha, it takes the left bank of Platte River as far as the mouth of the North Fort follows the South Fork, crosses the Laramie Territory, and the Wahsatch Mountains, turns Salt Lake, arrives at Salt Lake City, the capital of the Mormons, buries itself in the Tuilla Valley, crosses the American Desert, the Cedar and Humboldt Mountains, Humboldt River, the Sierra Nevada, and redescends via Sacramento to the Pacific, its

146

grade, even in crossing the Rocky Mountains, not exceeding one hundred and twelve feet to the mile.

Such was this long artery which the trains would pass over in seven days, and which would permit the Honourable Phileas Fogg—at least he hoped so—to take the Liverpool steamer, on the 11th, at New York.

The car occupied by Phileas Fogg was a sort of long omnibus, resting on two trucks, each with four wheels, whose ease of motion permits of going round short curves. There were no compartments inside; two rows of seats placed on each side, perpendicularly to the axle, and between which was reserved an aisle, leading to the dressing-rooms and others, with which each car is provided. Through the whole length of the train the cars communicated by platforms, and the passengers could move about from one end to the other of the train, which placed at their disposal palace, balcony, restaurant, and smoking-cars. All that is wanting is a theatre-car. But there will be one, some day.

On the platforms book and news dealers were constantly circulating, dealing out their merchandise; and vendors of liquors, eatables, and cigars were not wanting in customers.

The travellers left Oakland Station at six o'clock. It was already night, cold and dreary, with an overcast sky, threatening snow. The train did not move with great rapidity. Counting the stops, it did not run more than a speed which ought, however, to enable it to cross the United States in the fixed time.

They talked but little in the car. Sleep soon overcame the passengers. Passepartout sat near the detective, but he did not speak to him. Since the late events, their relations had become somewhat cold. No more sympathy or intimacy. Fix had not changed his manner, but Passepartout retained an extreme reserve, ready at the least suspicion to choke his old friend.

An hour after the starting of the train a fine snow commenced to fall, which fortunately could not delay the progress of the train. Through the windows nothing was seen but an immense white sheet, against which the clouds of steam from the locomotive looked greyish.

147

At eight o'clock a steward entered the car, and announced to the passengers that the hour for retiring had come. This was a sleeping-car, which in a few minutes was transformed into a dormitory. The backs of the seats unfolded, beds carefully packed away were unrolled by an ingenious system, berths were improvised in a few moments, and each passenger had soon at his disposal a comfortable bed, which thick curtains protected from all indiscreet looks. The sheets were clean and the pillows soft. Nothing more to be done but to lie down and sleep—which everyone did, as if he had been in the comfortable cabin of a steamer—while the train moved on under full head of steam across the State of California

In that portion of the country between San Francisco and Sacramento the ground is not very hilly. This portion of the railroad, under the name of the Central Pacific, originally had Sacramento for its starting-point, and went towards the east to meet that starting from Omaha From San Francisco to the capital of California the line ran directly to the north-east, along American River, which empties into San Pablo Bay. The one hundred and twenty miles included between these two important cities were accomplished in six hours, and towards midnight, while they were getting their first sleep, the travellers passed through Sacramento. They saw nothing of that large city, the seat of the state government of California, nor its fine wharves, its broad streets, its splendid hotels, its squares, nor its churches.

Leaving Sacramento, the train having passed Junction, Roclin, Auburn, and Colfax Stations, plunged into the Sierra Nevada It was seven o'clock in the morning when Cisco Station was passed. An hour afterwards the dormitory had become an ordinary car, and the passengers could get through the windows a glimpse of the picturesque views of this mountainous country. The route of the train followed the windings of the Sierra, here clinging to the sides of the mountains, there suspended above precipices, avoiding sharp angles by bold curves, plunging into narrow gorges from which there seemed to be no exit. The locomotive, flashing fire like a chased animal, its large smoke-pipe throwing out lurid lights, its sharp bell, its cow-catcher, extending out like a spur, mingled its shrieks and bellowings with the noise of the torrents and cascades, and twined its smoke in the dark branches of the firs.

There were few or no tunnels or bridges on the route. The railroad turned the flank of the mountains, not seeking in a straight line the shortest route from one point to another, and not doing violence to nature.

About nine o'clock the train entered the State of Nevada, through the Carson Valley, always following a north-easterly direction. At noon it left Reno, where the passengers had twenty minutes for breakfast.

From this point, the iron road, skirting Humboldt River, passed a few miles to the north. Then it bent to the east, and did not leave the stream until it reached the Humboldt range, where the river takes its source, nearly in the eastern end of the State of Nevada.

After breakfasting, Mr. Fogg, Mrs. Aouda, and their companions took their seats again in the car. Phileas Fogg, the young woman, Fix, and Passepartout, comfortably seated, looked at the varied country passing before their sight, vast prairies, mountains whose profiles were shown upon the horizon, and creeks tumbling down, a foaming mass of water. Sometimes, a large herd of bison, gathering in the distance, appeared like a moving dam. These innumerable armies of grazing animals frequently oppose an insurmountable obstacle to the passage of trains. Thousands of these animals have been seen moving on for several hours in close ranks across the railroad. The locomotive is then forced to stop and wait until the path is clear again.

The same thing happened on this occasion. About three o'clock in the afternoon a herd of ten or twelve thousand blocked the rail-road. The engine, having slackened its speed, tried to plunge its spur into the flank of the immense column, but it had to stop before the impenetrable mass.

They saw these buffaloes, as the Americans improperly call them, moving with their steady gait, frequently bellowing terribly. They had a larger body than those of the bulls of

149

Europe, short legs and tail, a projecting saddle forming a muscular bump, horns separated at the base, their heads, necks, and shoulders covered with long, shaggy hair. The could not think of stopping this moving mass. When the bison have adopted a course, nothing could swerve them from it or modify it. They are a torrent of living flesh which no dam could hold.

The travellers, scattered on the platforms, looked at this curious spectacle. But Phileas Fogg, who ought to be the most in a hurry, had remained in his seat, and was waiting philosophically until it should please the buffaloes to open a passage. Passepartout was furious at the delay caused by this mass of animals. He wanted to fire all the revolvers at them.

"What a country!" he cried. "Mere cattle stop trains, and move along in procession without hurrying? as if they did not impede travel! *Parbleu!* I would like to know if Mr. Fogg had foreseen this mischance in his programme! And what an engineer, who does not dare to rush his engine through this impeding mass of beasts!"

The engineer had not attempted to overcome the obstacle, and he acted wisely. He would undoubtedly have crushed the first buffaloes he struck by the cow-catcher; but, powerful as it was, the engine would have soon been stopped, and the train thrown off the track and wrecked.

The best course, then, was to wait patiently, ready to make up the lost time by an increase of the speed of the train. The passage of the bison lasted three full hours, and the road was not clear again until nightfall. At this moment the last ranks of the herd crossed the rails, whilst the first were disappearing below the southern horizon.

It was then eight o'clock, when the train passed through the defiles of the Humboldt range, and half-past nine when it entered Utah Territory, the region of the Great Salt Lake, the curious Mormon country.

CHAPTER 27

In which Passepartout follows, with a Speed of Twenty Miles an Hour, a Course of Mormon History

During the night of the 5th, to the 6th of December, the train went for fifty miles to the south-east, then it ran upwards about as far northerly, approaching the Great Salt Lake.

Passepartout, about nine o'clock in the morning, went on the platform to take the air. The weather was cold, the sky grey, but it had stopped snowing. The disc of the sun, enlarged by the mist, looked like an enormous piece of gold, and Passepartout was busy calculating its value in pounds sterling, when his attention was taken from this useful work by the appearance of a very strange personage.

This personage, who took the train at Elko Station, was tall, very brown, had a black moustache, black stockings, a black silk hat, black waistcoat, black pantaloons, white cravat, and black dog-skin gloves. He might have been taken for a clergyman. He went from one end of the train to the other, and on the door of each car fastened with wafers a written notice.

Passepartout approached and read on one of these notices that Elder William Hitch, taking advantage of his presence on train No. 48, would, from eleven to twelve o'clock, deliver an address on Mormonism in car No. 117—inviting to hear him all desirous of being instructed concerning the mysteries of the religion of the "Latter Day Saints."

"Certainly, I will go," said Passepartout to himself, who knew nothing of Mormonism but its custom of polygamy, the base of Mormon society.

The news spread rapidly through the train, which carried about one hundred passengers. Of this number thirty at most, attracted by the notice of the meeting, occupied at eleven o'clock the seats in car No.117. Passepartout was prominent in the front rank of the faithful. Neither his master nor Fix thought it worth while to take the trouble.

At the appointed hour Elder William Hitch rose, and in quite an irritated voice, as if he had been contradicted in advance, he cried:

"I tell you that Joe Smith is a martyr, that his brother Hiram is a martyr, and that the persecution by the United States Government of the prophets will also make a martyr of Brigham Young. Who dares to maintain the contrary."

No one ventured to contradict the missionary, whose excitement contrasted with his naturally calm physiognomy. But, without doubt, his anger was explained by the fact that Mormonism was now subjected to severe trials. The United States Government had, not without difficulty, just reduced these independent fanatics. It had made itself master of Utah, and had subjected it to the laws of the Union, after imprisoning Brigham Young, accused of rebellion and polygamy. Since that period, the disciples of the prophet redoubled their efforts, and whilst not coming to acts, resisted in words the demands of Congress.

We see that Elder William Hitch was trying to proselyte even on the trains.

And then he related, emphasising his narrative by his loud voice and the violence of his gestures, the history of Mormonism from *Bible* times: "How in Israel, a Mormon prophet of the tribe of Joseph, published the annals of the new religion and bequeathed them to his son Morom; how, many centuries later, a translation of this precious book, written in Egyptian characters, was made by Joseph Smith, Jr., a farmer in the State of Vermont, who revealed himself as a mythical prophet in 1825; how, finally, a celestial messenger appeared to him in an illuminated forest and gave him the annals of the Lord."

At this moment some of his hearers, not much interested in the retrospective narrative of the missionary, left the car; but William Hitch, continuing, related, "how Smith, Jr., with his father, his two brothers, and a few disciples, founded the religion of the Latter Day Saints—a religion which, adopted not only in America, but in England, in Scandinavia, and in Germany, counts among its faithful, artisans and also a number of people engaged in the liberal professions; how a colony was founded in Ohio; how a temple was built at a cost of two hundred thousand dollars, and a city built at Kirkland; how Smith became an enterprising banker, and received from a simple mummy showman a papyrus scroll containing a narrative written by Abraham and other celebrated Egyptians."

This narrative becoming a little long, the ranks of his hearers thinned out still more, and the audience only consisted of twenty persons.

But the Elder, undisturbed by this desertion, related the details of "how Joe Smith became bankrupt in 1837; how his ruined stockholders gave him a coat of tar and feathers; how he appeared again, more honourable and more honoured than ever, a few years after, at Independence, in Missouri, at the head of a flourishing community, which counted not less than three thousand disciples; and that then, pursued by the hatred of the Gentiles, he had to fly to the far West."

Ten hearers were still there, and among them the honest Passepartout, who listened with all his ears. Thus he learned "how, after long persecutions, Smith appeared in Illinois, and in 1839 founded, on the banks of the Mississippi, Nauvoo, the beautiful, whose population rose to twenty-five thousand souls; how Smith became the Mayor, Chief Justice, and General-in-Chief; how in 1843 he announced himself as candidate for the Presidency of the United States; and how, finally, he was drawn into an ambuscade at Carthage, thrown into prison, and assassinated by a band of masked men."

At this moment Passepartout was the only hearer in the car, and the elder, looking him in the face, fascinating him by his words, recalled to his mind that, two years after the assassination of Smith, his successor, the inspired prophet, Brigham Young, leaving Nauvoo, established himself on the banks of Salt Lake, and that there, in that splendid territory, in the midst of that fertile country, on the road which the emigrants take in crossing Utah to reach California, the new colony, thanks to the Mormon principles of polygamy, had increased enormously.

"And this," added William Hitch, "is why the jealousy of Congress has been aroused against us? why the United States soldiers have invaded the soil of Utah! why our chief, the prophet Brigham Young, has been imprisoned in defiance of all justice. Shall we give up to force? Never! Driven from Vermont, driven from Illinois, driven from Ohio, driven from Missouri, driven from Utah, we shall find some independent territory yet where we shall pitch our tents. And you, my brother," added the Elder, fixing his angry look on his single hearer, "will you plant yours in the shadow of our flag?"

"No," replied Passepartout bravely, flying in his turn, leaving the fanatic to preach in the desert.

But, during this discourse, the train had advanced rapidly, and about half-past twelve it touched the north-west corner of the Great Salt Lake. Thence could be embraced in a vast circumstance the aspect of this inland lake, which also bears the name of the Dead Sea, and into which empties an American Jordan. A beautiful lake, hemmed in by craggy rocks of broad surface, encrusted with white salt, a superb sheet of water which formerly covered a larger space; but in time its shores, rising by degrees, reduced its superficial area and increased its depth.

The Salt Lake, about seventy miles long, and thirty-five wide, is situated three thousand eight hundred feet above the level of the sea. Very different from Lake Asphaltite, whose depression is twelve hundred feet below the sea, it holds considerable salt in solution, and one-fourth the weight of the water is solid matter. Its specific gravity is 1170, that of distilled water being 1000. Fishes cannot live in it. Those that the Jordan, Weber, and other creeks carry into it soon perish; but it is not true that the density of its waters is such that a man cannot dive into it.

Around the lake the country was admirably tilled; for the Mormons understand agricultural pursuits; ranches and corrals for domestic animals; fields of wheat, corn, sorghum, luxuriant prairies, and everywhere hedges of wild roses, clumps of acacias and euphorbias, such would have been the appearance of this country six months later; but at this moment the ground was covered with a thin sheet of snow, descending lightly upon it.

At two o'clock the travellers got out at Ogden. The train stopping for six hours, Mr. Fogg, Mrs. Aouda, and their two companions had time to repair to the City of the Saints by the short branch from Ogden. Two hours were sufficient to visit this absolutely American town, and as such, built after the pattern of all the cities of the Union, vast checkerboards with long cold lines, "with the sombre sadness of right angles," according to Victor Hugo's expression. The founder of the City of the Saints could not escape from the need for symmetry which distinguishes the Anglo-Saxons. In this singular country, where the men are certainly not up to the level of their institutions, everything is done "squarely," cities, houses, and follies.

At three o'clock, the travellers were promenading through the streets of the town, built between the banks of the Jordan and the first rise of the Wahsatch Mountains. They noticed there few or no churches, but as monuments, the prophet's house, the court-house, and the arsenal; then houses of bluish bricks, with verandas and porches, surrounded by gardens bordered with acacias, palms, and locusts. A wall of clay and pebbles, built in 1853, surrounded the town. In the principal street, where the market is, were some hotels adorned with pavilions, and among others Salt Lake House.

Mr. Fogg and his companions did not find the town thickly peopled. The streets were almost deserted, save perhaps the part where the Temple was, which they reached only after having traversed several quarters surrounded by palisades. The women were pretty numerous, which was explained by the singular composition of Mormon households. It must not be supposed, however, that all Mormons are polygamists. They are free, but it is well to remark that all the females in Utah are anxious to be married; for, according to the religion of the country, the Mormon heaven does not admit to the possession of its beatitudes the unmarried of the feminine sex. These poor creatures neither seemed well off, nor happy. Some, the richer ones, doubtless, wore a short, low-cut, black silk dress, under a hood or a very modest shawl. The others were dressed in Indian fashion.

Passepartout, in his position as one convinced, did not regard without a certain fright these Mormon women, charged, in groups, with making a single Mormon happy. With his good sense, it was the husband whom he specially pitied. It seemed to him terrible to have to guide so many wives at once through the vicissitudes of life, conduct them, as it were, in a body to the Mormon paradise, with the prospect of finding them to all eternity in the company of the glorious Smith, who was to be the ornament of this place of delights. Certainly, he did not feel called, and he thought—perhaps he was mistaken—that the women of Salt Lake City cast rather embarrassing looks at his person. Very fortunately, his stay in the City of the Saints was not prolonged. At a few minutes past four the travellers were again at the station, and took their seats in the cars.

The whistle sounded; but at the moment that the driving-wheels of the locomotive, slipping upon the rails, commenced to impart some movement to the train, the cry, "Stop! stop!" was heard.

They do not stop trains just started. The gentleman who uttered the cry was evidently a Mormon behind time. He was breathless from running. Fortunately for him the station had neither gates nor barriers. He rushed, then, on the track, jumped upon the steps of the last car, and fell, out of breath, on one of the seats.

Passepartout, who had followed with emotion the incidents of this gymnastic feat, went to look at the tardy one, in whom he took a lively interest, when he learned that this citizen of Utah had thus taken flight in consequence of a household scene.

When the Mormon had recovered his breath, Passepartout ventured to ask him politely how many wives he had to himself—and from the manner in which he had just run away he would suppose that he had at least twenty of them.

156

"One, sir!" replied the Mormon, raising his arms heaven-
ward. "One, and that was enough!"

CHAPTER 28

In which Passepartout could not Succeed in making anyone listen to Reason

The train leaving Great Salt Lake and the station at Ogden,
rose for an hour towards the north, as far as Weber River,
having accomplished about nine hundred miles from San
Francisco. Leaving this point, it resumed the easterly direction
across the rocky hills of the Wahsatch Mountains. It is in this
part of the Territory, comprised between these mountains and
the Rocky Mountains properly so called, that the American
engineers were caught with the greatest difficulties. On this
portion of the route the subsidy of the United States
Government was raised to forty-eight thousand dollars per
mile, whilst on the plains it was only sixteen thousand dollars;
but the engineers, as has already been said, have not done
violence to nature—they have played with her, going round
the difficulties. To reach the great basin, only one tunnel,
fourteen thousand feet long, was bored in the entire route of
the railroad.

At Salt Lake the road had up to this time reached its greatest altitude. From this point its profile described a very long
curve, descending towards Bitter Creek Valley, then re-ascend-
ing to the dividing ridge of the waters between the Atlantic
and the Pacific. The creeks were numerous in this mountainous region. It was necessary to cross the Muddy, the Green,
and others, on culverts. Passepartout became more impatient
in proportion as he approached the end of his journey. Fix in

157

his turn would have been very glad to get out of this rough country. He feared delays, he dreaded accidents, and was more in a hurry than Phileas Fogg himself to set foot upon English soil!

At ten o'clock at night the train stopped at Fort Bridger station, which it left almost immediately, and twenty miles farther on it entered Wyoming Territory—following the entire valley of the Bitter Creek, whence flow a portion of the streams forming the water system of Colorado.

The next day, the 7th of December, there was a stop of a quarter-hour at Green River station. The snow had fallen quite heavily through the night, but mingled with rain and half-melted it could not interfere with the progress of the train. But this bad weather kept Passepartout in constant uneasiness, for the accumulation of the snow clogging the car wheels would certainly endanger the journey.

"What an idea," he said to himself, "for my master to travel during the winter! Could he not wait for the fine season of the year to increase his chances.?"

But at this moment, while the good fellow was busy only with the condition of the sky and the lowering of the temperature, Mrs. Aouda was experiencing more serious fears, which proceeded from quite another cause.

Some of the passengers had got out of the cars, and were walking on the platform of the Green River station, waiting for the train to leave. The young woman, looking through the window pane, recognised among them Colonel Stamp Proctor, the American who had behaved so rudely to Phileas Fogg at the time of the political meeting in San Francisco. Mrs. Aouda, not wishing to be seen, drew back from the window.

This circumstance made a lively impression upon the young woman. She was attached to the man who, however coldly, gave her every day tokens of the most absolute devotion. She doubtless did not comprehend the entire depth of the sentiment which her deliverer inspired in her, and to this sentiment she gave as yet only the name of gratitude; but unknown to herself it was more than that. Her heart was therefore wrung at the sight of the rough fellow of whom Mr. Fogg would, sooner or later, demand satisfaction. Evidently it was chance alone that had brought Colonel Proctor into this train; but he was there, and Phileas Fogg must be prevented at any cost from seeing his adversary.

When the train had started again, Mrs. Aouda took advantage for a moment, when Mr. Fogg was sleeping, to post Fix and Passepartout as to the situation.

"That Proctor is on the train!" cried Fix. "Well, compose yourself, madame; before dealing with the gentleman—with Mr. Fogg—he will have to deal with me! It seems to me that in all this business I have received the greatest insults!"

"And moreover," added Passepartout, "I will take care of him, Colonel as he is."

"Mr. Fix," continued Mrs. Aouda, "Mr. Fogg will allow no one to avenge him. He has said that he will return to America to find this ruffian. If, then, he sees Colonel Proctor, we cannot prevent an encounter, which may lead to deplorable results. He must therefore not see him."

"You are right, madame," replied Fox; "an encounter might ruin everything. Conquerer or conquered, Mr. Fogg would be delayed, and—"

"And," added Passepartout, "that would win the bet of the gentlemen of the Reform Club. In four days we shall be in New York! Well, then, if my master does not leave his car for four days, we may hope that chance will not put him face to face with this cursed American, confound him! Now, we can easily prevent him— "

The conversation was interrupted. Mr. Fogg had waked up, and was looking at the country through the window pane obscured by the snow. But later, and without being heard by his master or Mrs. Aouda, Passepartout said to the detective:

"Would you truly fight for him?"

"I would do anything to take him back to Europe alive!" simply replied Fix, in a tone which indicated an unbroken will.

Passepartout felt a shudder over him, but his convictions as to the honesty of his master were not weakened.

And now, were there any means by which Mr. Fogg could be detained in this car, so as to prevent any encounter between him and the colonel? That could not be difficult, as the gentleman was naturally not excitable or inquisitive. At all events, the detective thought he had found this means, for a few moments later he said to Phileas Fogg: "These are long and slow hours that we pass thus on the railway."

"Indeed they are," replied the gentleman, "but they pass."

"On board the steamers," continued the detective, "you used to take a turn at whist?"

"Yes," replied Phileas Fogg, "but here it would be difficult. I have neither cards nor partners."

"Oh! as for the cards, we will find it easy to buy them. They are sold on all trains in America. As for partners, if perchance, madame—"

"Certainly, sir," replied the young woman quickly, "I understand whist. That is part of the English education."

"And I," continued Fix, "have some pretensions to playing a good game. Now, with us three and a dummy—"

"As you please, sir," replied Phileas Fogg, delighted at resuming his favourite game, even on the railroad.

Passepartout was dispatched in search of the steward, and he soon returned with two complete decks of cards, counters, and a shelf covered with cloth. Nothing was wanting. The game commenced. Mrs. Aouda understood whist well enough, and she even was complimented sometimes by the severe Phileas Fogg. As for the detective, he was simply an adept, and worthy of holding his head up with this gentleman.

"Now," said Passepartout to himself, "we will keep him. He will not budge any more!"

At eleven o'clock in the morning, the train had reached the dividing ridge of the waters of the two oceans. It was at Bridger Pass, at a height of seven thousand five hundred and twenty-four English feet above the level of the sea, one of the highest points touched by the profile of the route in this passage across the Rocky Mountains. After going about two hundred miles, the travellers finally found themselves on the vast plains extending as far as the Atlantic, and which nature made so propitious for laying a railroad.

On the slopes of the Atlantic basin already appeared the first

streams, tributaries of the North Platte River. The entire northern and eastern horizon was covered by the immense semi-
circular curtain, which forms the southern portion of the Rocky
Mountains, the highest being Laramie's Peak. Between this
curve and the line of the road extended vast and plentifully
watered plains. On the right of the road rose the first spurs of
the mountainous mass, rounding off to the south as far as the
sources of the Arkansas river, one of the large tributaries of the
Mississippi.

At half-past twelve, the travellers caught sight for an-instant
of Fort Halleck, which commands this country. A few hours
more, and the crossing of the Rocky Mountains would be
accomplished. It was to be hoped, then, that no accident would
mark the passage of the train through this difficult region. The
snow had stopped falling. The weather became cold and dry.
Large birds, frightened by the locomotive, were flying in the
distance. Not a deer, a bear, or a wolf, showed itself on the
plain. It was the desert in all its barrenness.

After a very comfortable breakfast, served up in the car, Mr.
Fogg and his partners had just resumed their interminable
whist, when sharp whistles were heard. The train stopped.

Passepartout put his head out of the door, and saw nothing
which could explain this stop. No station was in sight.

Mrs. Aouda and Fix feared for an instant that Mr. Fogg
would think of going out on the track. But the gentleman
contented himself with saying to his servant:

"See then what it is."

Passepartout rushed out of the car. About forty passengers
had left their seats, and among them Colonel Stamp Proctor.

The train had stopped in front of a red signal which blocked
the way. The engineer and conductor, having got out,
discussed quite excitedly with a signalman, whom the station-
master at Medicine Bow, the next station, had sent in advance
of the train. Some of the passengers approached and took part
in the discussion, among others the aforesaid Colonel Proctor,
with his loud voice and imperious gestures.

Passepartout, having rejoined the group, heard the signalman say:

"No! there is no means of passing. The bridge at Medicine Bow is shaky and will not bear the weight of the train."

The bridge in question was a suspension bridge over the rapids, about a mile from the place where the train had stopped. According to the signalman, it threatened to fall, several of the wires having snapped, and it was impossible to risk its passage. He did not exaggerate in any way, then, in asserting that they could not pass over the bridge. And besides, with the careless habits of the Americans, we may say that when they are prudent, we would be very foolish not to be so.

Passepartout, not daring to go to inform his master, listened with set teeth, immovable as a statue.

"Ah, indeed!" cried Colonel Proctor, "we are not going, I imagine, to remain here, and take root in the snow!"

"Colonel," replied the conductor," we have telegraphed to Omaha for a train, but it is not probable that it will arrive at Medicine Bow before six hours."

"Six hours!" cried Passepartout.

"Without doubt," replied the conductor. "Besides, that time will be necessary for us to reach the station on foot."

"But it is only a mile from here," said one of the passengers.

"A mile, in fact, but on the other side of the river."

And cannot the river be crossed in a boat?" asked the colonel.

"Impossible. The creek is swollen with the rains. It is a torrent, and we will be compelled to make a detour of ten miles to the north to find a ford."

The colonel launched a volley of oaths, blaming the company and the conductor, and Passepartout, furious, was not far from joining with him. There was a material obstacle against which, this time, all his master's bank-notes, would be of no avail.

The disappointment was general among the passengers, who, without counting the delay, saw themselves obliged to foot it fifteen miles across the plain covered with snow. There was a hub-bub, exclamations, loud and deep, which would certainly have attracted Phileas Fogg's attention, if that gentleman had not been absorbed in his game.

But Passepartout found himself compelled to inform him, and, with drooping head, he turned towards the car, when the engineer of the train, a genuine Yankee, named Forster, raising his voice, said:

"Gentlemen, there might be a way of passing."

"On the bridge?" asked a passenger.

"On the bridge."

"With our train?" asked the colonel.

"With our train."

Passepartout stopped, and devoured the engineer's words.

"But the bridge threatens to fall!" continued the conductor.

"It don't matter," replied Forster. "I believe that by rushing the train over at its maximum of speed we would have some chances of passing."

"The devil!" exclaimed Passepartout.

But a certain number of the passengers were immediately carried away by the proposition. It pleased Colonel Proctor particularly. That hot-head found the thing very feasible. He recalled, even, that engineers had had the idea of passing rivers without bridges, with trains closely coupled, rushing at the height of their speed, etc. And finally, all those interested took sides with the engineer's views.

"We have fifty chances for passing," said one:

"Sixty," said another.

"Eighty! Ninety out of one hundred!"

Passepartout was perplexed, although he was willing to try anything to accomplish the passage of Medicine Creek, but the attempt seemed to him a little too "American."

"Besides," he thought, "there is a much simpler thing to do, and these people don't even think of it—Monsieur," he said to one of the passengers, "the way proposed by the engineer seems a little hazardous to me, but—"

"Eighty chances!" replied the passenger, turning his back to him.

"I know very well," replied Passepartout, addressing another gentleman, abut a simple reflection—"

"No reflection, it is useless!" replied the American addressed, shrugging his shoulders, "since the engineer assures us that we will pass!"

163

'Without doubt," continued Passepartout, "we will pass, but it would perhaps be more prudent—"

"What prudent!" cried Colonel Proctor, jumping at this word, heard by chance. "At full speed, you have been told! Don't you understand? At full speed!"

"I know—I understand," repeated Passepartout, whom no one would allow to finish his phrase; abut it would be, if not more prudent, since the word offends you, at least more natural—"

"Who? What? How? What is the matter with this fellow'" was heard from all directions.

The poor fellow did not know whom to address.

"Are you afraid?" Colonel Proctor asked him.

"I, afraid?" cried Passepartout. "Well, so be it! I will show these people that a Frenchman can be as American as they!"

"All aboard! All aboard!" cried the conductor.

"Yes, all aboard," replied Passepartout; "all aboard! and right away! But they can't prevent me from thinking that it would have been more natural for us to have gone over the bridge afoot, and then brought the train afterwards!"

But no one heard this sage reflection, and no one would have acknowledged its justness.

The passengers took their seats again in the cars. Passepartout resumed his, without saying anything of what had occurred. The players were entirely absorbed in their game.

The locomotive whistled vigorously. The engineer reversed his engine, and backed for about a mile—returned like a jumper who is going to take a leap.

Then, to a second whistle, they commenced to move forwards, the speed increased; it soon became frightful: but a single puffing was heard from the locomotive; the pistons worked twenty strokes to the second; the axles smoked in the journals. They felt, so to speak, that the entire train, moving at the rate of one hundred miles to the hour, did not bear upon the rails. The speed destroyed the weight.

And they passed! And it was like a flash of lightning. They saw nothing of the bridge. The train leaped, it might be said, from one bank to the other, and the engineer could not stop his train for five miles beyond the station.

But the train had scarcely crossed the river than the bridge, already about to fall, went down with a crash into the rapids of Medicine Bow.

CHAPTER 29

In which certain Incidents are Related, only to be met with on the Railroads of the United States

That same evening the train continued its course without obstructions, passed Fort Sanders, crossed the Cheyenne Pass and arrived at Evans Pass. At this point, the railroad reached the highest point - on the route, i.e. eight thousand and ninety-one feet above the level of the ocean. The travellers now only had to descend to the Atlantic over those boundless plains levelled by nature.

There was the branch from the "Grand Trunk" to Denver City, the principal town of Colorado. This territory is rich in gold and silver mines, and more than fifty thousand inhabitants have already settled there.

At this moment thirteen hundred and eighty-two miles had been made from San Francisco in three days and three nights. Four nights and four days, if nothing interfered, ought to be sufficient to reach New York. Phileas Fogg was then still within his time.

During the night they passed to the left of Camp Walbach. Lodge Pole Creek ran parallel to the road, following the straight boundary between the Territories of Wyoming and

Colorado. At eleven o'clock they entered Nebraska, passing near Sedgwick, and they touched at Julesburg, on the South Fork of the Platte River.

It was at this point that the Union Pacific Road was inaugurated on the 23rd of October, 1867, by its chief engineer, General G. M. Dodge. There stopped the two powerful locomotives, drawing the nine cars of invited guests, prominent among whom was the Vice-President of the road, Thomas C. Durant; three cheers were given; there the Sioux and Pawnees gave an imitation Indian battle; there the fireworks were set off; there, finally, was struck off by means of a portable printing press the first number of the *Railway Pioneer*. Thus was celebrated the inauguration of this great railroad, an instrument of progress and civilisation, thrown across the desert, and destined to bind together towns and cities not yet in existence. The whistle of the locomotive, more powerful than the lyre of Amphion, was soon to make them rise from the American soil.

At eight o'clock in the morning Fort M'Pherson was left behind. Three hundred and fifty-seven miles separate this point from Omaha The railroad followed, on its left bank the capricious windings of the South Fork of Platte River. At nine o'clock they arrived at the important town of North Platte, built between the two arms of the main stream, which join each other around it, forming a single artery—a large tributary—whose waters mingle with those of the Missouri a little above Omaha.

The one hundred and first meridian was passed.

Mr. Fogg and his partner had resumed their play. Neither of them complained of the length of the route—not even the dummy. Mr. Fix had won a few guineas at first, which he was in a fair way to lose, but he was not less deeply interested than Mr. Fogg. During this morning chance singularly favoured this gentleman. Trumps and honours were showered into his hands. At a certain moment, after having made a bold combination, he was about to play a spade, when behind the seat a voice was heard, saying:

"I should play a diamond."

Mr. Fogg, Mrs. Aouda, and Fix raised their heads. Colonel Proctor was near them.

Stamp Proctor and Phileas Fogg recognised each other at once.

"Ah, it is you, Englishman," cried the colonel; "it's you who are going to play a spade."

"And who plays it," replied Phileas Fogg coldly, laying down a ten of that colour.

"Well, it suits me to have it diamonds," replied Colonel Proctor, in an irritated voice.

And he made a motion as if to pick up the card played, adding:

"You don't understand anything of this game."

"Perhaps I will be more skillful at another," said Phileas Fogg,

"You have only to try it, son of John Bull!" replied the coarse fellow.

Mrs. Aouda became pale. All the blood went to her heart. She seized Phileas Fogg's arm, and he gently repulsed her. Passepartout was ready to throw himself on the colonel, who was looking at his adversary with the most insulting air. But Fix had risen, and going to Colonel Proctor, said to him:

"You forget that you have me to deal with; me whom you have not only insulted, but struck!"

"Mr. Fix," said Mr. Fogg, "I beg your pardon, but it concerns me alone. In insisting that I was wrong in playing a spade, the colonel has insulted me anew, and he shall give me satisfaction."

"When you will, and where you will," replied the American, "and with whatever weapon you please!"

Mrs. Aouda tried in vain to restrain Mr. Fogg. The detective uselessly endeavoured to take up the quarrel on his own account. Passepartout wanted to throw the colonel out of the door, but a sign from his master stopped him. Phileas Fogg went out of the car, and the American followed him on the platform.

"Sir," said Mr. Fogg to his adversary, "I am very much in a hurry to return to Europe, and any delay whatever would be very prejudicial to my interest."

"Well! what does that concern me?" replied Colonel Proctor.

"Sir," replied Mr. Fogg, very politely, "after our meeting in San Francisco, I formed the plan to come back to America to find you, as soon as I had completed the business which calls me to the Old World."

"Truly!"

"Will you appoint a meeting with me in six months?"

"Why not in six years?"

"I say six months," replied Mr. Fogg, "and I will be prompt to meet you."

"All evasions!" cried Stamp Proctor. "Immediately, or not at all."

"All right," replied Mr. Fogg. "You are going to New York?"

"No."

"To Chicago?"

"No."

"To Omaha?"

"It concerns you very little! Do you know Plum Creek station.?"

"No," replied Mr. Fogg.

"It is the next station. The train will be there in an hour. It will stop ten minutes. In ten minutes we can exchange a few shots with our revolvers."

"Let it be so," replied Mr. Fogg. "I will stop at Plum Creek."

"And I believe that you will remain there!" added the American, with unparalleled insolence.

"Who knows, sir?" replied Mr. Fogg, and he re-entered the car as coolly as usual.

That gentleman commenced to reassure Mrs. Aouda, saying to her that blusterers were never to be feared. Then he begged Fix to act as his second in the encounter which was going to take place. Fix could not refuse, and Phileas Fogg resumed quietly his interrupted game, playing a spade with perfect serenity.

At eleven o'clock the whistle of the locomotive announced that they were near Plum Creek station. Mr. Fogg rose, and followed by Fix, he went out on the platform. Passepartout accompanied him, carrying a pair of revolvers. Mrs. Aouda remained in the car, pale as death.

At this moment the door of the next car opened, and Colonel Proctor appeared likewise upon the platform, followed by his second, a Yankee of his own stamp. But at the moment that the two adversaries were going to step off the train, the conductor ran up to them and cried:

"You can't get off, gentlemen."

"Why not?" asked the colonel.

"We are twenty minutes behind time, and the train does not stop."

"But I am going to fight a duel with this gentleman."

"I regret it," replied the conductor, "but we are going to start again immediately. Hear the bell ringing!"

The bell was ringing, and the train moved on.

"I am really very sorry, gentlemen," said the conductor. "Under any other circumstances, I could have obliged you. But, after all, since you had not the time to fight here, who hinders you from fighting while the train is in motion?"

"Perhaps that will not suit the gentleman!" said Colonel Proctor, with a jeering air.

"That suits me perfectly" replied Phileas Fogg.

"Well, we are decidedly in America!" thought Passepartout, "and the conductor is a gentleman of the first order."

Having said this, he followed his master.

The two combatants and their seconds, preceded by the conductor, repaired to the rear of the train, passing through the cars. The last car was only occupied by about ten or a dozen passengers. The conductor asked them if they would be kind enough to vacate for a few moments for two gentlemen who had an affair of honour to settle.

Why not? The passengers were only too happy to be able to accommodate the two gentlemen, and they retired on the platforms.

The car, fifty feet long, accommodated itself very conveniently to the purpose. The two adversaries might march on each other in the aisle, and fire at their ease. There never was a duel easier to arrange. Mr. Fogg and Colonel Proctor, each furnished with two six-barrelled revolvers, entered the car. Their seconds, remaining outside, shut them in. At the first whistle of the locomotive, they were to commence firing. Then after a lapse of two minutes what remained of the two gentlemen would be taken out of the car. Truly, there could be nothing simpler. It was even so simple that Fix and Passepartout felt their hearts beating almost as if they would break.

They were waiting for the whistle agreed upon, when suddenly savage cries resounded. Reports accompanied them, but they did not come from the car reserved for the duellists. These reports continued, on the contrary, as far as the front and along the whole line of the train. Cries of fright made themselves heard from the inside of the cars.

Colonel Proctor and Mr. Fogg, with their revolvers in hand, went out of the car immediately, and rushed forward where the reports and cries resounded more noisily.

They understood that the train had been attacked by a band of Sioux.

It was not the first attempt of these daring Indians. More than once already they had stopped the trains. According to their habit, without waiting for the stopping of the train, rushing upon the steps to the number of a hundred, they had scaled the cars like a clown does a horse at full gallop.

These Sioux were provided with guns. Thence the reports, to which the passengers, nearly all armed, replied sharply by shots from their revolvers. At first the Indians rushed upon the engine. The engineer and firemen were half-stunned with blows from their muskets. A Sioux chief, wishing to stop the train, but not knowing how to manoeuvre the handle of the regulator, had opened wide the steam valve instead of closing it, and the locomotive, beyond control, ran on with frightful rapidity.

At the same time, the Sioux entered the cars, they ran like enraged monkeys over the roofs, they drove in the doors and fought hand to hand with the passengers. The trunks, broken open and robbed, were thrown out of the baggage car on the road. Cries and shots did not cease.

But the passengers defended themselves courageously. Some of the cars, barricaded, sustained a siege, like real

170

moving forts, borne on at a speed of one hundred miles an hour.

From the commencement of the attack, Mrs. Aouda had behaved courageously. With revolver in hand, she defended herself heroically, firing through the broken panes when some savage presented himself. About twenty Sioux, mortally wounded, fell upon the track, and the car wheels crushed like worms those that slipped on to the rails from the top of the platforms.

Several passengers, severely wounded by bullets or clubs, lay upon the seats.

But an end must be put to this. This combat had lasted already for ten minutes, and could only end to the advantage of the Sioux, if the train was not stopped. In fact, Fort Kearney station was not two miles distant. There was a military post, but that passed, between Fort Kearney and the next station the Sioux would be masters of the train.

The conductor was fighting at Mr. Fogg's side, when a ball struck him and he fell. As he fell, he cried: "We are lost if the train is not stopped inside of five minutes!"

"It shall be stopped!" said Phileas Fogg, who was about to rush out of the car.

"Remain, Monsieur," Passepartout cried to him. "That is my business."

Phileas Fogg had not the time to stop the courageous young man, who, opening a door without being seen by the Indians, succeeded in slipping under the car. Whilst the struggle continued, and whilst the balls were crossing each other above his head, recovering his agility, his suppleness as a clown, he made his way under the cars. Clinging to the chains, assisting himself by the lever of the brakes and the edges of the window-sashes, climbing from one car to another with marvellous skill he thus reached the front of the train. He had not been seen; he could not have been.

There, suspended by one hand between the baggage car and the tender, with the other he loosened the couplings, but in consequence of the traction, he would never have been able to pull out the yoking-bar if a sudden jolt of the engine had not made the bar jump out, and the train, detached, was left farther and farther be, hind, while the locomotive flew on with new speed.

Carried on by the force acquired, the train still rolled on for a few minutes, but the brakes were manoeuvred from the inside of the cars, and the train finally stopped, less than one hundred paces from Kearney station.

The soldiers of the fort, attracted by the firing, ran hastily to the train. The Sioux did not wait for them, before the train stopped entirely the whole band had decamped.

But when the passengers counted each other on the platform of the station, they noticed that several were missing, and among others the courageous Frenchman, whose devotion had just saved them.

CHAPTER 30

In which Phileas Fogg simply does his duty

Three passengers, including Passepartout, had disappeared. Had they been killed in the fight? Were they taken prisoners by the Sioux? As yet it could not be told.

The wounded were quite numerous, but none mortally. The one most seriously was Colonel Proctor, who had fought bravely, and who fell struck by a ball in the groin. He was carried to the station with the other passengers, whose condition demanded immediate care.

Mrs. Aouda was safe. Phileas Fogg, who had not spared himself, had not a scratch. Fix was wounded in the arm—but it was an unimportant wound. But Passepartout was missing, and tears flowed from the young woman's eyes.

Meanwhile, all the passengers had left the train. The wheels of the cars were stained with blood. To the hubs and spokes hung ragged pieces of flesh As far as the eye could reach long red trails were seen on the white plain. The last Indians were then disappearing in the south, along the banks of Republican River.

Mr. Fogg, with folded arms, stood motionless. He had a serious decision to make. Mrs. Aouda, near him, looked at him without uttering a word. He understood her look. If his servant was a prisoner ought he not to risk everything to rescue him from the Indians?

"I will find him dead or alive," he said simply, to Mrs. Aouda.

"Ah! Mr. Fogg—Mr. Fogg!" cried the young woman, seizing her companion's hands and covering them with tears.

"Alive!" added Mr. Fogg, "if we do not lose a minute!"

With this resolution Phileas Fogg sacrificed himself entirely. He had just pronounced his ruin. A single day's delay would make him miss the steamer from New York. His bet would be irrevocably lost. But in the face of the thought, "It is my duty!" he did not hesitate.

The captain commanding Fort Kearney was there. His soldiers—about a hundred men—had put themselves on the defensive in the event of the Sioux making a direct attack upon the station.

"Sir," said Mr. Fogg to the captain, "three passengers have disappeared."

"Killed?" asked the captain.

"Killed or prisoners," replied Mr. Fogg. "That is an uncertainty which we must bring to an end. It is your intention to pursue the Sioux?"

"It is a grave matter, sir," said the captain. "These Indians may fly beyond the Arkansas! I could not abandon the fort entrusted to me."

"Sir," replied Phileas Fogg, "it is a question of the life of three men."

"Doubtless—but can I risk the life of fifty to save three?"

"I do not know whether you can, but you ought."

"Sir," replied the captain, "and one here has the right to tell me what my duty is."

"Let it be so!" said Phileas Fogg coldly, "I will go alone!"

"You, sir!" cried Fix, who approached, "go alone in pursuit of the Indians!"

"Do you wish me then to allow to perish the unfortunate man to whom every one of us that is living owes his life? I shall go."

"Well, no, you shall not go alone!" cried the captain, moved in spite of himself. "No! You are a brave heart! Thirty volunteers!" he added, turning to his soldiers.

The whole company advanced in a body. The captain had to select from these brave fellows. Thirty soldiers were picked out, and an old sergeant put at their head.

"Thanks, Captain!" said Mr. Fogg.

"You will permit me to accompany you?" Fix asked the gentleman.

"You will do as you please," replied Phileas Fogg. "But if you wish to do me a service, you will remain by Mrs. Aouda In case anything should happen to me—"

A sudden paleness overcast the detective's face. To separate himself from the man whom he had followed step by step and with so much persistence! To let him venture so much in the desert. Fix looked closely at the gentleman, and whatever he may have thought, in spite of his prejudices, in spite of his inward struggle, he dropped his eyes before that quiet, frank look.

"I will remain," he said.

A few moments after, Mr. Fogg pressed the young woman's hand: then, having placed in her care his precious travelling bag, he set out with the sergeant and his little band.

But before starting, he said to the soldiers:

"My friends, there are five thousand dollars for you if you save the prisoners!"

It was then a few minutes past noon.

Mrs. Aouda retired into a sitting-room of the station, and there, alone, she waited, thinking of Phileas Fogg, his simple and grand generosity, his quiet courage. Mr. Fogg had sacrificed his fortune, and now he was staking his life—and all this without hesitation, from a sense of duty, without words. Phileas Fogg was a hero in her eyes.

The detective (Fix) was not thinking thus, and he could not restrain his agitation. He walked feverishly up and down the platform of the station, one moment vanquished, he became himself again. Fogg having gone, he comprehended his foolishness in letting him go. What! Had he consented to be separated from the man that he had just been following around the world! His natural disposition got the upper hand; he criminated and accused himself; he treated himself as if he had been the director of the Metropolitan police reproving an agent caught at a very green trick.

"I have been a silly fellow!" he thought. "The other fellow would have told him who I was! He was gone; he will not return! Where can I capture him now? But how have I (Fix) so allowed myself to be fascinated, when I have a warrant for his arrest in my pocket! I am decidedly only an ass!"

Thus reasoned the detective, while the hours slipped on too slowly for his liking. He did not know what to do. Sometimes, he felt like telling Mrs. Aouda everything. But he understood how he would be received by the young woman. What course should he take? He was tempted to go in pursuit of this Fogg across the immense white plains. It did not seem impossible for him to find him. The footprints of the detachment were still imprinted upon the snow! But, under a fresh covering, every track would soon be effaced.

Fix was discouraged. He felt an almost insurmountable desire to abandon the party. This very occasion of leaving Kearney station and of prosecuting the journey, so fruitful of mishaps, was opened to him.

About two o'clock in the afternoon, while the snow was falling in large flakes, long whistles were heard coming from the east. An enormous shadow, preceded by a lurid light, slowly advanced, considerably increased by the mist, which gave it a fantastic appearance.

But no train was expected yet from the east. The help asked for by telegraph could not arrive so soon, and the train from Omaha to San Francisco would not pass until the next day. They were soon enlightened.

This locomotive, moving under a small head of steam, and

whistling very loud, was the one which, after being detached from the train, had continued its course with such frightful speed, carrying the unconscious fireman and engineer. It had run on for several miles; then the fire had gone down for want of fuel; the steam had slackened, and an hour afterwards, relaxing its speed by degrees, the engine finally stopped twenty miles beyond Kearney station.

Neither the engineer nor the fireman was dead, and after a very long swoon they revived.

The engine had stopped. When he saw himself in the desert, and the locomotive without cars attached to it, the engineer understood what had happened. e could not guess how the locomotive had been detached from the train, but he did not doubt that the train, left behind, was in distress.

The engineer did not hesitate as to what he ought to do. To continue his course in the direction of Omaha was prudent, to return towards the train, which the Indians were perhaps yet robbing, was dangerous. No matter! Coal and wood were thrown into the furnace, the fire started up again, the head of steam increased again, and about two o'clock in the afternoon the engine returned, running backwards to Kearney station. This was the whistling they heard in the mist.

It was a great satisfaction for the travellers, when they saw the locomotive put at the head of the train. They were going to be able to continue their journey so unfortunately interrupted.

On the arrival of the engine, Mrs. Aouda came out of the station, and addressing the conductor, she asked:

"You are going to start?"

"This very instant, madame."

"But the prisoners—our unfortunate companions— "

"I cannot interrupt the trip," replied the conductor. "We are already three hours behind time."

"And when will the next train coming from San Francisco pass?"

"To-morrow evening, madame."

"To-morrow evening! But it will be too late. We must wait—"

"Impossible," replied the conductor. "If you are going, get aboard the car."

"I will not go," replied the young woman.

Fix heard this conversation. A few moments before, when every means of locomotion failed him, he had decided to quit Kearney, and now that the train was there, ready to continue its course, and he only had to seat himself in the car, an irresistible force fixed him to the ground. The platform of the station burned his feet, and he could not tear himself away from it. The conflict within himself recommenced. His anger at his want of success choked him. He was going to struggle on to the end.

Meanwhile the passengers and some of the wounded—among others Colonel Proctor, whose condition was very serious—had taken seats in the cars. The buzzing of the overheated boiler was heard; the steam escaped through the valves; the engineer whistled, the train started, and soon disappeared, mingling its white smoke with the whirling of the snow.

The detective Fix had remained.

Some hours passed. The weather was very bad, the cold very keen. Fix, seated on a bench in the station, was motionless. It might have been supposed that he was sleeping. Notwithstanding the storm, Mrs. Aouda left every moment the room which had been placed at her disposal. She went to the end of the platform, trying to look through the tempest of snow, wishing to pierce the mist which narrowed the horizon around her, listening if she could hear any sound. But there was nothing. She went in then, chilled through, to return a few moments later, and always in vain.

Evening came. The little detachment had not returned. Where was it at this moment? Had it been able to overtake the Indians? Had there been a fight, or were these soldiers, lost in the mist, wandering at a venture? The captain of Fort Kearney was very uneasy, although he did not wish to let his uneasiness appear.

Night came; the snow fell less heavily, but the intensity of the cold increased. The most intrepid glance would not have looked at this vast, obscure space without terror. An absolute silence prevailed over the plain. Neither the flight of a bird nor the passage of a wild beast disturbed the unbroken quiet.

177

During the whole night, Mrs. Aouda, her mind full of dark presentiments, her heart filled with anguish, wandered on the border of the prairie. Her imagination carried her afar off and showed her a thousand dangers. What she suffered during those long hours could not be expressed.

Fix, still immovable in the same spot, did not sleep. At a certain moment, a man approached and spoke to him, but the detective sent him away, after replying to him by a negative sign.

Thus the night passed. At dawn, the half-concealed disc of the sun rose from a misty horizon. Still the eye might reach as far as two miles. Phileas Fogg and the detachment had gone to the south. The south was entirely deserted. It was then seven o'clock in the morning.

The captain, extremely anxious, did not know what course to take. Ought he to send a second detachment to help the first? Ought he to sacrifice fresh men with so few chances of saving those who were sacrificed at first? But his hesitation did not last, and with a gesture calling one of his lieutenants, he gave him the order to throw out a reconnaissance to the south, when shots were heard. Was it a signal? The soldiers rushed out of the fort, and half a mile distant they perceived a small band returning in good order.

Phileas Fogg marched at the head, and near him Passepartout and the two passengers, rescued from the hands of the Sioux.

There was a fight ten miles south of Fort Kearney. Passepartout and his two companions were already struggling against their captors, and the Frenchman had knocked down three of them with his fist, when his master and the soldiers rushed to their rescue.

All—the deliverers and the delivered—were received with cries of joy, and Phileas Fogg divided among the soldiers the reward he had promised them, whilst Passepartout repeated to himself, not without reason:

"I must confess that I am certainly costing my master very dearly."

Fix, without uttering a word, looked at Mr. Fogg, and it

would have been difficult to analyse the impression struggling within him. As for Mrs. Aouda, she took the gentleman's hand, and pressed it in hers, without being able to utter a word!

In the meantime Passepartout, upon his arrival, was looking for the train at the station, He thought he would find it there, ready to start for Omaha, and he hoped they could still make up the lost time.

"The train, the train!" he cried.

"Gone," replied Fix.

"And when will the next train pass?" asked Phileas Fogg.

"Not until this evening."

"Ah!" simply replied the impassible gentleman.

CHAPTER 31

In which the Detective Fix takes seriously in charge Phileas Fogg's Interests

Phileas Fogg found himself twenty hours behind time. Passepartout, the involuntary cause of this delay, was desperate. He had certainly ruined his master!

At this moment the detective approached Mr. Fogg, and looking closely in his face, asked:

"Very seriously, sir, you are in a hurry?"

"Very seriously," replied Phileas Fogg.

"I insist," continued Fix. "It is very much to your interest to be in New York on the 11th, before nine o'clock in the evening, the time of departure of the Liverpool steamer."

"I have a very great interest."

"And if your journey had not been interrupted by this Indian attack you would have arrived in New York on the morning of the 11th."

"Yes, twelve hours before the departure of the steamer."

"Well, you are now twenty hours behind time. The difference between twenty and twelve is eight. Eight hours are to be made up. Do you wish to try to do it?"

"On foot?" asked Mr. Fogg.

"No, on a sledge," replied Fix, "on a sledge with sails. A man has proposed this means of conveyance to me."

It was the man who had spoken to the detective during the night and whose offer he had refused.

Phileas Fogg did not reply to Fix; but Fix having shown him the man in question, who was walking up and down before the station, the gentleman went to him. An instant after, Phileas Fogg and this American, named Mudge, entered a hut built at the foot of Fort Kearney.

There Mr. Fogg examined a very singular vehicle, a sort of frame laid on two long beams, a little raised in front, like the runners of a sledge, and upon which five or six persons could be seated. On the front of the frame was fastened a very high mast, to which an immense brigantine sail was attached. The mast, firmly held by metallic fastenings, held an iron stay, which served to hoist a large jibsail. At the rear a sort of rudder allowed the apparatus to be steered.

As could be seen, it was a sledge sloop-rigged. During the winter, on the icy plains, when the trains are blocked up by the snow, these vehicles make extremely rapid trips from one station to another. They carry a tremendous press of sail, far more than a cutter, and, with the wind behind, they glide over the surface of the prairie with a speed equal to, if not greater than, that of an express train.

In a few moments, the bargain was concluded between Mr. Fogg and the owner of this land craft. The wind was good. It blew with a strong breeze from the west. The snow had hardened, and Mudge was certain that he could take Mr. Fogg in a few hours to Omaha. There the trains are frequent, and the routes leading to Chicago and New York numerous. It was not impossible to make up the time lost. There should be no hesitation in making the attempt.

Mr. Fogg, not wishing to expose Mrs. Aouda to the discomforts of a trip in the open air, with the cold rendered more unbearable by the speed, proposed to her to remain under Passepartout's care at Kearney station. The honest fellow would undertake to bring her to Europe by a better route and under more acceptable conditions.

Mrs. Aouda refused to be separated from Mr. Fogg, and Passepartout felt very happy at this determination. Indeed, nothing in the world would have induced him to leave his master, since Fix was to accompany him.

As to what the detective then thought, it would be difficult to say. Had his convictions been shaken by Phileas Fogg's return, or rather did he consider him a very shrewd rogue, who, having accomplished his tour of the world, believed that he would be entirely safe in England? Perhaps Fix's opinion concerning Phileas Fogg was really modified. But he was none the less decided to do his duty, and more impatient than all of them to hasten with all his might the return to England.

At eight o'clock the sledge was ready to start. The travellers—we were tempted to say the passengers—took their places, and wrapped themselves closely in their travelling cloaks. The two immense sails were hoisted, and, under the pressure of the wind, the vehicle slipped over the hardened snow with a speed of forty miles an hours.

The distance between Fort Kearney and Omaha is, in a straight line—in a bee-line, as the Americans say—two hundred miles at the most. If the wind continued, this distance could be accomplished in five hours. If no accident happened, the sledge ought to reach Omaha at one o'clock in the afternoon.

What a journey! The travellers, huddled up against each other, could not speak. The cold, increased by the speed, cut off their words. The sledge glided as lightly over the surface of the plain as a vessel over the surface of the water—with the swell at least. When the breeze came, skimming the earth, it seemed as if the sledge was lifted from the ground by its sails, which were like huge wings. Mudge, at the rudder kept the straight line, and with a turn of the tiller he corrected the lurches which the apparatus had a tendency to make. All sail was carried. The jib had been arranged so that it no longer was screened by the brigantine. A top-mast was hoisted, and another jib stretched to the wind added its force to that of the other sails. It could not be exactly estimated, but certainly the speed of the sledge could not be less than forty miles an hour.

"If nothing breaks," said Mudge, "we shall arrive!"

It was Mudge's interest to arrive at the time agreed upon, for Mr. Fogg, adhering to his plan, had stimulated him by the promise of a handsome reward.

The prairie, which the sledge was crossing in a straight line, was as flat as a sea It might have been called a frozen pond. The railroad which ran through this section, ascended from south-west to north-west by Grand Island, Columbus, an important Nebraska town, Schuyler, Fremont, then Omaha During its entire course, it followed the right bank of Platte River. The sledge shortening this route, took the chord of the arc described by the railroad. Mudge did not fear being stopped by the Platte River, at the short bend in front of Fremont, as it was frozen over. The way was then entirely free of obstructions, and Phileas Fogg had only two things to fear: an accident to the apparatus, a change or a calm of the wind.

But the breeze did not abate. On the contrary, it blew so hard that it bent the mast, which the iron fastenings kept firm. These metal fastenings, like the chords of an instrument, resounded as if a violin-bow had produced their vibrations. The sledge slid along in the midst of a plaintive harmony, of a very peculiar intensity.

"These chords give the fifth and the octave," said Mr. Fogg.

And these were the only words he uttered during this trip. Mrs. Aouda carefully wrapped in furs and cloaks, was preserved as much as possible from the attacks of the cold.

Passepartout, his face red as the solar disc when it sets in the midst, drew in the biting air. With the depth of unshaken confidence that he possessed, he was ready to hope again. Instead of arriving in New York in the morning, they would arrive there in the evening, but there might be some chances that it would be before the departure of the Liverpool steamer.

Passepartout even experienced a strong desire to grasp the hand of his ally Fix. He did not forget that it was the detective himself who had procured the sledge with sails, and consequently the only means there was to reach Omaha in good time. But by some unknown presentiment, he kept himself in his accustomed reserve.

At all events, one thing which Passepartout would never forget, was the sacrifice which Mr. Fogg had unhesitatingly made to rescue him from the hands of the Sioux. As for that, Mr. Fogg had risked his fortune and his life—No! his servant would not forget him!

Whilst each one of the travellers allowed himself to wander off in such various reflections the sledge flew over the immense carpet of snow. If it passed over creeks, tributaries, or sub-tributaries of Little Blue River, they did not perceive it. The fields and the streams disappeared under a uniform whiteness.

The plain was absolutely deserted. Comprised between the Union Pacific Road and the branch uniting Kearney to St. Joseph, it formed as it were a large uninhabited island. Not a village, not a station, not even a fort. From time to time they saw passing like a flash some grimacing tree, whose white skeleton was twisted about by the wind. Sometimes flocks of wild birds rose; sometimes, also, prairie wolves in large bands, gaunt, famished, urged by a ferocious demand of nature, vied with the sledge in swiftness. Then Passepartout, with revolver in hand, held himself ready to fire upon those that came nearest. If any accident had then stopped the sledge, the travellers, attacked by these ferocious carnivorous beasts, would have run the greatest risks. But the sledge kept on in its course; it was not long in getting ahead, and soon the whole howling band was left behind.

At noon, Mudge recognised by certain landmarks that he was crossing the frozen course of the Platte River. He said nothing, but he was sure that in twenty miles more he would reach Omaha.

And, indeed, one hour afterwards this skillful guide, abandoning the helm, hastened to the halyards of the sails and furled them, whilst the sledge, carried on by its irresistible force, accomplished another half-mile under bare ropes. Finally it stopped, and Mudge pointing out a mass of roofs white with snow, said: "We have arrived."

Arrived! Arrived indeed at the station which, by numerous trains, is in daily communication with the eastern part of the United States!

Passepartout and Fix jumped to the ground and shook their stiffened limbs. They helped Mr. Fogg and the young woman to descend from the sledge. Phileas Fogg settled generously with Mudge, whose hand Passepartout shook like a friend's and all hurried towards the depot in Omaha.

The Pacific Railroad, properly so called, has its terminus at this important city in Nebraska, placing the Mississippi base in connection with the great ocean. To go from Omaha to Chicago, the Chicago, Rock Island and Pacific road is taken, running directly to the east, and passing fifty stations.

A through train was ready to start. Phileas Fogg and his companions had only time to hurry into a car. They had seen nothing of Omaha; but Passepartout acknowledged to himself that it was not to be regretted, as they were not on a sight-seeing tour.

The train passed with very great speed into the State of Iowa, through Council Bluffs, Des Moines, and Iowa City. During the night it crossed the Mississippi at Davenport, and, entered Illinois at Rock Island. The next day the 10th, at four o'clock in the afternoon, they arrived at Chicago, already risen from its ruins, and sitting more proudly than ever on the shores of the beautiful Lake Michigan.

Nine hundred miles separated Chicago from New York. Trains are not wanting at Chicago. Mr. Fogg passed immediately from one to the other. The nimble locomotive of the Pittsburg, Fort Wayne, and Chicago Railway started at full speed, as if it understood that the honourable gentleman "had no time to lose." It traversed Indiana and Ohio, passing by populous cities and over wide expanses of agricultural land, with but few pauses; and, sixteen hours after leaving Chicago, the Ohio was reached.

At thirty-five minutes after nine, on the evening of the 11th, the train entered the great depot at Jersey City, the walls of which are washed by the Hudson River. From this station, the eastern terminus of a railroad system of great magnitude, fifty-one passenger and eighty-one freight trains depart every twenty-four hours, and an equal number arrive. Steamers and sailing vessels lined the miles of docks extending on both sides of the station, and the mighty river was filled with craft of all kinds engaged in the commerce of New York, which rose in front of the travellers as they emerged upon the broad, covered way running in front of the depot, where the gigantic ferryboats of the railroad company receive and land their myriads of travellers, pausing not in their work day or night.

At thirty-five minutes after nine at night, the train stopped in the depot, near the very pier of the Cunard line of steamers, otherwise called the British and North American Royal Mail Steam Packet Company.

The *China*, bound for Liverpool, left thirty-five minutes before!

CHAPTER 32

In which Phileas Fogg engages in a Direct Struggle with Ill Luck

The *China*, in leaving, seemed to have carried away with her Phileas Fogg's last hope.

In fact, none of the other steamers in the direct service between America and Europe, neither the French Transatlantic steamers, nor the ships of the White Star line, nor those of the Inman Company, nor those of the Hamburg line, nor any others, could serve the gentleman's project.

The *Pereire*, of the French Atlantic Company, would not start until the 14th of December. And besides, like those of the Hamburg Company, she would not go directly to Liverpool or London, but to Havre, and this additional trip from Havre to Southampton, delaying Phileas Fogg, would have rendered his last efforts of no avail.

The gentleman posted himself thoroughly about all this by consulting his Bradshaw, which gave him, day by day, the movements of the trans-oceanic vessels.

Passepartout was annihilated. It killed him to miss the steamer by thirty-five minutes. It was his fault—he who, instead of aiding his master, had not ceased to scatter obstacles in his way! And when he reviewed in his mind all the incidents of the journey; when he calculated the sums spent, which were a pure loss, and for his own interest; when he thought that this enormous bet, added to the heavy expenses of this now useless journey, would completely ruin Mr. Fogg, he overwhelmed himself with opprobrium.

Mr. Fogg did not reproach him at all, and leaving the pier of the ocean steamers, he said only these words:

"We will consult to-morrow. Come."

Mr. Fogg, Mrs. Aouda, Fix, and Passepartout crossed the Hudson from Jersey City in the ferry-boat, and got into a carriage, which took them to the St. Nicholas Hotel, on Broadway. Rooms were put at their disposal, and the night passed—a very short one for Phileas Fogg, who slept soundly, but very long for Mrs. Aouda and her companions, whose agitation did not allow them to rest.

The next day was the 12th of December. From the 12th, at seven in the morning, to the 21st, at eight forty-five in the evening, there remained nine days, thirteen hours, and forty-five minutes. If, then, Phileas Fogg had left the night before in the *China* one of the best sailers of the Cunard line, he would have arrived at Liverpool, and then in London, in the desired time!

Phileas Fogg left the hotel alone, having recommended his servant to wait for him, and to notify Mrs. Aouda to hold herself in readiness at any moment.

Mr. Fogg repaired to the banks of the Hudson, and among the ships moored to the wharf, or anchored in the stream, he sought with care those which were about to leave. Several vessels had their signals for departure up and were preparing to put to sea at the morning high tide, for in this immense and admirable port, there is not a day when a hundred vessels do not set sail for every quarter of the globe; but the most of them were sailing vessels, and they would not suit Phileas Fogg.

This gentleman was seeming to fail in his last attempt, when he perceived, moored in front of the Battery, at a cable's length at most, a merchantman, with screw, of one outlines, whose smokestack, emitting clouds of smoke, indicated that she was preparing to sail.

Phileas Fogg hailed a boat, got in it, and with a few strokes of the oar, he found himself at the ladder of the *Henrietta*, an iron-hulled steamer, with her upper parts of wood.

The captain of the *Henrietta* was on board. Phileas Fogg went up on deck and asked for the captain, who presented himself immediately.

He was a man fifty years old, a sort of sea wolf, a grumbler who would not be very accommodating. His large eyes, his complexion oxydised copper, his red hair, his large chest and shoulders, indicating nothing of the appearance of a man of the world.

"The captain?" asked Mr. Fogg.

"I am he."

"I am Phileas Fogg, of London."

"And I am Andrew Speedy, of Cardiff."

"You are going to start?"

"In an hour."

"You are loaded for—?"

"Bordeaux."

"And your cargo?"

"Gravel in the hold. I have no eight. I sail in ballast."

"You have passengers?"

"No passengers. Never have passengers. A merchandise that's in the way and reasons."

"Your vessel sails swiftly?"

187

"Between eleven and twelve knots. The *Henrietta* is well known."

"Do you wish to convey me to Liverpool, myself and three persons?"

"To Liverpool? Why not to China?"

"I said Liverpool."

"No!"

"No?"

"No. I am setting out for Bordeaux, and I shall go to Bordeaux."

"It doesn't matter what price?"

"It don't matter what price!"

The captain spoke in a tone which did not admit of a reply.

"But the owners of the *Henrietta*—" replied Phileas Fogg.

"The owners of the *Henrietta* are myself," replied the captain. "The vessel belongs to me."

"I will freight it for you."

"No."

"No?"

"I will buy it from you."

Phileas Fogg did not change countenance. But the situation was serious. It was not at New York as at Hong-Kong, nor with the captain of the *Henrietta* as with the captain of the *Tankadere*. Until the present the gentleman's money had always overcome obstacles. This time the money failed.

But the means of crossing the Atlantic in a vessel must be found, unless they went across in a balloon, which would have been very venturesome, and which, besides, was not practicable.

Phileas Fogg, however, appeared to have an idea, for he said to the captain:

"Well, will you take me to Bordeaux?"

"No, even if you would pay me two hundred dollars."

"I offer you two thousand."

"For each person?"

"For each person."

"And there are four of you?"

"Four."

Captain Speedy commenced to scratch his forehead as if he would tear the skin off. Eight thousand dollars to be made without changing his course; it was well worth the trouble of putting aside his decided antipathy for every kind of passenger. Passengers at two thousand dollars apiece, besides, are no longer passengers, but valuable merchandise.

"I leave at nine o'clock," said Captain Speedy simply, "and you and yours will be there?"

"At nine o'clock we will be on board!" simply replied Mr. Fogg.

It was half-past eight. To land from the *Henrietta*, get in a carriage, repair to the St. Nicholas Hotel, and take back with him, Mrs. Aouda, Passepartout, and even the inseparable Fix, to whom he graciously offered a passage, this was all done by the gentleman with the quiet which never deserted him under any circumstances.

At the moment that the *Henrietta* was ready to sail, all four were aboard.

When Passepartout learned what this last voyage would cost he uttered one of those prolonged "Oh's!" which run through all the spaces of the descending chromatic scale!

As for Detective Fix, he said to himself that the Bank of England would not come out whole from this affair. In fact, by the time of their arrival, and admitting that this Mr. Fogg would not throw a few handfuls besides into the sea, more than seven thousand pounds would be missing from the banknotes in the travelling bag!

CHAPTER 33

In which Phileas Fogg shows Himself equal to Circumstances

An hour afterwards the steamer *Henrietta* passed the lightboat which marks the entrance of the Hudson, turned Sandy Hook point, and put to sea. During the day she skirted Long Island, in the offing of the Fire Island Light, and rapidly ran towards the east.

At noon the next day, the 13th of December, a man went upon the bridge to take charge of the vessel. It would certainly be supposed that this man was Captain Speedy! Not at all. It was Phileas Fogg.

As for Captain Speedy, he was very snugly locked up in his cabin, and was howling at a rate that denoted an anger very pardonable, which amounted to a paroxysm.

What had happened was very simple. Phileas Fogg wanted to go to Liverpool; the captain would not take him there. Then Phileas Fogg had agreed to take passage for Bordeaux, and during the thirty hours that he had been on board, he had manoeuvred so well with his bank-notes, that the crew, sailors, and firemen—an occasional crew, on bad terms with the captain—belonged to him. And this is why Phileas Fogg commanded in the place of Captain Speedy, while the captain was shut up in his cabin, and why, finally, the *Henrietta* was steering her course toward Liverpool. It was very clear, seeing Mr. Fogg's manoeuvre, that he had been a sailor.

Now, how the adventure would come out, would be known later. Mrs. Aouda's uneasiness did not cease, although she said nothing. Fix was stunned at first-Passepartout found the thing simply splendid.

"Between eleven and twelve knots," Captain Speedy had said, and the *Henrietta* did indeed maintain this average of speed.

If then—how many "ifs" yet?—if the sea did not become too rough, if the wind did not rise in the east, if no mishap occurred to the vessel, no accident to the engine, the *Henrietta* in the nine days, counting from the 12th of December to the 21st, could accomplish the three thousand miles separating New York from Liverpool. It is true that once arrived, the *Henrietta* affair on top of the Bank affair might take the gentleman a little farther than he would like.

During the first few days they went along under excellent conditions. The wind was not too rough; the wind seemed stationary in the north-east; the sails were hoisted, and with them the *Henrietta* sailed like a genuine transatlantic steamer.

Passepartout was delighted. The last exploit of his master, the consequences of which he preferred not to consider, filled him with enthusiasm. The crew had never seen a gayer, more agile fellow. He made a thousand friendships with the sailors and astonished them by his acrobatic feats. He lavished upon them the best names and the most attractive drinks. He thought that they manoeuvred like gentlemen, and that the firemen coaled up like heroes. His good humour was very communicative, and impressed itself upon all. He had forgotten the past, with its annoyances and its perils. He thought only of the end, so nearly reached, and sometimes he boiled over with impatience, as if he had been heated by the furnace of the *Henrietta* Frequently, also, the worthy fellow revolved around Fix; he looked at him with a distrustful eye, but he did not speak to him, for there no longer existed any intimacy between these two old friends.

Besides, Fix, it must be confessed, did not understand this thing at all. The conquest of the *Henrietta*, the purchase of her crew, and Fogg manoeuvring like an accomplished seaman—this combination of things confused him. He did not know what to think. But, after all, a man who commenced by stealing fifty-five thousand pounds could finish by stealing a vessel. And Fix was naturally led to believe that the *Henrietta*, directed by Fogg, was not going to Liverpool at all, but into some quarter of the world where the robber, become a pirate, would quietly place himself in safety! This hypothesis, it must be confessed, could not be more plausible, and the detective commenced to regret very seriously having entered upon this affair.

As for Captain Speedy, he continued to howl in his cabin, and Passepartout, whose duty it was to provide his meals, did it only with the greatest precautions, although he was so strong. Mr. Fogg had no longer the appearance of even suspecting that there was a captain on board.

On the 13th they passed the edge of the Banks of Newfoundland Those are bad latitudes. During the winter, especially, the fogs are frequent there, the blows dreadful. Since the day before, the barometer, suddenly fallen, indicated an approaching change in the atmosphere. In fact, during the night the temperature varied, the cold became keener, and at the same time the wind shifted into the south-east.

This was a misfortune. Mr. Fogg, in order not to be driven out of his course, had to reef his sails and increase his steam. But the progress of the ship was slackened, owing to the condition of the sea, whose long waves broke against her stern. She was violently tossed about, and to the detriment of her speed. The breeze increased by degrees to a hurricane, and it was already a probable event that the *Henrietta* might not be able to hold herself upright against the waves. Now, if she had to fly before the storm, the unknown, with all its bad chances, threatened them.

Passepartout's face darkened at the same time as the sky, and for two days the good fellow was in mortal dread. But Phileas Fogg was a bold sailor, who knew how to keep head against the sea, and he kept on his course, without even putting the vessel under a small head of steam. The *Henrietta*, whenever she could rise with the wave, passed over it, but her deck was swept from end to end. Sometimes, too, when a mountain wave raised the stern out of the water, the screw came out of the water, beating the air with its blades, but the ship still moved right on.

Still the wind did not become as severe as might have been feared. It was not one of those hurricanes which sweep on with a velocity of ninety miles an hour. It continued quite fresh, but unfortunately it blew obstinately from the south-east, and did not allow the sails to be hoisted. And yet, as we will see, it would have been very useful if they could have come to the aid of the steam!

The 16th of December was the seventy-fifth day that had elapsed since leaving London. The *Henrietta* had not yet seen seriously delayed. The half of the voyage was nearly accomplished, and the worst localities had been passed. In summer, success would have been certain. In winter they were at the mercy of the bad weather. Passepartout did not speak. Secretly he hoped, and if the wind failed them he counted at least upon the steam.

Now, on this day, the engineer ascended to the deck, met Mr. Fogg, and talked very earnestly with him.

Without knowing why—by a presentiment, doubtless—Passepartout felt a sort of vague uneasiness. He would have given one of his ears to have heard with the other what was said. But he could catch a few words, these among others, uttered by his master:

"You are certain of what you say?"

"I am certain, sir," replied the engineer. "Do not forget that, since our departure, all our furnaces have been going, and although we had enough coal to go under a small head of steam from New York to Bordeaux, we have not enough for a full head of steam from New York to Liverpool!"

"I will take the matter under consideration," replied Mr. Fogg. Passepartout understood. A mortal fear took possession of him.

The coal was about to give out.

"Ah! if my master wards that off," he said to himself, "he will certainly be a famous man!"

And having met Fix, he could not help posting him as to the situation.

"Then," replied the detective, with set teeth, "you believe that we are going to Liverpool.?"

"I do, indeed!"

"Idiot!" replied the detective, shrugging his shoulders as he turned away.

Passepartout was on the point of sharply resenting the epithet, whose true signification he could not understand; but he said to himself that the unfortunate Fix must be very much disappointed, and humiliated in his self-esteem, having so awkwardly followed a false scent around the world, and he refrained from condemning him.

And now what course was Phileas Fogg going to take? It was difficult to guess. But it appeared that the phlegmatic gentleman decided upon one, for that evening he sent for the engineer and said to him:

"Keep up your fires and continue on your course until the complete exhaustion of the fuel."

A few moments after, the smoke stack of the *Henrietta* was vomiting torrents of smoke.

The vessel continued, then, to sail under full steam; but, as he had announced, two days later, the 18th, the engineer informed him that the coal would give out during the day.

"Don't let the fires go out," replied Mr. Fogg. "On the contrary, let the valves be charged."

About noon of this day, having taken observations and calculated the position of the vessel, Phileas Fogg sent for Passepartout and ordered him to go for Captain Speedy. This good fellow felt as if he had been commanded to unchain a tiger, and he descended into the poop, saying to himself:

"Positively I shall find a madman!"

In fact, a few minutes later a bomb came on the poop-deck, in the midst of cries and oaths. This bomb was Captain Speedy. It was evident that it was going to burst.

"Where are we?" were the first words he uttered in the midst of his choking anger, and certainly if the worthy man had been apoplectic, he would never have recovered from it.

"Where are we?" he repeated, his face purple.

"Seven hundred and seventy miles from Liverpool," replied Mr. Fogg, with imperturbable calmness.

"Pirate!" cried Andrew Speedy.

"I have sent for you, sir—"

"Sea-skimmer!"

—"Sir," continued Phileas Fogg, "to ask you to sell me your ship."

"No! by all the devils, no!"

"I shall be obliged to burn her."

"To burn my ship!"

"At least her upper portions, for we are out of fuel."

"Burn my ship !" cried Captain Speedy, who could no longer pronounce his syllables. "A ship that is worth fifty thousand dollars!"

"Here are sixty thousand!" replied Phileas Fogg, offering him a roll of bank-notes.

This produced a powerful effect upon Andrew Speedy. No American is without emotion at the sight of sixty thousand dollars. The captain forgot in an instant his anger, his imprisonment, all his grievances from his passenger. His ship was twenty years old. It might be quite a bargain! The bomb could not explode. Mr. Fogg had withdrawn the fuse.

"And the iron hull will be left me," he said in a singularly softened tone.

"The iron hull and the engine, sir. It is a bargain?"

"A bargain."

And Andrew Speedy, snatching the roll of bank-notes, counted them and slipped them into his pocket.

During this scene, Passepartout was white as a sheet. As for Fix he narrowly escaped an apoplectic fit. Nearly twenty thousand pounds spent, and yet this Fogg was going to relinquish to the seller the hull and the engine, that is, nearly the entire value of the vessel! It is true that the sum stolen from the bank amounted to fifty-five thousand pounds!

When Andrew Speedy had pocketed his money, Mr. Fogg said to him:

"Sir, don't let all this astonish you. Know that I lose twenty thousand pounds if I am not in London on the 21st of December, at a quarter before nine in the evening. Now, I had missed the steamer from New York, and as you refused to take me to Liverpool—"

"And I have done well, by all the imps of the lower regions," cried Andrew Speedy, "since I make by it at least forty thousand dollars."

Then he added, more calmly:

"Do you know one thing, Captain—!"

"Fogg."

"Well, Captain Fogg, there is something of the Yankee in you."

And having paid his passenger what he thought to be a compliment, he went away, when Phileas Fogg said to him:

"Now this ship belongs to me?"

"Certainly, from the keel to the truck of the masts, all the wood, understand."

"Very well. Cut away the inside arrangements and fire up with the debris."

It may be judged how much of this dry wood was necessary to maintain the steam at sufficient pressure. This day, the poop-deck, the cabins, the bunks, and the spare deck all went.

The next day, the 19th of December, they burned the masts, the rafts, and the spars. They cut down the masts, and delivered them to the axe. The crew displayed an incredible zeal. Passepartout, hewing, cutting, sawing, did the work of ten men. It was a perfect fury of demolition.

The next day, the 20th, the railings, the armour, all of the ship above water, the greater part of the deck, were consumed. The *Henrietta* was now a vessel cut down like a pontoon.

But on this day they sighted the coast of Ireland and Fastnet Light.

However at ten o'clock in the evening the ship was only passing Queenstown. Phileas Fogg had only twenty-four hours to reach London. Now, this was the time the *Henrietta* needed to reach Liverpool, even under full headway. And the steam was about to fail the bold gentleman!

"Sir," said Captain Speedy to him then, who had come to be interested in his projects, "I really pity you. Everything is against you. We are yet only in front of Queenstown."

"Ah!" said Mr. Fogg, "that is Queenstown, the place where we perceive the light?"

"Yes."

"Can we enter the harbour?"

"Not for three hours. Only at high tide."

"Let us wait," Phileas Fogg replied calmly, without letting it be seen on his face that, by a last inspiration, he was going to try to conquer once more his contrary fate!

Queenstown is a port on the coast of Ireland, at which the transatlantic steamers coming from the United States deposit their mail-bag. These letters are carried to Dublin by express trains always ready to start. From Dublin they arrive in Liverpool by very swift vessels, thus gaining twelve hours over the most rapid sailers of the ocean companies.

These twelve hours which the America couriers gained, Phileas Fogg intended to gain too. Instead of arriving by the *Henrietta* in the evening of the next day, at Liverpool, he would be there by noon, and, consequently, he would have time enough to reach London before a quarter of nine in the evening.

Towards one o'clock in the morning, the *Henrietta* entered Queenstown harbour at high tide, and Phileas Fogg, having received a vigorous shake of the hand from Captain Speedy, left him on the levelled hulk of his vessel, still worth the half of what he had sold it for!

The passengers landed immediately. Fix at this moment, had a fierce desire to arrest Mr. Fogg. He did not do it, however. Why? What conflict was going on within him? Had he changed his mind with reference to Mr. Fogg? Did he finally perceive that he was mistaken? Fix, however, did not leave Mr. Fogg. With him, Mrs. Aouda, and Passepartout, who did not take time to breathe, he jumped into a train a Queenstown at half-past one in the morning, arrived at Dublin at break of day, and immediately embarked on one of those steamers—regular steel spindles, all engine—which, disdaining to rise with the waves, invariably pass right through them.

At twenty minutes before noon, the 21st of December, Phileas Fogg finally landed on the quay at Liverpool. He was now only six hours from London.

But at this moment Fix approached him, put his hand on his shoulder, and, showing his warrant, said:

"You are really Phileas Fogg?"

"Yes, sir."

"I arrest you in the name of the Queen."

CHAPTER 34

Which gives Passepartout the opportunity of letting out some atrocious, but perhaps Unpublished, Words

Phileas Fogg was in prison. He had been shut up in the Custom House in Liverpool, and was to pass the night there, awaiting his transfer to London.

At the moment of his arrest, Passepartout wished to rush upon the detective. Some policemen held him back. Mrs. Aouda, frightened by the brutality of the act, and knowing nothing about it, could not understand it. Passepartout explained the situation to her. Mr. Fogg, this honest and courageous gentleman, to whom she owed her life, was arrested as a robber. The young woman protested against such an allegation, her heart rose with indignation, and tears flowed from her eyes when she saw that she could not do anything, or attempt anything to save her deliverer.

As for Fix, he had arrested the gentleman because his duty commanded him to, whether he was guilty or not. The courts would decide the question.

But then a thought came to Passepartout—the terrible thought that he was certainly the cause of all this misfortune! Indeed, why had he concealed this adventure from Mr. Fogg? When Fix had revealed both his capacity as a detective and the mission into which he was charged, why had he decided not to warn his master? The latter, informed, would without doubt have given Fix proofs of his innocence; he would have demonstrated to him his error; at any rate, he would not have conveyed at his expense and on his tracks this unfortunate detective, whose first care was to arrest him the moment he set foot on the soil of the United Kingdom. Thinking of his faults and his imprudence, the poor fellow was overwhelmed with

198

remorse. He wept, so that it was painful to look at him. He felt like blowing his brains out.

Mrs. Aouda and he remained, notwithstanding the cold, under the porch of the Custom House. Neither of them wished to leave the place. They wanted to see Mr. Fogg once more.

As for that gentleman, he was really ruined, and at the very moment that he was about to reach his end. This arrest would ruin him irrecoverably. Having arrived at Liverpool at twenty minutes before twelve, noon, on the 21st of December, he had until quarter of nine in the evening to appear at the Reform Club—that is, nine hours and five minutes, and he only needed six to reach London. At this moment, anyone entering the Custom House would have found Mr. Fogg seated motionless, on a wooden bench, without anger, imperturbable. He could not have been said to be resigned, but this blow had not been able to move him, in appearance at least. Was he fostering within himself one of those secret spells of anger, terrible because they are pent up, and which breaks out only at the last moment with irresistible force? We do not know. But Phileas Fogg was there, calm, waiting for—what? Did he cherish some hope? Did he still believe in success, when the door of his prison was closed upon him?

However that may be, Mr. Fogg carefully put his watch on the table, and watched the hands move. Not a word escaped from his lips, but his look had a singular fixedness.

In any event, the situation was terrible, and for anyone that could read his thoughts, they ran thus:

An honest man, Phileas Fogg, was ruined.

A dishonest man, he was caught.

Did he think of escaping? Did he think of looking to see whether there was a practicable outlet from his prison? Did he think of flying? We would be tempted to believe so; for, once he took the tour of the room. But the door was securely locked and the windows had iron bars. He sat down again, and took from his pocket-book the diary of his journey. On the line which bore these words;

"December 21st, Saturday, Liverpool," he added:

"Eightieth day, 11.40 am.," and he waited.

The Custom House dock struck one. Mr. Fogg observed that his watch was two hours fast by this clock.

Two hours! Admitting that he should jump aboard an express train at this moment he could still arrive in London and at the Reform Club before quarter of nine in the evening. A light frown passed over his forehead.

At thirty-three minutes after two o'clock a noise sounded outside, a bustle from the opening of doors. The voice of Passepartout was heard, and also that of Fix.

Phileas Fogg's look brightened up a moment.

The door opened, and he saw Mrs. Aouda, Passepartout, Fix, rushing towards him.

Fix was out of breath, his hair all disordered, and he could not speak.

"Sir," he stammered, "sir—pardon—an unfortunate resemblance—robber arrested three days ago—you—free—!"

Phileas Fogg was free! He went to the detective, looked him well in the face, and with the only rapid movement that he ever had made or ever would make in his life, he drew both his arms back, and then, with the precision of an automaton, he struck the unfortunate detective with both his fists.

"Well Sir" cried Passepartout, who, allowing himself an atrocious flow of words, quite worthy of a Frenchman, added: "Zounds! this is what might be called a fine application of English fists!"

Fix, prostrate, did not utter a word. He only got what he deserved. But Mr. Fogg, Mrs. Aouda, and Passepartout immediately left the Custom House. They jumped into a carriage and in a few minutes arrived at the depot.

Phileas Fogg asked if there was an express train ready to start for London.

It was forty minutes past two. The express left thirty-five minutes before.

Phileas Fogg then ordered a special train.

There were several locomotives of great speed with steam up; but, owing to the exigencies of the service, the special train could not leave the depot before three o'clock.

At three o'clock, Phileas Fogg, after saying a few words to

the engineer about a certain reward to be won, moved on in the direction of London, in the company of the young woman and his faithful servant.

The distance which separates Liverpool from London must be accomplished in five hours and a half—a very feasible thing when the road is clear on the whole route. But there were compulsory delays, and when the gentleman arrived at the depot all the clocks in London were striking ten minutes of nine.

Phileas Fogg, after having accomplished this tour of the world, arrived, five minutes behind time!

He had lost his bet.

Chapter 35

In which Passepartout does not have repeated to Him twice the Order His Master gives Him

The next day the residents of Saville Row would have been much surprised if they had been told that Phileas Fogg had returned to his dwelling. The doors and windows were all closed. No change had taken place outside.

After leaving the depot Phileas Fogg gave Passepartout an order to buy some provisions, and he had gone into his house.

This gentleman received with his habitual impassibility the blow which struck him. Ruined! and by the fault of that awkward detective! After moving on with steady step during this long trip, overturning a thousand obstacles, braving a thousand dangers, and having still found time to do some good on his route, to fail before a brutal act, which he could not foresee, and against which he was defenceless—that was terrible! He had left only an insignificant remnant of the large sum which he had taken away with him when he started on his journey. His fortune now only consisted of the twenty thousand pounds deposited at Baring Brothers, and those twenty thousand pounds he owed to his colleagues of the Reform Club. Having incurred so many expenses, if he had won the bet he would not have been enriched; and it is probable that he had not sought to enrich himself, being of that class of men who bet for the sake of honour—but this bet lost would ruin him entirely. The gentleman's decision was taken. He knew what remained for him to do.

A room in the house in Saville Row was set apart for Mrs. Aouda. The young woman was desperate. From certain words which Mr.Fogg let drop, she understood that he contemplated some fatal design.

It is known, indeed, to what lamentable extremities these Englishmen are carried sometimes under the pressure of a fixed area. Thus, Passepartout, without seeming to do so, was closely watching his master.

But first the good fellow descended to his room and turned off the burner which had been burning for eighty days. He found in the letter-box a note from the gas company, and the thought that it was more than time to stop the expenses for which he was responsible.

The night passed. Mr. Fogg had retired; but had he slept? As for Mrs. Aouda, she could not take a single moment's rest. Passepartout had watched, like a dog, at his master's door.

The next morning Mr. Fogg sent for him, and ordered him very briefly to prepare Mrs. Aouda's breakfast. As for himself, he would be satisfied with a cup of tea and a piece of toast. Mrs. Aouda would be kind enough to excuse him from breakfast and dinner, for all his time would be devoted to arranging his affairs. He would not come down. He would only ask Mrs. Aouda's permission to have a few moment's conversation with her in the evening.

Passepartout, having been given the programme for the day, had nothing to do but to conform to it. He looked at his master, still so impassible, and he could not make up his mind to quit his room. His heart was full, and his conscience weighed down with remorse, for he accused himself more than ever for this irreparable disaster. Yes! if he had warned Mr. Fogg, if he had disclosed to him the plans of the detective Fix, Mr. Fogg would not have dragged the detective Fix with him as far as Liverpool, and then . . .

Passepartout could not hold in any longer.

"My master! Monsieur Fogg!" he cried, "curse me. It is through my fault that — "

"I blame no one," replied Phileas Fogg in the calmest tone. "Go."

Passepartout left the room and went to find the young woman, to whom he made known his master's intentions.

"Madame," he added, "I can do nothing by myself, nothing at all. I have no influence over my master's mind. You, perhaps—"

"What influence would I have," replied Mrs. Aouda "Mr.Fogg is subject to none. Has he ever understood that my gratitude for him was overflowing? Has he ever read my heart? My friend, you must not leave him a single instant. You say that he has shown a desire to speak to me this evening?"

"Yes, madame. It is no doubt with reference to making your position in England comfortable."

"Let us wait," replied the young woman, who was quite pensive.

Thus during this day, Sunday, the house in Saville Row was as if uninhabited, and for the first time since he lived there, Phileas Fogg did not go to his club, when the Parliament House clock struck half-past eleven.

And why should this gentleman have presented himself at the Reform Club? His colleagues no longer expected him. Since Phileas Fogg did not appear in the saloon of the Reform Club the evening of the day before, on this fatal date, Saturday, December 21st, at quarter before nine, his bet was lost. It was not even necessary that he should go to his banker's to draw this sum of twenty thousand pounds. His opponents had in their hands a cheque signed by him, and it only needed a simple writing to go to Baring Brothers in order that the twenty thousand pounds might be carried to their credit.

Mr. Fogg had then nothing to take him out, and he did not go out. He remained in his room, putting his affairs in order. Passepartout was continually going up and down stairs. The hours did not move for this poor fellow. He listened at the door of his master's room, and in doing so, did not think he committed the least indiscretion. He looked through the keyhole, and imagined that he had this right. Passepartout feared at every moment some catastrophe. Sometimes he thought of Fix, but a change had taken place in his mind. He no longer blamed the detective. Fix had been deceived, like everybody else, with respect to Phileas Fogg, and in following him and arresting him he had only done his duty, while he . . . This thought overwhelmed him, and he considered himself the most wretched of human beings.

When, finally, Passepartout would be too unhappy to be alone, he would knock at Mrs. Aouda's door, enter her room, and sit down in a corner without saying a word, and look at the young woman with a pensive air.

About half-past seven in the evening, Mr. Fogg sent to ask Mrs. Aouda if she could receive him, and in a few moments after the young woman and he were alone in the room.

Phileas Fogg took a chair and sat down near the fireplace opposite Mrs. Aouda. His face reflected no emotion. Fogg returned was exactly the Fogg who had gone away. The same calmness, the same impassibility.

He remained without speaking for five minutes. Then, raising his eyes to Mrs. Aouda, he said:

"Madame, will you pardon me for having brought you to England?"

"I, Mr. Fogg!" replied Mrs. Aouda, suppressing the throbbings of her heart.

"Be kind enough to allow me to finish," continued Mr. Fogg. "When I thought of taking you so far away from that country, become so dangerous for you, I was rich, and I counted on placing a portion of my fortune at your disposal. Your life would have been happy and free. Now, I am ruined."

"I know it, Mr. Fogg," replied the young woman, "and I in turn will ask you—Will you pardon me for having followed you, and— who knows? for having perhaps assisted in your ruin by delaying you?"

"Madame, you could not remain in India, and your safety was only assured by removing you so far that those fanatics could not retake you."

"So, Mr. Fogg," replied Mrs. Aouda, "not satisfied with rescuing me from a horrible death, you believe you were obliged to assure my position abroad?"

"Yes, madame, replied Fogg, "but events have turned against me. However, I ask your permission to dispose of the little I have left in your favour."

"But you, Mr. Fogg, what will become of you?" asked Mrs. Aouda.

"I, madame," replied the gentleman coldly, "I do not need anything."

"But how, sir, do you look upon the fate that awaits you.?"

"As I ought to look at it," replied Mr. Fogg.

"In any event," continued Mrs. Aouda, "want could not reach such a man as you. Your friends—"

"I have no friends, madame."

"Your relatives—"

"I have no relatives now."

"I pity you, then, Mr. Fogg, for solitude is a sad thing. What! have you not one heart into which to pour your troubles? They say, however, that with two, misery itself is bearable!"

"They say so, madame."

"Mr. Fogg," then said Mrs. Aouda, rising and holding out her hand to the gentleman, ado you wish at once a relative and a friend? Will you have me for your wife?"

Mr. Fogg, at this, rose in his turn. There seemed to be an unusual reaction in his eyes, a trembling of his lips. Mrs. Aouda looked at him. The sincerity, rectitude, firmness, and sweetness of this soft look of a noble woman, who dared everything to save him to whom she owed everything, first astonished him, then penetrated him. He closed his eyes for an instant, as if to prevent this look from penetrating deeper. When he opened them again, he simply said:

"I love you. Yes, in truth, by everything most sacred in the world, I love you, and I am entirely yours!"

"Ah!" cried Mrs. Aouda, pressing his hand to her heart.

He rang for Passepartout. He came immediately. Mr. Fogg was still holding Mrs. Aouda's hand in his. Passepartout understood, and his broad face shone like the sun in the zenith of tropical regions.

Mr. Fogg asked him if he would be too late to notify Rev. Samuel Wilson, of Mary-le-Bone Parish.

Passepartout gave his most genial smile.

"Never too late," he said.

It was then five minutes after eight.

"It will be for to-morrow, Monday," he said.

"For to-morrow, Monday?" asked Mr. Fogg, looking at the young woman.

"For to-morrow, Monday!" replied Mrs. Aouda

Passepartout went out, running as hard as he could.

CHAPTER 36

In which "Phileas Fogg" is again at a Premium in the Market

It is time to tell here what a change of opinion was produced in the United Kingdom when they learned of the arrest of the true robber of the bank, a certain James Strand, which took place in Edinburgh on the 17th of December.

Three days before, Phileas Fogg was a criminal whom the police were pursuing to the utmost, and now he was the most honest gentleman, accomplishing mathematically his eccentric tour round the world.

What an effect, what an excitement in the papers! All the betters for or against, who had already forgotten this affair, revived as if by magic. All the transactions became of value. All the engagements were renewed, and it must be said that betting was resumed with new energy. The name of Phileas Fogg was again at a premium on the market.

The five colleagues of the gentleman, at the Reform Club, passed these three days in some uneasiness. Would this Phileas Fogg, whom they had forgotten, reappear before their eyes? Where was he at this moment? On the 17th of December—the day that James Strand was arrested—it was seventy-six days since Phileas Fogg started, and no news from him! Was be dead? Had he given up the effort, or was he continuing his course as agreed upon? And would he appear on Saturday, the 21st of December, at a quarter before nine in the evening, the very impersonation of exactness, on the threshold of the saloon of the Reform Club?

We must give up the effort to depict the anxiety in which for three days all of London society lived. They sent dispatches to America, to Asia, to get news of Phileas Fogg. They sent morning and evening to watch the house in Saville Row. Nothing there. The police themselves did not know what had become of the detective Fix, who had so unfortunately thrown himself on a false scent. This did not prevent bets from being entered into anew on a larger scale. Phileas Fogg, like a racehorse, was coming to the last turn. He was quoted no longer at one hundred, but at twenty, ten, five; and the old paralytic Lord Albemarle bet even in his favour.

So that on Saturday evening there was a crowd in Pall Mall and in the neighbouring streets. It might have been supposed that there was an immense crowd of brokers permanently established around the Reform Club. Circulation was impeded. They discussed, disputed, and cried the prices of "Phileas Fogg," like they did those of English Consuls. The policemen had much difficulty in keeping the crowd back, and in proportion as the hour approached at which Phileas Fogg ought to arrive, the excitement took incredible proportions.

This evening, the five colleagues of the gentleman were assembled in the grand saloon of the Reform Club. The two bankers, John Sullivan and Samuel Fallentin, the engineer Andrew Stuart, Gauthier Ralph, the director of the Bank of England, and the brewer, Thomas Flanagan, all waited with anxiety.

At the moment that the clock in the grand saloon indicated twenty-five minutes past eight, Andrew Stuart, rising, said:

"Gentlemen, in twenty minutes the time agreed upon between Mr. Phileas Fogg and ourselves will have expired."

"At what hour did the last train arrive from Liverpool asked Thomas Flanagan.

"At twenty-three minutes after seven," replied Gauthier Ralph, "and the next train does not arrive until ten minutes after twelve, midnight."

"Well, gentlemen," continued Andrew Stuart, "if Phileas Fogg had arrived in the train at twenty-three minutes after seven, he would already be here. We can then consider we have won the bet."

"Let us wait before deciding," replied Samuel Fallentin. "You know that our colleague is an oddity of the first order. His exactness in everything is well known. He never arrives too late or too soon, and he will appear here at the very last minute, or I shall be very much surprised."

"And I," said Andrew Stuart, who was, as always, very nervous, "would not believe it was he if I saw him."

"In fact," replied Thomas Flanagan, "Phileas Fogg's project was a senseless one. However exact he might be, he could not prevent the occurrence of inevitable delays, and a delay of but two or three days would be sufficient to compromise the tour."

"You will notice besides," added John Sullivan "that we have received no news from our colleague, and yet telegraph lines were not wanting upon his route."

"Gentlemen, he has lost," replied Andrew Stuart, "he has lost a hundred times! You know, besides, that the *China*—the only steamer from New York that he could take for Liverpool

208

to be of any use to him—arrived yesterday. Now, here is the list of passengers, published by the *Shipping Gazette*, and the name of Phileas Fogg is not among them. Admitting the most favourable chances, our colleague has scarcely reached America! I calculate twenty days, at least, as the time that he will be behind, and old Lord Albermarle will be minus his five thousand pounds!"

"It is evident," replied Gauthier Ralph, "and to-morrow we have only to present to Baring Brothers Mr. Fogg's cheque."

At this moment, the clock in the saloon struck forty minutes after eight.

"Five minutes yet," said Andrew Stuart.

The five colleagues looked at each other. It may be believed that their hearts beat a little more rapidly, for, even for good players, it was a great risk. But they did not betray themselves, for at Samuel Fallentin's suggestion, they seated themselves at a card table.

"I would not give my part of four thousand pounds in the bet," said Andrew Stuart, seating himself, "even if I was offered three thousand nine hundred and ninety-nine!"

At this moment the hands noted forty-two minutes after eight.

The players took up their cards, but their eyes were constantly fixed upon the clock. It may be asserted that notwithstanding their security, the minutes had never seemed so long to them!

"Forty-three minutes after eight," said Thomas Flanagan, cutting the cards which Gauthier Ralph presented to him.

Then there was a moment's silence. The immense saloon of the Club was quiet. But outside they heard the hubbub of the crowd, above which were sometimes heard loud cries. The pendulum of the clock was beating the seconds with mathematical regularity, and every player could count them as they struck his ear.

"Forty-four minutes after eight," said John Sullivan, in a voice in which was heard an involuntary emotion.

One more minute and the bet would be won. Andrew Stuart and his colleagues played no longer. They had abandoned their cards! They were counting the seconds!

At the fortieth second, nothing. At the fiftieth still nothing!

At the fifty-fifth, there was a roaring like that of thunder outside, shouts, hurrahs, and even curses kept up in one prolonged roll.

The players rose.

At the fifty-seventh second, the door of the saloon opened, and the pendulum had not beat the sixtieth second, when Phileas Fogg appeared, followed by an excited crowd, who had forced an entrance into the Club, and in his calm voice he said:

"Gentlemen, here I am!"

CHAPTER 37

In which it is Proved that Phileas Fogg has gained nothing by making this Tour of the World, unless it be Happiness

Yes! Phileas Fogg in person.

It will be remembered that at five minutes after eight in the evening, about twenty-five hours after the arrival of the travellers in London, Passepartout was charged by his master to inform Rev. Samuel Wilson in reference to a certain marriage which was to take place the next day.

Passepartout went, delighted. He repaired with rapid steps to the residence of Rev. Samuel Wilson, who had not come home. Of course Passepartout waited, but he waited full twenty minutes at east. In short, it was thirty-five minutes past eight when he left the clergyman's house. But in what a condition! His hair disordered, hatless, running, running as has never been seen in the memory of man, upsetting passers-by, rushing along the sidewalks like a water-spout.

In three minutes, he had returned to the house in Saville Row, and fell out of breath, in Mr. Fogg's room.

He could not speak.

"What is the matter?" asked Mr. Fogg.

"Master"—stammered Passepartout—"Marriage—impossible!"

"Impossible-?"

"Impossible—to-morrow."

"Why?"

"Because to-morrow is—Sunday."

"Monday," replied Mr. Fogg.

"No—to-day—Saturday."

"Saturday? Impossible!"

"Yes, yes, yes!" cried Passepartout. "You have made a mistake of one day. We arrived twenty-four hours in advance—but there are not ten minutes left!"

Passepartout seized his master by the collar, and dragged him along with irresistible force!

Phileas Fogg, thus taken, without having time to reflect, left the room, went out of his house, jumped into a cab, promised one hundred pounds to the driver, and, after running over two dogs and running into five carriages, arrived at the Reform Club.

The clock indicated quarter of nine when he appeared in the grand saloon.

Phileas Fogg had accomplished this tour of the world in eighty days!

Phileas Fogg had won his bet of twenty thousand pounds!

And now, how could so exact and cautious a man have made the mistake of a day? How did he think that it was the evening of Saturday, December 21st, when it was only Friday, December 20th, only seventy-nine days after his departure.

This is the reason for this mistake. It is very simple.

Phileas Fogg had, without suspecting it, gained a day on his journey—only because he had made the tour of the world going to the *east*, and on the contrary, he would have lost a day going in the contrary direction, that is, towards the *west*.

Indeed, journeying towards the east, Phileas Fogg was going towards the sun, and consequently the days became as many times four minutes less for him, as he crossed degrees in that direction. Now there are three hundred and sixty degrees in the earth's circumference, and these three hundred and sixty degrees, multiplied by four minutes, give precisely twenty-four hours—that is to say, the day unconsciously gained. In other words, while Phileas Fogg, travelling towards the east, saw the sun pass the meridian *eighty* times, his colleagues, remaining in London, saw it pass only *seventy-nine* times. Therefore this very day, which was Saturday, and not Sunday, as Mr. Fogg thought, his friends were waiting for him in the saloon of the Reform Club.

And Passepartout's famous watch, which had always kept London time, would have shown this, if it had indicated days, as well as the minutes and hours!

Phileas Fogg then had won the twenty thousand pounds. But as he had spent in his journey about nineteen thousand, the pecuniary result was small. However, as has been said, the eccentric gentleman had sought in his bet to gain the victory and not to make money. And even the thousand pounds remaining he divided between Passepartout and the unfortunate Fix, against whom he could not cherish a grudge. Only for the sake of exactness, he retained from his servant the cost of the gas burned through his fault for nineteen hundred and twenty hours.

This very evening Mr. Fogg, as impassible and as phlegmatic as ever, said to Mrs. Aouda:

"This marriage is still agreeable to you?"

"Mr. Fogg," replied Mrs. Aouda, "it is for me to ask you that question. You were ruined; now you are rich—"

"Pardon me, madame; my fortune belongs to you. If you had not thought of the marriage, my servant would not have gone to the house of Rev. Samuel Wilson. I would not have been apprised of my mistake, and—"

"Dear Mr. Fogg—" said the young woman.

"Dear Aouda," replied Phileas Fogg.

It is readily understood that the marriage took place forty-eight hours later, and Passepartout, superb, resplendent, dazzling, was present as the young woman's witness. Had he not saved her, and did they not owe him that honour?

At daylight the next morning, Passepartout knocked noisily at his master's door.

The door opened, and the impassible gentleman appeared.

"What is the matter, Passepartout?"

"What's the matter, sir! I have just found out this moment—

"What?"

"That we could make the tour of the world in seventy-eight days."

"Doubtless," replied Mr. Fogg, "by not crossing India But if I had not crossed India, I would not have saved Mrs. Aouda, she would not be my wife, and—"

And Mr. Fogg quietly shut the door.

Thus Phileas Fogg won his bet. In eighty days he had accomplished the tour around the world!

To do this he had employed every means of conveyance, steamers, railways, carriages, yachts, merchant vessels, sledges, elephants. The eccentric gentleman had displayed in this affair his wonderful qualities of coolness and exactness.

But what then? What had he gained by leaving home? What had he brought back from his journey?

Nothing, do you say? Nothing, perhaps, but a charming woman, who—improbable as it may appear—made him the happiest of men!

Truly, would you not, for less than that, make the tour of the world?

Landmark Visitors Guide

The Best of

Lancashire

Includes Manchester & Liverpool

Mike Smith

Mike Smith is a magazine journalist and travel writer. He contributes monthly features to both
Lancashire Life and Derbyshire Life, and his books include Dordogne, Exploring Northern
France and Spirit of the High Peak, all published by Landmark.

Published by

Landmark Publishing

The Oaks, Moor Farm Road West, Ashbourne, Derbyshire DE6 1HD

Published in the UK by
Landmark Publishing Ltd,
The Oaks, Moor Farm Road West, Ashbourne, DE6 1HD
Tel: 01335 347349   email: landmark@clara.net
website: landmarkpublishing.co.uk

ISBN 13: 978-1-84306-434-3

Front cover: Downham village (courtesy of Lancashire Life www.lancashirelife.co.uk)
Back cover, top: Yellow Duckmarine, Albert Dock, Liverpool
Back cover, bottom: Millennium Bridge, Salford Quays (Paul Reid – Shutterstock)
Back cover, right: Lytham Windmill (Tom Curtis – Shutterstock)

Picture Credits

Images below are from Shutterstock with copyright to:

Jane McIlroy: p.7 top **Dave McAleavy:** p.7 middle **G Beanland:** p.7 bottom **Samot:** p.23 bottom
Paul Reid: p.27 bottom **Tom Curtis:** p.50 **Victor Burnside:** p.71 right **Andrew Barker:** p.94
Jeff Dalton: p.95 **John Hemmings:** p.99 top-right

Courtesy of Ashton Underlined: p.35 top & inset

Courtesy of Lancaster City Council: p.42 & p.58

Uncredited photographs by Mike Smith

DISCLAIMER

While every care has been taken to ensure that the information in this book is as accurate as possible at the time of publication, the publishers and author accept no responsibility for any loss, injury or inconvenience sustained by anyone using this book.
Maps in this book are for location only. You are recommended to buy a road map.